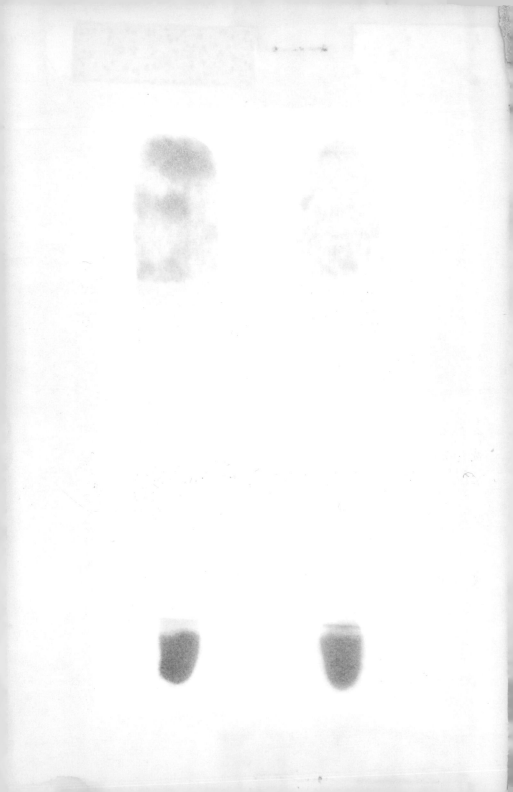

Beautiful Kate

LITTLE, BROWN AND COMPANY
Boston   *Toronto*

Beautiful Kate

Newton Thornburg

FIRST EDITION

Library of Congress Cataloging in Publication Data

Thornburg, Newton.
  Beautiful Kate.

  I. Title.
PS3570.H649B4   813'.54   81–23677
ISBN 0–316–84394–6   AACR2

BP

Designed by Janis Capone

Published simultaneously in Canada
by Little, Brown & Company (Canada) Limited

PRINTED IN THE UNITED STATES OF AMERICA

Once Again
To Karin

Beautiful Kate

one

I have been back all of three days now, back in my father's house. So where else would I find myself at this moment but alone upstairs in the old bedroom sitting at the old desk, Bic in hand, trying to exorcise the same demons that drove me out of here in the first place, at the fearless age of eighteen. Goddamn his ancient ass, but I do find it hard to like the man, even now, when I can barely afford to feed myself, let alone indulge some grizzled animosity of the blood. It has been eleven years since I was here last—to see my mother into the ground then—and in all that time he has not changed any more than the bronze doughboy posturing down at the town square. Oh, the hair is whiter and his step is less sure and he is thinner than ever. But for me it is the eyes that count, and they are just the same, only blacker and harder, if that is possible, twin points of burning moral certitude in a world clouded by weakness and doubt and corruption—*my* sort of world, he would tell you. And best of all, you would not even have to ask, for he has never been shy about expressing himself on the subject of his moral inferiors, who happily are so numerous that all he has ever had to do is look up from whatever cranky tome or pamphlet currently deemed worthy of his interest, and there we are, wretched sinners against his word.

Jason, his name is, Jason Cutter Kendall, seventy years old, asthmatic and arthritic and arteriosclerotic, not even rich or powerful anymore, yet here I sit at my perennial legal pad venting my spleen against the old bastard as if I couldn't punch him out if the spirit moved me, or as if I had no choice at all in coming back here. But then, as you will no doubt discover, logic and strength of character are not exactly my strong points, which might explain why I have been traveling with Toni, a paragon of the simpler virtues.

I remember four nights ago as we rattled across the Mississippi and headed into Illinois in my venerable Triumph, both of us tired and cold and irritable. All I hoped for was a few hours of silence from her, long enough for us to reach Woodglen and — I hoped — safety. Instead she picked up again the tiresome litany of bitching that had plagued me all the way from Hollywood.

"You could stop somewhere," she said. "Any one of these little burgs ought to have a bar where we could score. Just one lousy joint, that's all I'm asking."

I told her to shut up.

"I'll make us crash." She reached for the wheel, only to get shoved back against the car door for her trouble.

"God, I hate you," she wept. "Miserable old washed-up fart. What the hell am I doing here with you anyway? Middle of nowhere, with nothing! I should've stayed with Dandy — he could've got a part for me, I know he could."

"Sure, in some stroke opera for the Princess thee-ay-ters."

It was not a nice thing to say, and not really fair either, for she has appeared in only one porno film and that was almost five years ago, when she was in her teens. But that *miserable old washed-up fart* still rankled. Forty-three wasn't that old, I thought, smiling grimly to myself because I could not dispute any other part of her epithet. I expected her to kick me or at least go for the wheel again, though all she did was look over at me with those show-biz eyes of hers while pulling her mouth down into a sexy pout. But whatever she was trying to communicate did not quite come through, such is the general effect of her appearance, that pert face and long bleached hair and tan California body, which together send out a message so clear and constant that all lesser communications tend to get lost in the process.

"I hope they catch you," she said. "I hope you wind up in Soledad."

I pointed out that being wanted as a material witness didn't exactly qualify me as public enemy number one.

"That's bull. It was your boat and you knowingly rented it to the poor bastards. So you're just as guilty as they were. The narcs aren't gonna forget about you. Ever."

"If you say so."

"I say so."

We had just driven through a small town and now were going past a roadhouse with a bright neon sign simulating a bubbling glass of champagne.

"*There!*" Toni cried. "They're bound to have stuff in there! Please, Greg! You can stay in the car. I'll do it myself."

It was a scene she had already performed, probably a half-dozen times in the last few hours. At first I patiently had explained to her that a country bar in the Midwest was not the same as an L.A. disco and that all we were likely to score in them was beer nuts and boilermakers. But now I simply drove on past, saying nothing.

"God, I wish I was back in Venice," she lamented.

At two in the morning we reached the far southwest suburbs of Chicago and finally Woodglen itself, which over the years had not undergone change so much as decimation. The town square still existed, but only as an arbitrary and purposeless street arrangement, considering that the court-house had been razed long ago and the four rows of stores which once had surrounded it now stood empty or had been torn down and converted into parking garages — for whose cars I could not imagine, since the entire area was similarly blighted and empty. It was only as we went out of town on Main Street that the city began to show some life again, in the

5

form of bars and fast food franchises and supermarkets, all shuttered and dark at that late hour.

Farther on we came to Woodglen Estates, a sprawl of tract houses on land that once had been part of old Jason's country-gentleman farm—and my home, the place where I had grown up with Cliff and Kate. As on my last return here, I began to feel an odd oppressiveness in the air, almost as if memory were a storm moving in upon me. The "estates," I saw, were in even worse shape than they had been eleven years before, identical tiny wooden ranch houses on sixty-foot lots, once gaily painted yellow and pink and light green and inhabited by young white-collar couples on their way up in the world, but run-down now, gray and ramshackle, a number of them abandoned. On the occasion of my mother's funeral, the area was already beginning to turn black and Latino, and I could see now that it was probably solid minorities, a suburban slum surrounding the startling anachronism of Jason's big old white house and barn—which suddenly now came looming out of the darkness like a feudal manse in the midst of the spreading huts of its serfs. Only as you drove nearer could you see that the manse was equally ramshackle, and not all that large either, just an old-fashioned two-story nine-room house. Across from it a half-dozen young blacks stood drinking wine on the street corner.

"Christ," Toni said. "I don't see anyone but spades."

"Maybe that's all there is."

"Beautiful."

"That's what they call it."

As we pulled into the driveway, she shook her head in disbelief. "This is *it*? This is what we drove halfway across the fucking continent for?"

"It's called home," I told her. "A place of refuge and succor."

In response she gave me a pitying look and struggled out of the tiny car, sighing like a condemned woman. I had parked at the side entrance to the house. In front of us the driveway curved back to the barn, which was unpainted and covered with spray-can graffiti. In the gloom I could make out only the largest message: *the Lords rule.*

"Why not honk the horn?" Toni said. "Stir 'em up a little."
Instead I knocked on the door and waited, then knocked again, louder and longer until finally a light went on inside.

Toni sighed. "Well, it's about time. They must all be stoned."

"Or asleep. Do you think that could be it?"

The porchlight came on and the door opened—on Junior, my younger brother by a decade, once known as Tan Pants, for the soaking diapers he had worn till the age of four or five. Now though he stood before me very much a man, husky like me, but bearded and longhaired, a hippie diehard in an old bathrobe. As he stepped onto the porch, a smirk pulled at his mouth.

"Well, I'll be pissed—the big screenwriter, no less. And with the usual Beautiful Person in tow."

I introduced them. "My brother Junior—and this is Toni. Toni's an actress."

"Of course she is," Junior said.

But Toni liked combat. "*Junior?* Nobody's called Junior."

"Make it Little Jason, then. Will that do?"

Toni smiled at him. "How about some grass? You got any grass?"

Junior looked at me. "Well, at least she ain't a stuffed shirt like the last one."

Behind him, in the kitchen, the back stairway door opened and Sarah stood there blinking against the light and frowning. She had her hair up in curlers and she was tugging an old chenille housecoat tightly around the dumpy thickness of her body. But now her eyes opened wide and a joyous smile spread on her face.

"Greg? Greg! Oh Jesus!"

She came running into my arms and I picked her up and hugged her and kissed her. I have always believed that there should be a law that every man have at least one Sarah in his life, a sister or mother or whatever who thinks he's simply the greatest and loves him doggedly and unquestioningly, no matter how little he may have done to merit such devotion. Sarah, a thirty-five-year-old spinster schoolteacher, evidently feels that

7

I've done all the things that she has only dreamed of, from leaving home early and writing screenplays to traveling abroad and bedding the rich and the beautiful. And I don't think it bothers her in the least that none of these "accomplishments" has prevented me from washing up on her doorstep now like any other flotsam. But then that's what I mean by *unquestioning* love. A gift.

Anyway, that was the scene when I made it back here four nights ago, with Toni. Sarah embraced us and fed us and fell all over us, asking so many questions that the ever tactful Toni finally suggested that she give us a little space.

"Jesus, there's still tomorrow, isn't there?" my love remonstrated.

Sarah sat there in the kitchen like a squashed bug, unable to respond even after I apologized for Toni, saying that we'd had a long hard trip and the girl just wasn't herself. I tried to pump Sarah about her teaching job at the high school, but she seemed not even to hear me, so great was her awareness of Toni by then. She kept glancing furtively at her, as if she feared not just another reprimand but possibly corporal punishment as well. And when Toni renewed her inquiries about marijuana, flirting openly with Junior in her quest for the stuff, I was afraid that Sarah was about to crawl under the table and stay there. So I took her by the arm and had her show me to my old room upstairs, just down the hall from Jason's. Till then, not much had been said about the old man's failure to get up and greet us himself. Sarah had gone into his room to see if he was all right, which he evidently was. But he chose not to get up. It had been eleven years since he had seen me last, I overheard, and he could endure the privation one night more. I told Sarah that it was just as well, because I too would most likely survive the night.

In the eighteen months Toni has been living with me I have not done any writing, so she is somewhat annoyed at my new habit of coming up here alone to our room to scratch out a few words. She keeps asking me how my "diary" is coming and did I mention the great head she had given me last night? Did I record how "utterly bored" she is on this "ghetto farm"? Naturally, in her boredom she has taken to doing what she does best, which is to keep all available males in a state of high sexual turmoil. Junior, for instance, is suddenly much clumsier than I remember his being. He keeps spilling things and is always tripping over himself, especially when Toni is flouncing around in my shorty samurai robe. And unbelievably, she seems to have even old Jason's juices running stronger, to the point now where he is getting out of bed at eight in the morning instead of at noon, as he has been for years, according to Junior.

On our first day here, though, a Saturday, it was almost one o'clock before the old man blew his little whistle and Sarah went scurrying up to his room, which caused Junior to snort with derision.

"Weekdays I have the privilege," he said. "I get to take him breakfast in bed."

Toni was incredulous. "Why don't you just put him away somewhere?"

"Because I live off him. Because I'm a leech."

"What a neat family," Toni said. "And here I always thought mine was the pits."

Sarah appeared at the top of the stairs. "He'll see you now," she announced.

Toni laughed. "Well, hot damn! Aren't we fortunate!"

But suddenly I had no time for her or her pragmatic sarcasms, because my heart was beginning to pound at me and the old dryness was powdering my throat. Even if I had wanted to, which I did not, I doubt if I could have explained to her the special character of the relationship between my father and me. To love someone without liking him, to fear him without respecting him, that was only part of the problem, as was his long-standing but erroneous conviction that he knew me totally, in all the secret chambers of my soul. More to the point was the fact that I knew he always had blamed me in some willful and senseless way for what had happened to Cliff and Kate, as if I had not loved them more than life. But he never knew that, you see. Together, the two of us spoke only the language of contention.

As I followed Sarah into his room I experienced again the old feeling of growing smaller in his presence, of shrinking back to some childhood moment of guilt and confrontation. Over the years—in my four brief visits here—it has been such a recurrent phenomenon that I even have a name for it, *diminishing returns,* as if humor could mitigate the humiliation I feel in such moments. Toni had followed me into the room, but I was not aware of her or anything else except those laserlike black eyes following my progress to the foot of his bed.

"Well, the prodigal returns once more," he said, in a voice much frailer than I remembered it. "What happened? Did your Santa Barbara millionairess dump you?"

"A few years ago, yes."

"And this is your new one?"

"This is Toni," I told him. "Toni, meet my old man."

"Jason," Sarah amended.

Toni for once had nothing to say, an affliction that my father unhappily has never experienced.

"A very pretty girl. But then you always could pick 'em, couldn't you, Greg?" He grinned at Toni. "His only problem is holding on to them. You all get his number eventually."

"And what number is that?" Toni asked, having found her voice now.

Jason pretended innocence. "Don't ask me—I'm not a girl."

"You want to know why we're here?" I asked him.

"You want to tell me?"

"Not particularly, but I suppose I should. You remember Janet?"

"The one before the millionairess?"

"Yes, that one. She's got the police on me for nonsupport," I lied. "And I'm broke. I had nowhere else to go."

It was a speech that Jason relished. His seamed face settled into an expression of patrician disdain as he looked up at Sarah now. "And this is your hero? This is the man who's—what is it you always say—the man who's had it all?"

Sarah took a deep breath and suggested to him that, since we were all going to be living together for a while, it might be a good idea if we tried to get along.

"Of course, it would," Toni interjected. "But you know men. They like to think they're boys. And boys fight."

Jason was not amused. "Are you reprimanding me, young lady?"

"Why not? The two of you don't sound like a father and son—more like a couple of kids."

I could see in Jason's eyes that he was teetering between outrage and feigned indulgence. And I'm convinced it was only Toni's looks that made the difference, that easy, disarming sexiness which made the old martinet break into a brittle laugh finally.

"Well, maybe we do at that," he said. "Maybe we'll have to clean up our act, eh, Greg?"

I said nothing, as usual unable to give the man any quarter at all.

That evening, after Jason had gone to bed, the four of us sat around the kitchen table drinking beer and eating popcorn. Sarah had got out the family photo albums and Toni for some reason was captivated by them. Normally she had a hard time evincing interest in anything that did not relate in some way to herself, but the albums proved to be an exception. What seemed to intrigue her most of all were the early snapshots of Cliff, Kate, and me as children on the farm and how totally different that world was from the one outside our windows now. The open fields looked immense and beautifully peaceful, with cattle and horses on them instead of cheerless ranks of deteriorating tract houses. And the house and barn and corrals in the photos were a startling white and so well kept it beggared belief that they too could have turned to ruin in a single generation. Yet they had—don't ask me why. It's as if all of us—the people in Woodglen Estates the same as the Kendalls—fell into some sort of pernicious time warp in which a millennium of degeneration was miraculously compressed into a few decades.

But as Toni continued to leaf through the pages of the albums, firing questions at us, I realized that it was not decline that fascinated her but Kate.

"You know who she looks like here? A young Vivian Leigh. Only blond."

"No way." For some reason, the comparison irked me unreasonably.

"Oh yes she does," Toni insisted. "She's got that same—I don't know what."

"Wildness?" Sarah asked. "She was always pretty wild, wasn't she, Greg?"

It was not a subject I liked, that of my twin sister, flesh and spirit once so close to mine, so inseverable, that I sometimes lost sight of that arbitrary line where she left off and I began, even to the point where I found myself wondering whether she was half male or I half female. No, that's both silly and inaccurate, for what we really were together—with Cliff—was something almost asexual, a troika yoked by spirit and empathy, not sex. Not then, anyway.

"Wild?" I said. "Yeah, I guess you could say that."

Junior was laughing, wiping the beer foam from his beard. "I remember she had a name for everybody. Chief Tan Pants for me." He smiled ruefully at Sarah. "And remember what she called the two of us? *Emily's kids.* Which meant, I guess, that she and Greg and Cliff were Jason's."

"Well, we did come along pretty late," Sarah said. "I really don't remember that much about her. Except that I always wanted to look like her. And sound like her. And—"

Her face reddened as she broke off.

"She was very attractive," Sarah finished. "Very unusual."

Toni was smiling at me. "And she was *your* twin?"

"Not identical," I said.

"I'd say not."

But Sarah would not have me denigrated, even by my lover. She flipped the album to a snapshot of me sitting on the corral.

"He was just as attractive," she said. "And he still is."

Continuing to smile, Toni looked me over, like a used-car buyer. "Hmm, I don't know—twenty-five years *is* twenty-five years."

"No, it isn't—it's more," I said.

As the evening wore on, Junior kept at his beer as if he were being paid by the can. And with each one he emptied—and crumpled—he seemed to recover a bit more of that bitchy belligerence he had greeted us with on our arrival, before the sight of Toni in her samurai robe had begun to play tricks with his head. He kept going on about the "trinity" as he called us— Cliff, Kate, and me—and what a drag it had been growing up as a member of "Emily's family." And Kate had been so right, he said, dubbing them that, because that was exactly how Jason had always treated them, as if they were poor relations. It had always been "Cliff this" and "Kate that" even after the two of them were both dead and buried.

"And it really stuck in my craw," Junior said. "You'd have thought Sarah and I were just some niggers who worked here, somebody who didn't count, you know? And *you*—" Looking at me, he sneered openly, not unlike a silent screen villain. "The old man always goes on like you're his biggest disappointment, you know? Like he hates your guts. But in the next breath he's mumbling about what an athlete you were and how talented and all that shit, like you could've been somebody famous if it wasn't for your weakness, as he calls it. His word for cunt."

I had pushed back my chair, getting ready to leave. But he reached out and took hold of my wrist.

"Now, come on—stick around," he advised. "Toni likes all this dirty linen, don't you, sweetheart?"

"Sure, I really dig it," she said, laughing at the look I gave her.

With my free hand I took hold of Junior's wrist and squeezed until he let go of mine.

"See? Just what I said—the great athlete!" He stopped rubbing his wrist long enough to pop another can. "Never mind that Sarah and I've been taking care of him all these years,

13

while you just drop in for funerals and spend the rest of your time living off women and pretending you're a writer. Never mind who keeps this place going and keeps the dudes from burning us out. No, that's not important. No way. It's the *past*, that's all that matters with him. You and *them* — a suicide and a lunatic."

I did get up then, resisting a powerful urge to punch my little brother's drunken face.

"Come on," I said to Toni. "We're going to bed."

Her face was a pout. "Aw, just when it was getting interesting."

Our room upstairs once had been the guest room, where Jason put up all the cranks and phonies who shared his passionate views on organic gardening, agrarian populism, and the vital importance of securing elective office for Jason Kendall. In the forties Governor Stratton had appointed him to fill a vacancy in the state senate, but when he ran for the same office two years later he was soundly defeated in the primaries. He was similarly slaughtered in a bid for a U.S. congressional seat, the main reason being his generously expressed contempt for all politicians and "public leeches," whether Democrat or Republican. This sorry political record seemed to have no effect on his houseguests, however, who through the years doggedly addressed him as Senator, possibly because his mail still went out under the letterhead of Illinois State Senator Jason Cutter Kendall.

In time, though, their visits became increasingly infrequent — why, I never knew. Perhaps they tired of the master-slave relationship favored by Jason, or maybe like most people they prospered sufficiently during the boom years of the late forties and fifties so that the old causes no longer seemed quite so important. In any case, as the room stood empty more and more, Cliff and I campaigned to get it for our own, not only because it was larger than the one we had then but also because it had its own private door to the upstairs bathroom. It was a change Jason would not hear of, however, not until Kate began to work on him with her considerable weaponry. And all she demanded from us in payment was two weeks free from milking the three cows we kept on the farm. So Cliff and I got the room and had it until the end. And now, with so many rooms in the house vacant, it once more had been designated the guest room, and thus was mine again, mine and Toni's.

As the two of us came in here that night, after Junior's drunken show of belligerence, she promptly began to pump me about Kate and Cliff: what had Junior meant about their being "a suicide and a lunatic"?

"He's just smashed," I told her. "Who knows what he means? They were in a car crash, like I told you. Cliff crawled out and made it home before he died of loss of blood. I guess he thought Kate was already dead. But she wasn't. She died in the hospital some time later."

It was not the truth of course, or at least not the whole truth. But then I had never been able to talk easily about their deaths with anyone—not Jason or my mother or any of my lovers and wives over the years—so I saw no reason to start now, with Toni. If I have anything in me like a soul, I figure that it resides in my memory of the two of them, Kate and Cliff. And if I have any religion it is simply not to profane that memory. So I lie or change the subject.

"Let's take a bath," I said.

"Together?"

I made like Charles Boyer. "But of course."

"The bed's softer."

"Don't argue. I'll punch you out."

In the bathroom, naked but still dry, we kissed and fondled and did other unspeakable things until the tub was full and then we slipped into it. With Toni, the basic problem in sex is simply in trying to make the damned thing last, like a kid with the most delicious ice-cream cone ever fashioned. The inventive little things she does with her body—that perfect ass and those sinewy legs and high small incomparable breasts—I'm sure would turn even the Pope into a red-eyed ravening monster of lust. And I'm no Holy Father. So in a short time—too short a

15

time—we were lying there together in the tub, twined and sated, indifferently soaping each other, occasionally kissing. Finally Toni spoke.

"Where do they get their money?"

"What money?"

"What do they live on—Sarah's salary?"

"I suppose so—that, and bank interest. Jason used to have a nest egg in the bank. That's what we lived on, not farm income. The farm never made a dime, as I remember."

"How much of a nest egg?"

"It earned five or six thousand, something like that."

"And he's kept it in the bank all this time? With inflation and everything?"

"How do I know? I haven't been home for over ten years, remember?"

Toni was frowning, drumming her fingers on my hip. "Five or six thousand—then, that must mean about a hundred thousand nest egg, right?" I couldn't help laughing, she was so transparent in her greed. "You want to heist it?" I asked, nibbling her ear.

She rolled onto me, straddling my waist and leaning down so we were eyeball to eyeball, in the Defense Secretary's deathless phrase. I'm sure I blinked.

"Part of it will soon be yours anyway, won't it?" she said.

"That depends."

"On what?"

"On whether it even exists. On how long he lives. And on whether he leaves any of it to me—which I seriously doubt he will."

She shook her head thoughtfully, summoning all her thespian talents. "God, I get scared, Greg. I mean, what if the police do trace you back here? What if they say you were in on the deal too? You could serve time."

"You think so?"

"And what would I do? Where would I go?"

"There's always Dandy."

"Screw Dandy. I'm talking about my man, not some lousy agent."

"So what do you suggest?" I asked, though of course I already knew. A cretin would have known.

"We've got to get our hands on some money, Greg. We really do. We've got to get the hell out of here. Go to Florida or someplace. You know it's gonna be *winter* here soon?" She enunciated the word as if it meant certain death for us.

"*Some* money, huh? Like whose?"

She saw then that I was laughing at her, and that was all it took. Immediately she was scrambling out of the tub and fighting off my hands. In her fury, she even swatted my cock, which had grown hard again under her weight. She began to towel off.

"That's it, buster. You've had it. It's gonna be a cold day in hell before you get me into the tub again. Or anywhere else."

"Deny me anything but that," I mourned.

"Yeah, you'll see."

She angrily flounced out of the bathroom, leaving me with the vision of that splendid tush, as though to rub it in, all that I would be losing.

"Hey baby," I called to her. "I'm sorry. I really am. I see things more clearly now."

Later that night I lay awake in the too-soft brass bed, with Toni sleeping soundly against me, her right leg draped over mine. And in the penumbral dark, the room seemed slowly to come alive around me, partially lit by the same old farmyard polelight, its rays slanting past the edge of the window shade, forming that remembered pane of whiteness in which even the swimming dust motes were not of now, like the ceiling water stains and the mythic figures I had always seen in them and saw again: Otto Graham passing the football and the even more formidable torso of Anita Ekberg, both having waited all these years just to be seen again by me, to be freed for one more night before melding back into the stains that even Kate had never been able to see as anything other than what they were.

Often she would sneak in at night and join us, in summer sitting on Cliff's twin bed or mine, but in winter diving under the covers to stay warm, oblivious of any turmoil such proximity caused us.

The time I am thinking of, she was thirteen and just beginning to develop, as Cliff was, at fifteen, both of them late bloomers, in sexual development anyway. (In my own case the magic occurred at fourteen, which meant that though I was not as tardy as they were, I was still behind them by a full year — a year that I remember now as the most painful of my young life, a sort of training ground for later. Suddenly the two most important persons in my life, and with whom I had hitherto shared that life as an equal, now treated me as the little guy, the snotnose, and it made me preternaturally nasty. All it would take is one wrong word or condescending look and I would tear into them, trying to reassert my lost equality.)

But getting back to that particular night. It was shortly after Cliff and I had gone to bed when Kate came slipping in, from the bathroom, as was her habit. And this night, it was my bed she sat on.

"We gotta do something," she said. "We just gotta do something."

"About what?"

"*Him,* you jerk! Your brother. Don't you know what Jason's been doing to him?"

"What about me?" I protested. "Jason's been working my butt off too."

"Bull!" she said. "He's always got Cliff doing more. And now there's the book work besides."

I shrugged. "It's his own fault. It's your own fault, ain't it, Cliff."

Cliff was lying there with his usual look of battered noblesse oblige, a boy who was not just a good scout but an Eagle Scout, so unfailingly generous and noble and right-thinking that I often wondered how he could make it in the world without Kate and me to protect him.

"I guess so," he said. "But I still think it's important what Jason's trying to do — teach us the stuff we don't get in school."

Kate looked to the ceiling for strength. "Sweet Jesus, Cliff, it ain't just the French and Russian Lit — it's the freaking farm too. Look what he's got lined up for you there — a few summer chores, he calls it — and it's more damn work than him and Stinking Joe have done in five years."

Cliff did not protest. He was too tired. From ten that morning till after dark the two of us had been bucking hay, tossing the filthy heavy itchy bastards up onto the hay wagon and then unloading them into the barn — while Stinking Joe, the hired man, drove the tractor and Jason himself sat in his air-conditioned library preparing our daily tests in Beginning French and Russian Literature. The difference between us was that Cliff sat in bed now with his light on and Menard's French grammar propped on his lap.

"Sweet Jesus," Kate said, "you're really gonna study it. Can't you for once go in there like we do and just tell him. *Sorry, father dear, but I just didn't have the time.*"

"He won't take that from me."

"Because you never make him, dumbo!" Kate said it loud enough to wake the house.

"It's important," Cliff insisted. "We should learn French. We should know it. We should be grateful we have a father who can teach it to us."

To keep her head from exploding, Kate pressed her hands over her ears and fell back onto the bed. She was wearing a pair of Cliff's outgrown pajamas, with a button missing in front, which prompted me to scrunch down as low as I could get, hoping for a glimpse of one of her budding jugs, as we elegantly called them then. Though I think she sensed what I was up to, she ignored it — Greg after all was still just a snotnose kid.

She sat up again, wagging her head. "Okay, that's it. Cliff is so keen on all this, that's his business. But me and Greg, we just don't give a dog's turd about French or *The Brothers Karamazov.* And we sure ain't gonna do the freaking chicken house on top of it."

This was another of Jason's summer projects for the three of us: scraping and repainting a superfluous chicken house that he intended to turn into a "theater" in which we were to perform those same ancient French plays we refused to study.

"We just ain't gonna scrape all the paint off that thing," Kate said. "And we ain't gonna scrub it and repaint it either. And above all, we ain't gonna convert the freaking place into—what the devil does he call it?—a theatuh in the round! Who for, I'd like to know? Stinking Joe and Emily's kids? I'm not sure they're ready for Tartuffe."

Cliff tried to explain, pointing out how few visitors were dropping in to see Jason now, and consequently how much time he had on his hands.

"Fine," Kate said. "Then let *him* paint the damn thing. We'll conjugate his precious French verbs."

Cliff could barely hold his eyes open. "Please leave, okay?" he asked her. "I still gotta go through my vocabulary."

Kate shook her head and sighed. As she got up I copped the peek I wanted, the bottom curve of one of her tiny jugs. At the bathroom door she stopped.

"Just let me say this, *mes frères*. Old Jason's gonna have to make a choice this summer. His theater or his *français*. He ain't gonna get both."

I had no idea what she had meant by that pronouncement until a few days later, when the two of us were busy scraping paint off the chicken house in ninety-five-degree heat. Cliff was out mending fence with Stinking Joe, Mother was busy with "her" family, and Jason as usual was involved in some vital intellectual pursuit in the air-conditioned comfort of his library. Because the day was so muggy and hot and the labor ahead of us so long and tiresome, I had tried to "turn off my head," which was how I thought of it then, the task of trying to outlast agony. So I was not really aware of what Kate was up to until she was well along with her plans. I did know that she was not scraping her share of the paint, but I didn't know why, not even when a line of laying hens began to file past me, clucking and pecking at the ground as they spread out into the barnyard. I immediately ran around to the front to see how they had escaped from their pen, which adjoined the building. And what I found was Kate crouched inside the wire walls, herding out the last few stragglers. She shushed me with her finger.

"What's up?" I asked.

"You sure you want to know?"

"Tell me."

"Just watch."

With all the chickens liberated, I followed her from the pen into the small building. On a platform against one wall six cans of white exterior paint and two gallons of turpentine had been stacked. Kate picked up one of the bottles of turpentine and emptied it onto some bales of straw, also stacked against the wall. She recapped the bottle, put it back on the platform, and repeated the process with the second bottle. By then I knew what she was doing, but I didn't say a word, possibly because it was so damned mesmerizing, standing there watching a *girl*, my twin sister, casually going about the business of doing what I would never have had the guts to do, not even if I'd had a hundred chicken houses to paint. Finishing with the turpentine, she pulled out a pack of Camels and lit one.

"It'll be my fault," she said, dragging deeply. "I was taking an illegal smoke break, and — "

Casually she flipped the cigarette onto the straw and a sheet of flame roared up the wall.

"And *poof!*" she finished. "There went our *theatuh in the round!*"

We were both running out of the building by then, breathless and excited and scared. At least I was scared. As we ran toward the house I glanced at Kate and saw that she was smiling, a wild joyous smile that struck in my heart the first fear I had ever felt for her. But it failed to last. Within minutes, as I stood with her and the rest of the family watching the chicken house disappear in a tower of flame, all I felt was an awed sense of pride. What other snotnose, I wondered, ever had such a sister as mine?

Two.

The next morning, leaving Toni still asleep in bed, I went downstairs and found Sarah and Junior at the kitchen table reading the Sunday paper and looking for all the world like a typical married couple, silent and weary and bored. Sarah had her hair up in curlers again and was wearing her bulky chenille housecoat, a combination that would have made Cheryl Tiegs look dowdy. As I got a cup of coffee and sat down, she excused herself and hurried back upstairs, saying something about being late for church, which not unexpectedly drew a smirk from Junior.

"Me, it's okay to look like a bum in front of. But big brother—now, that's a different story."

I reminded him that she had to get ready for church, which only made him laugh.

"Listen, I know her better than she knows herself. And for some reason, she actually thinks you're hot shit. Now, ain't that a laugh?"

I toasted him with my coffee. "You're a sweet kid, Junior. You brighten your little corner."

"Amen, brother."

That bitchy exchange must have satisfied him, given the muscles of his animus sufficient workout for the time being, for he became almost pleasant from that point on. I scrambled some eggs and made toast and a glass of reconstituted orange juice. And, sitting down to eat, I scoured the *Tribune* as if I expected to find my story bannered in it: *Unemployed Screenwriter Flees California under Suspicious Circumstances.* But once again the world had failed to take note of my comings and goings, almost as if it had better things to do, such as chronicling the previous night's inventory of mayhem, all the beatings and rapes and shootings and robberies that had occupied the citizenry since the last issue of the paper, twenty-four hours before.

Putting the paper down, I took note of the beautiful day outside.

"Think I'll take a walk around the place," I said. "See how it's holding up."

Junior looked at the clock. "Yeah, you still got time. I'll go with you."

"What do you mean, got time?"

"Before the Lords show up. The barn, it's their clubhouse."

"What *Lords?*"

"The Congo Lords. A gang of neighborhood black kids, teenagers mostly. The barn and the grounds too — it's all pretty much theirs."

"What do you mean — they rent it?"

"After a fashion, yeah. They agree not to burn us out and we agree to let 'em have the barn."

"Beautiful."

Junior shrugged. "Maybe not. But it is survival. And these days, that's the name of the game."

I could not argue that point. And anyway, Toni had just come down the stairs, wearing her own robe for a change, a long green Dragon Lady affair with a split up the side, showing not only her leg but a sizable portion of her derriere as well. Junior noticed.

"Be a good idea, though, if she stays inside," he said. "At least today, when most of 'em show up. No sense stirring up the Lords any more than you have to."

Looking half asleep still, Toni apparently had not heard him.

23

She asked where Sarah was.

"Getting ready for church," I told her.

"You're kidding. What's for breakfast?" She was sitting down, waiting to be served.

I pushed a box of cornflakes over to her. "Nothing fancy."

"But I smell eggs!" she complained.

Junior was already on his feet. "And you shall have some, milady," he said, in a plucky attempt at charm. "And why not some bacon too?"

Toni smiled at him. "Why not?"

Minutes later Sarah came downstairs wearing a flowered dress with sleeves and a flowered hat pinned into her tightly curled hair. As she saw Toni, with no makeup and her hair uncombed and half her ass hanging out, she stumbled off the last stair and almost fell. Her face was crimson as she hurried past, heading for the garage.

"Got to rush," she said. "Sunday school's in twenty minutes."

"Yeah, and it's all of a half mile away." Junior observed.

When she was gone, Toni looked at me in consternation. "How old did you say she is?"

"Thirty-five."

"You could've fooled me."

Outside I found the day much colder than it had looked from the kitchen. A membrane of ice covered the water puddles in the driveway and my breath plumed in the air. Nevertheless it was every inch a beautiful Midwest fall day, bright and crisp, perfect for football. And, oddly, it was that very perfection my eyes found so harsh, for it pitilessly pointed up how ugly everything else had become, in this once lovely place I called home. The lawn that Cliff and I had kept short and smooth with a push mower and weed knife now looked more like a field of beaten-down brush. And the trees were gone too, the dozens of high-rise elms that had shaded the lawn and the driveway as it curved past the house, back to the barn. Now only a few stumps were left, big as poker tables, sad reminders of how virulent the Dutch elm disease of the sixties had been. And, looking down the street and out past the barn at the once handsome hills and fields now scored with roads and cluttered with ramshackle houses and abandoned cars and other junk, I found myself wishing that some simple disease had caused all that too, a disease with a name. Poverty somehow did not quite measure up.

Junior, walking next to me, said that we could go through the barn if I wanted.

"Part of it anyway," he went on. "All except their club rooms."

"What do they do in there?"

"Who knows? I guess they oil their weapons and practice karate and talk about The Day."

"What day?"

"*Our* day. The day we get it."

"That one, eh?"

"And they swap girl friends," he said. "And drink beer and smoke dope. They've had four fires I know about. Fortunately they put 'em all out in time."

Inside, I barely glanced at the opening to the mow, knowing I would see things that were not there. Swallowing my anguish, I sauntered on. And I noticed that the place did not even smell like a barn anymore. The milking stalls, with their open stanchions and dungless floors, looked almost sinister in their emptiness. Our old Holsteins once had filled them like berthed ships, twice a day giving full buckets of warm rich milk, most of which had been fed to our Angus calves, whose mothers had been bred down to such fashionable blockiness that they could not give enough milk even to sustain their own offspring. Farther on, in the loafing shed part of the barn, I looked up through the opening above a manger and saw the great rafters vaulting toward the roof beam and the rail below it, from which the old rusted hayfork hung like some giant spider waiting through the generations to feed again. I thought of the time with the sparrows, that night of death and high excitement.

"Bring back memories?" Junior asked.

"Yeah—lousy ones," I lied. "Did you ever have to milk?"

He shook his head. "Naw — by the time I was old enough to do anything, the cows were gone. Jason had sold them off."

We left the barn through the rear door and started down the path toward the pond, which once had lain like an emerald amid the thick sand of oak and hickory trees that had separated the barnyard from the main pasture. Now most of those trees were gone also, probably because they had lain too close to one of the new roads, across which a row of ranch houses now faced us. I came to the last rise in the path and went over it, expecting to see the pond again, icy at its fringes. Instead there was only a sinkhole, a depression littered from one side to the other with old tires and empty cans and paper and garbage as well as the skeletons of a dog and a burned-out Lincoln Continental.

"Not quite like it was, huh?" Junior said.

"No, it's changed."

He grinned. "Yeah, we don't swim here much anymore. Not enough privacy."

Across the road, a tiny black boy was throwing stones at us, stones that kept dropping short, into the sinkhole. Junior shook his fist at him.

"Debbil gonna git you, boy!" he shouted. "Debbil gonna eat your ass!"

The kid turned and ran, both hands covering his backside. Junior was laughing.

"You know what they call me?" he said. "*Mister* Kendall. Been so long since they seen Jason, they don't even know he's still alive."

On the way back I asked him the inevitable question — why he had stayed on here all these years — and he gave me the same crap that he had given Toni, saying he was a leech and preferred to live off Jason.

"What about women?" I asked.

"I can take 'em or leave 'em."

"But too smart to leave home over them?"

"That's it. I'm too smart."

Talking to him was like playing tennis with a pro: everything came back at you, just out of reach.

As we rounded the barn, heading for the house, I saw two young black men pausing at the barn door to give me the onceover. Junior raised his fist to them in a black power salute. "The Lords rule!" he shouted.

They nodded coolly. One of them said, "Right on, man. '

"This is my brother," Junior said. "My real, honest-to-God blood-brother."

They seemed to know he was having fun with them, but it apparently did not bother them. As we went on into the house, he explained them to me.

"The mean-looking dude is Captain Midnight. The meaner-looking one calls himself Sandman. He's an amateur fighter. They run the Lords. Not to mention the neighborhood."

"But they take sass from you?"

"Well, I'm a special case. I don't count, you see. They think I'm crazy." He said this with a grin, as though he were really getting away with something.

Later that morning, as I sat alone in my room writing some of the forgettable words above, Jason knocked on the door and immediately entered, as if he expected to catch me *flagrante delicto,* schlong in hand. He had come up from downstairs and was breathing hard from the effort, which in turn made him scowl as though his infirmity were somehow my fault. He wobbled across the room and sank into the bentwood rocker there like a man lowering himself into a hot bath.

"What do you do up here?" he asked.

"Sleep. Write. Make love."

He shook his head in knowing contempt. "Always the wiseacre. Even now, when you're—how old are you now?"

"Forty-three."

That made him snort. "Middle-aged. Almost old yourself. But still a wiseacre."

I asked him what he wanted, which made his bushy eyebrows ride up.

"What is this? Can't I visit my own son in my own house? Is that against the law now?"

"No, but I'm working," I explained.

"*Working?*"

"I'm writing. That's what I do. I'm a writer."

He pretended to be impressed by this bit of news. "Oh yes, now I remember. And what was that last motion picture you *wrote?* Last one I heard about anyway? *Passing Through,* wasn't that it? The one we couldn't take Mother to, because it was so filthy."

"The one that got a nomination, you mean. But that wasn't my last film, Jason."

"Oh? And did they get even dirtier after that?"

"Naturally. The most recent one was all fucking. No dialogue at all."

My response seemed to please him. "And still the wiseacre."

"That's me, all right. Listen, you wouldn't want to do this some other time, would you?"

"Why? Is what you're scribbling there so important?"

"It passes the time."

"Well, I can do that too, you know."

Accepting my fate then, I swiveled the desk chair to face him and lit a cigarette, only to hear him comment on the unwisdom of "that filthy habit." He then asked me about Toni, wondering why such a pretty young women would sell herself so cheap, living with a man without benefit of marriage. Why, a girl like that certainly should have been able to find herself a husband in Hollywood, he said, somebody more her own age, somebody rich and successful, maybe a producer of some kind. I suggested that perhaps she had a weakness for wiseacres, but Jason ignored that. He expressed a keen interest in my matrimonial history since my last home visit, for Mother's funeral, as if he didn't already know it by heart, and I dryly explained to him that I'd been married only twice in my life, once to Janet Murphy, who was suing me for nonsupport of my two teenage daughters (that lie again), and most recently to Ellen Brubaker, the Santa Barbara millionairess, as he habitually referred to her.

Had I liked it, living off a rich women like that? Hadn't it made me feel less of a man? Well no, not really. And what was it that made that marriage too go sour finally? Was it the usual, that I hadn't bothered to listen to my marriage vows and had gone on living the life of a "swinging Hollywood bachelor"?—yes, that was the very phrase he used. So what could I except nod and mumble that, yes, it possibly had been something like that, a failure of some sort or other. But I had made the lady happy, I said, so happy in fact that she had given me a boat—a yacht—as a divorce present.

"*Divorce* present! Never heard of such a thing before."

His black eyes seemed to glow with the effort to read me correctly. I could see the near-panic in him, the fear that he was being ridiculed in some subtle "Hollywood" way. And I could almost hear his mind turning over, seeking some safer ground from which to attack again. His hands, on the arms of the rocker, would not lie still. They stroked and drummed the wood.

"You know, Gregory, we never did talk much about that last summer, did we? The summer you left?"

I pretended that the floor was not opening under me. "What is there left to say?"

He forced a laugh out of his wheezing lungs. "*What is there to say?* Oh, I'd think quite a lot. Your brother and your twin are in a terrible accident. Clifford dies—" Even now he couldn't speak the truth of it, couldn't get his mouth around the more exact word. "—Kate is so terribly hurt."

"I know all this, Jason."

"And maybe you know *more* too. That's all I'm asking."

"What more?"

"Like what were they doing alone in the car? Where were their dates? It was early to be coming home from the dance, wasn't it?"

"It was a long time ago."

"Not for me. It's like yesterday."

I shrugged and squirmed, wishing his goddamn eyes would wander from mine for even a second. But they would not. "Well, I don't know what happened. I didn't understand then, and I don't understand now."

29

"I see." His hands continued to drum on the chair. "You don't understand any of that, eh? Well then, maybe you can help me with this—*why did you leave?* Why did you run off when Kate was still in a coma?"

He waited for my answer, long heavy seconds that went on and on. But I said nothing. And he continued.

"You know, there were times when she looked like she would come out of it."

"*Come out of it?*" I almost laughed at his choice of words. I almost cried.

"You don't know! You weren't there!"

"The hell I wasn't. I went to the hospital, Jason. I *saw* her."

"*Once!*"

"Twice."

"Big deal."

"It was enough."

"Didn't it ever occur to you that if you'd stayed, she might have hung on?"

"As what?"

"As a human being!" He flung the words at me like a curse.

"A vegetable, don't you mean? A faceless, brain-damaged, paraplegic Cyclops! What did such a creature as that have to do with Kate! I didn't leave Kate! I left—"

"*You left her to die!*" he broke in. "You left us to bury her! You left us with nothing."

I had gotten up by then, knocking over the desk chair in my haste to get out of the range of his eyes. Standing at the window, I shakily lit another cigarette. Outside I saw a tall black youth bouncing a tennis ball off the side of the barn, over the heads of other Congo Lords gathered around the door, loafing and sitting in the sun. One of them had his knife out and was busily carving letters into the wood, perhaps only his own initials and not some casual threat of death and destruction. As I watched, a door opened and Junior miraculously appeared, followed by a black kid who looked both edgy and angry. Junior said something to him, but the kid turned away and headed for the street. The one bouncing the tennis ball laughingly called out to him and got the finger in response. Junior ambled toward the house.

Without turning, I finally spoke. "Well, you've said it, old man. You got it all out. So why not leave now, okay? I've still got some 'scribbling' to do."

A few moments later I heard the rocker creaking as he pushed himself laboriously to his feet. He shuffled to the door and stopped, already breathing hard. I waited.

"Do you have any idea how much we needed you?" he asked.

I continued to stand at the window, looking out upon the bright November day. And I said nothing, not until I heard the door close behind him. And then I whispered the words. I fogged the window with them.

"Do you have any idea how much I needed to leave?"

It is growing dark now. Sarah is gone again, attending some function at her school, which she and her colleagues call Combat High. Toni and Junior meanwhile have been downstairs playing cards and drinking beer most of the afternoon. Occasionally she will come up to our room and work me over: *What is it, you too good for the rest of us? You gonna LIVE up here finally, take your meals here, for God's sake? Well that's fine, it's okay with me, you can sleep with that lousy diary if that's what you want. You can have sex with it.*

And then she is gone and I hear laughter in the kitchen, hers and especially Junior's, and I wonder if he's beginning now to dream the big dream, yokel that he is, not knowing what an Olympian cockteaser he's in with. Still, there is also the little matter of what I saw out the window earlier. If no other "Lords" had been around, no one except Junior and the slender kid emerging guiltily from the barn, then I might have had something more than this nasty, nettling suspicion that my little brother may be a bit of a pederast. But immediately I realize that the idea simply doesn't wash, basically because Junior otherwise certainly seems straight enough, perhaps even as relentlessly heterosexual as his cunt-crazed older brother if that is possible. So I discount the idea. I laugh at it. Almost.

From the barn, even as far away as it is, the sound of recorded soul music—Rick James, Brick, Michael Jackson—booms against my window. Occasionally there is shouting or laughter or a crash of some kind, though I have yet to hear the gunfire that Junior says erupts now and then, as the Lords, in brief bursts of high spirits, shoot holes in the barn roof. And I remember another time, when Stinking Joe came up with a solution to our persistent barn sparrow problem.

Joe was unchallengeably a member of the old school, especially when it came to dress, favoring overalls and heavy blue workshirts and woolen long johns that he did not believe in overwashing, to the extent that each morning's first sweat would waken the miasma already slumbering in the wool. It was in fact not unlike a diurnal uncapping of the septic tank—and the only remarkable thing about the man. Otherwise he was ruthlessly ordinary: middle-aged, average size, and no more stupid or lazy than our other hired men had been. It was only behind his back, however, that Kate and I called him *Stinking* Joe. But Cliff did not even approve of that.

"If he hears you, it'll hurt the man's feelings," he remonstrated. "Is that what you want?"

"It might get him to wash," Kate said.

"Why should he? He's just a farm worker."

"Yeah—a *stinking* farm worker."

Like most of our arguments, it was never resolved. Cliff would take the high road and Kate the low road, with me usually trailing along after her, for no better reason than that her way always seemed so much more fun than his.

In any event, on this occasion Stinking Joe said he knew a sure way to get rid of the sparrows inhabiting the barn and fouling the fresh hay bales stacked there. It had to be a nighttime operation, he said, and the only tools we would need were Ping-Pong paddles, a flashlight, and two pans to beat against each other. When he explained further, Cliff demurred, saying that it wasn't a humane way to kill the birds, which only confused Stinking Joe and exasperated Kate.

"For God's sake, Cliff, they're only freaking sparrows. How the devil should we kill them—with sleeping pills?"

"Well, I don't want any part of it."

"So what else is new? You can stay down here and work on some freaking merit badge for all we care." She turned to Stinking Joe. "Let's go. We're ready if you are."

With our flashlight and paddles and pans, the three of us went up the ladder into the mow and climbed the mountainous stacks of hay bales, Stinking Joe heading for one end of the barn while Kate and I made our way to the other. We had to get to the very top, at that point under the peak where the upper haymow doors were kept open, to vent the still-fresh hay. Following Joe's instructions, we closed and hooked the doors and fashioned a platform of hay bales to stand on. Kate had taken one paddle while I had the other one and the flashlight. Joe meanwhile had reached the opposite end; under the peak.

"You kids ready?" he called.

"Damn right we are!" was Kate's answer.

All along the rail above us we could hear the rustling of the birds, hundreds of them. And to my shame, I kept wondering if what we were about to do was wrong, if for no other reason than that my big brother disapproved of it. At the same time my heart raced with excitement and anticipation.

"Well, turn it on, stupid," I heard Kate say.

And I did just that, shining the flashlight straight ahead, toward Stinking Joe. Immediately he began to make a racket, yelling and banging the pans against each other, and within a few seconds the rustling of the sparrows became a roar, a dry desperate beating sound that made me grip the paddle tightly as the first of the birds arrived, right in front of me, winging toward the light which it thought promised escape and freedom. And I swung, hitting it like a shuttlecock, swatting it back and down. At the same time, I heard the splat of Kate's paddle striking another of the birds, and she let out a squeal of delight. But quickly there were more upon us and we both kept swinging, while Joe continued to shout and bang his pans

33

together at the other end of the haymow. The sparrows came at us in such numbers that most of them escaped, but only to fly back toward Joe and the racket which promptly made them turn again and head once more for the light. It seemed almost like a game for them, a game of death in which they kept trying over and over to score, until they finally did, almost all of them.

For a while I continued to think that it was excitement I was feeling, something kindred to Kate's reveling squeal. But then I began to realize that what I really felt was desperation, a cold-sweating, gut-clenching longing for it all to be over and done and for us to be out of there. And finally the birds did stop coming. What few were left must have called on some unknowing instinct for species survival as they fluttered to the safety of the rafters, perches where my flashlight's treacherous promise could not reach them. I lowered the light then, only to see the feathered carnage at our feet, and below, on the bales of hay there. At the same time, in the dimness, I saw Cliff's head peering up out of the ladder opening far below us, and in my mind I saw what he saw, the flash moving in the blackness, flickering over me and Kate and the scattered, the mounded, sparrows at our feet. I wanted to yell at him to get out, to run, but Kate's voice beat me.

"Boy, you missed it, Cliff! You really missed it!"

Coming down from the mow, Stinking Joe allowed that it had been a good job well done. His excitement was right up there with Kate's and I would not have been surprised if the two of them had performed a little jig in celebration. But Cliff as usual had a problem.

"What about all the dead ones?" he asked. "You just gonna leave them up there for the cats to eat?"

Kate gave me a wry look. "Jesus, there he goes again—his holiness himself."

"So the cats have a little feast tonight," Joe said. "What kin that hurt? Less for me to clean up in the morning."

Cliff turned away from us. He picked up a rock and winged it against a tree in the yard, an angry, deadly shot. Stinking Joe raised his hand in parting as he headed for his rattletrap pre-war Ford. And Kate gave me a punch on the arm.

"Come on, squirt, let's get rid of this sweat." She was already starting down the path toward the pond.

I motioned for Cliff to come along, but he just stood there under the polelight, blond and gangling and suffering, a spirit not really designed for life in this world of red teeth and claws. Finally, though, he shrugged and came along, following us through the trees to the pond, which rang in the warm night air with the racket of crickets and frogs and cicadas.

When we were younger, the three of us had often gone swimming nude, and without thinking much about it, this casual baring of our sexual difference. And I imagine that if Cliff or I had ever said anything to point up that difference, Kate would have taken a poke at us. In later years, however, and especially after Cliff and Kate reached puberty, we either swam in bathing clothes or peeled down to our underwear and dove in. And this last was what I had expected us to do that night, mostly because I didn't think there was any other alternative. But then I was not reckoning with the intensity of Kate's anger at Cliff, how deeply she resented his censure and how badly she needed to get even with him, in any way she could.

She and I had reached the pond first and were already shucking off our shirts and jeans when Cliff arrived. But Kate did not stop there. Clearly lit by the distant polelight, she slipped out of her bra and panties and stepped to the edge of the rickety dock, smiling insolently back at Cliff while I stood there and gawked in my jockey shorts. She still had the hardness of a boy, with long sleek legs and a flat belly, but there was a subtle curvaceousness to her now that I had never seen before, a difference symbolized by the diamond of dark hair between her legs. Her breasts were the size of peaches and so beautiful to me that I immediately had to dive into the pond to hide my swift erection. When I came to the surface I saw that she had disappeared too, though only for a few seconds as her head came popping up out of the water now between me and Cliff, who was still standing fully dressed on the grassy bank.

"Here I am again!" she cried. "Kate the bird-killer! The stripteaser!"

"You go too far," Cliff said to her. "Lately all you want to do is shock people. You don't seem to know right from wrong."

Still smiling at him, she treaded water. "Come on, Saint Clifford—take it off and join us. Take it all off."

While Cliff did nothing, I impulsively pulled off my own shorts and threw them up onto the dock, too late remembering how small and hairless I still was between my legs.

Kate laughed happily. "There! See, your holiness? It's easy— you just peel 'em off and jump in."

Cliff went over and got my shorts and threw them back to me in the water. "Don't you be an ass too, Greg," he said.

This time, for emphasis, I sailed the shorts over his head. He looked at Kate again.

"Now you've got *him* all screwed up. You proud of yourself? And he's just a kid."

"Fuck you, Cliff!" I yelled at him. "Why don't you go home and *study* something!"

"That's just what I'll do," he said, leaving the dock. "You two infants can stay here and shock one another. Big deal."

His leaving seemed the last straw for Kate. Yelling, she began to strike her fist against the water. "Go on, get out of here, you holy bastard! You freaking self-righteous bastard! You freaking asshole!"

When he was gone, she continued to flail away at the water, and finally I saw that she was crying. "Just a bunch of birds!" she got out. "A bunch of goddamn sparrows! And he can't even do that! He's too good! Too noble! Well, screw him! Just screw the freaking saint!"

In a fury, she swam back to the dock and took hold of the ladder, preparing to pull herself up. And without really knowing what I was doing, I had followed her there and now took hold of her from behind, on her hips, just as I'd done dozens of times before, to pull her back into the water. Only this time I found myself holding on to flesh—the bare flesh of a woman.

She turned in my hands and brutally shoved my head under water. Humilated, I pushed off from the ladder and didn't surface until I reached the center of the pond. By then, she was on the dock dressing.

"I'm sorry, little brother," she said. "I'm just so damn mad. Why can't he go along, like he used to? Just the three of us. But he won't. He's too weird. Just too freaking weird."

I could see the tears still shining in her eyes and I guess that was something I was not supposed to see, for she ran off then, swiftly, just like Cliff or me, just like one of the boys.

I don't know why it is that I remember that night so clearly, whether it was the dark trauma of the bird slaughter or my first real look at Kate as a woman. Either one of those things probably would have been sufficient to fix those hours in my mind, but together I see the two events now—and I see that night—as a kind of dividing line, a wall suddenly flung up across the paths of our lives. During those hours we lost some incalculable measure of innocence, and it seemed that from that point on Kate and Cliff cemented themselves ever more firmly into the positions they had taken then, with the result that things were never again quite the same between the three of us.

I also can't help thinking of the sparrows, all those doomed birds flying so eagerly toward their destruction, a memory that invariably brings to mind the verses in the Bible affirming that God has our hairs numbered and knows when even a sparrow falls. But I wonder—does He really? Those scores of tiny feathered corpses at my feet, were they numbered and remembered? Or is it that dinosaurs and civilizations pass on, and sparrows and stars and brothers and sisters—and the heavens never blink?

Three

Let me describe this place for you. As I said earlier, it is a typical two-story farmhouse, with nine rooms including the one in the basement. The porch runs across the front of the house and is about twelve feet deep, more than adequate for the old chain-hung swing that Kate and I used to fly like a spaceship, swinging it sideways higher and higher until it finally would strike the house at one end of its trajectory and bring Jason storming out of his library to punish us, usually with a tongue-lashing.

The double front doors open into a foyer dominated by the stairway to the second floor. To the left is the living room, which is reasonably spacious and filled with a small fortune in antique furniture. At the rear of the room is the doorway to Jason's library, a room I once considered the central locus of power on earth, specifically the huge oak desk from which he could look out upon his fields and cattle in one direction and upon his supplicants in the other, spread out over a black leather sofa and two matching chairs.

Returning to the foyer, one enters the dining room on the right and continues past the downstairs bathroom to the kitchen, which is almost as large as the living room, including a pantry that one could stock for Armageddon. There is an antique woodburning stove as well as an electric range and the usual applicances: a refrigerator, a sarcophagus-sized freezer, and so on. One doorway opens onto the side entry porch and another onto the back porch, which is as large as the one in front, but enclosed, a catch-all for a half century of family living. The narrow back stairway (the one on which Sarah almost fell the other day) also opens into the kitchen, making it even more the center of activity and traffic in the house.

The upstairs is equally spacious if equally unexciting: five bedrooms and the one bathroom as well as the "sleeping porch"—the screened-in upper level of the back porch, where Cliff, Kate, and I sometimes slept in the summer, on cots we often used as trampolines.

And there you have it, a brief tour of this place to which I've repaired in order to escape the fed-narcs and their fellow inquisitors in the L.A. Police Department. Now, you may wonder what kind of sense this makes, to hide out in one's ancestral home. But what you don't know is that after leaving here at eighteen, I had a somewhat unnatural passion for severing the ties that bind. Oh, I wrote to my mother occasionally or called her on the phone, kept her and Jason at least vaguely informed as to where I was and what I was doing. But otherwise—in any documents I signed and in any applications I made—I invariably referred to myself as an orphan, partially because it abbreviated the amount of writing and explaining I had to do, but also because it satisfied some puerile need I had for secrecy and self-dramatization—not to mention revenge. For I believed then, just as I do now, that if Jason had been less a martinet and more a father, Cliff would not have done what he did. But then I don't want to get into all that now (the sun is still out as I write this and my blood is running scared). Rather I'm just trying to explain why I gathered up Toni and my few belongings and came all this way: not only because the food and lodging are the right price but also because I trusted the sluggard federal functionaries not to trace me here.

In any case, here we are. And here I sit filling the old legal pads. Across the room, Toni is lying on her back in the unmade bed, making a game out of applying nail polish to her toes. Occasionally she sighs and gives me one of her sex-bomb looks or she will twist onto her side to accent the mind-bending curve of her hip in the white Dacron pajamas she's still wearing, in the middle of the afternoon. For her, sex is becoming a release from boredom, and I wonder if I will even be able to walk after a few more weeks. Forty-three is not twenty-three, but then I don't want to remind her of that. What's so great about walking anyway?

Last night, waking at Scott Fitzgerald's favorite hour, I went downstairs to make coffee and smoke some cigarettes (my own eccentric if unproven formula for getting back to sleep) and found that Sarah had already beaten me to the punch, so to speak—in this case, a bottle of Cutty Sark. As was her habit, she began to tug at her robe and fuss with her hair rollers.

"Well, you caught me," she said. "The secret toper."

"Now, that's a word you don't hear every day."

"You mean it's old-fashioned. Which I'm such an expert at."

I got a glass and sat down, pouring myself a few fingers of the scotch. "No, that's not what I meant," I told her. "I meant it's a good solid old Anglo-Saxon word, which most of us unfortunately are too inarticulate to use."

"But not me." She toasted herself. "The English teacher. The Burnout of Combat High."

"Burnout?"

"That's what we pedagogues call it, when you can't take it anymore. When you just give up and draw your salary and let 'em graduate illiterate. Most of my juniors couldn't read Dick and Jane, but they can push you around. And they can stab you. We've had one teacher stabbed and two beaten up just in the last semester."

"That bad, eh?"

She made a gesture of futility and tipped up her glass again. "Which is one of the reasons for our vote tonight. Your little sister is now on strike."

This was the first I had heard of any strike and I asked her why she hadn't told us about it earlier, when she came home from the teachers' meeting at the school. She shrugged and said there was no particular reason, except that she seemed to have a hard time getting a word in edgewise lately.

"No matter what I say, no one seems to hear anymore," she said. "Everybody just looks right through me. Like I wasn't there."

"Oh come on, Sarah," I protested. "That can't be true."

"Oh no? Listen, when your Toni's around, I might as well crawl in a hole. Which is exactly where I wish I were most of the time."

I pretended to be indignant, insisting that when I was with the two of them, I was just as aware of her as I was of Toni, and probably more so, because her interests were broader and she had more to say on a wider variety of subjects. But this only made her pat my hand indulgently.

"Good try, Greg," she said. "But I know what I am—boring and dowdy. Which is okay. I'm used to it. And I could live with it—until *she* came here."

"Toni doesn't mean anything, Sarah. She—"

"She just *is*—yeah. And that's the tough part. She probably doesn't even know how she looks at me."

"How's that?"

"Like I've been in a car wreck."

"Oh, come on. You're exaggerating."

She poured more scotch into our glasses. "Maybe so. But then there's Junior—the way she's turned him into a lap dog. The surliest bastard in Woodglen is suddenly all sweetness and smiles. Tell me—do you worry how much time he spends with her?"

"When I'm busy, what else is there for her to do?"

"That's no answer."

"All right, then—no, I don't worry. Toni likes to work the audience. She always has. But she's straight."

"Good point."

"How so?"

Sarah smiled impishly. "Because our dear brother ain't."

"Ain't what?"

"Ain't straight. As in ain't heterosexual."

"No kidding."

My reaction obviously disappointed her. "You don't seem all that surprised."

"I had an inkling."

"That's odd. He's usually so careful to hide it. Afraid Jason will find out, I guess."

"Why? Don't you think the old man would approve?"

Sarah laughed at that. "No, not hardly."

"Well, how's he kept it from him all these years? I would assume it isn't a recent aberration."

"I don't know. In fact, I didn't know it myself until a few years ago. He doesn't exactly flaunt it. I guess he was what you call a closet—well, you know."

"Queen."

She shrugged. "Somehow the word doesn't fit him."

"No, it doesn't."

"And yet I guess that's why he's stayed here all these years— because of all the boys around. All the *black* boys."

"Could be."

She sat there for a time smoking and sipping at her drink. Finally she stubbed out her cigarette.

"Greg," she said, "would you mind if I took off for a while? Say, a week or so?"

"Of course not. But where would you go?"

"Miami, I think. I've got some money saved. And I figure the strike will last for months. Maybe all year. We want a twenty-five-percent raise and the district is broke. So you figure it out."

"You'd go alone?"

"Sure. Alone I can handle. But this house I can't. Not right now anyway."

"I see."

Again she reached for my hand. "Oh listen, it isn't you. If you'd come back alone, you know I wouldn't leave. You do know that, don't you?"

"Sure, honey. We'll be fine. Don't worry about us."

"Well, I will worry—about you, anyway. And Jason. If you're gonna eat, Junior will just have to let loose of some of his shekels for a change and buy the groceries."

"Junior?"

"Sure. You didn't know he's the family moneybags?"

"Can't say I did."

What she told me then I found more than a little surprising. It seems that as far back as the seventy-four recession, Jason had convinced himself that the western world was going to suffer an economic collapse and that Woodglen Estates was going to become even more a jungle than it already was. His fear of the neighborhood blacks was such, Sarah claimed, that he had not set foot out of the house in over three years. And because he believed that Junior "had a way with them," he begged him to stay on. But Junior, never a slouch at divining his own best interests, would not commit himself until Jason finally agreed to meet his price.

"How much?" I asked.

Sarah shook her head. "All I know is that Jason's savings are gone. And I think he cashed in some Krugerrands he had too. I guess Junior got every one of them. Each year, as the old man got more paranoid, Junior must have simply raised the ante."

If the house had not been so still, I probably would have whistled, so impressed was I by my little brother's mendacity.

"But where do you come in?" I asked.

Sarah gestured at the walls around us. "The house. This decrepit old turkey. I guess it goes to me. And you—I'm afraid you only get his best wishes."

"That'll be the day. But then I never expected anything. At the same time, I don't like the idea of little Tan Pants winding up with it all either. And at your expense."

She shrugged indifferently. "He considers it income. His pay for staying on with us. And maybe he's right. I'm not sure Jason and I could have carried on here alone. I don't think the old man would've ever slept. Even now he worries all the time about being burned out."

It would have been nice if the conversation had ended there, but it did not. Sarah said nothing for a time, just sat there staring down at her drink. Then, with a pained smile, she finally looked up at me again.

"How come you never stayed before?" she asked. "I mean, the other times, it was just for a day or two."

"I was busier then, I guess. My scripts were more in demand."

She ignored the explanation. "Was it Cliff and Kate? Because of what happened to them? And you just couldn't stand it here after that?"

"Something like that."

She smiled happily. "I thought so. When I was little, I figured it was me. Or all of us. I figured that maybe you just didn't like us. And so you never came."

She waited, but I could not think of a thing to say. I poured another drink for myself.

"It's funny," she went on. "I barely remember you from when I was a kid, before you left. And then you dropped in—what was it—four times in all these years? And yet somehow I feel closer to you than I do to Junior. Does that make any sense?"

"Sure. The more you're with a male Kendall, the harder they are to take."

It was a limp attempt at levity, at lightening the moment, and all it got was a wan smile. But I think that Sarah did get my message: that I had no desire to talk about the whys and wherefores of my long exile from home.

After she had gone back to bed, I remained there in the kitchen for a while, working on the scotch and mulling over the other matters she had touched upon. Though I'd already had an inkling that Junior was homosexual—as I'd explained to her—I was still surprised at having the suspicion confirmed. Other people have gay brothers, not I. At the same time I have to admit that this alleged homosexuality of Junior's makes it easier for me to deal with the other part of Sarah's revelations— that he now holds the family purse strings—which could only have enhanced his appeal for Toni. Now, though, the matter seems moot. Junior's interest in her would appear to be sexual only in the narrow deviant sense, in that she is the kind of woman he has always wanted to be. Or at least that is how I interpret the curious adulation the gay community always seems to whip up for the Marilyns of the world.

But enough of my little brother. The thing that really fascinates me in all this is *how* he came into his bank account, the idea that Jason would simply surrender it to him out of fear and timidity. For whatever weaknesses I may have thought my father possessed, timidity was never one of them. In fact, of all the men I've ever known, I would say that Jason is easily the most cocksure, most overbearing, most arrogant sonofabitch of them all. Why then this sudden fever of self-doubt and cowardice? Could it have been simply a matter of age, an old man coming to terms with his diminished strength and faculties? If so, then I still can't think of a less likely candidate than Jason Kendall, if for no other reason than that in all the years I've known him, the man has never exhibited the slightest talent for self-knowledge. To the contrary, I think he always had himself convinced just as he did Cliff and Kate and me that it was his destiny to lead and to rule. The fact that he temporarily had to make do with ruling his family instead of a state or nation never confused us — or him, I'm sure — as to what his ultimate lot would be. He was our Napoleon waiting out his exile in the cool Elba of the library.

I don't imagine you would be surprised to learn that Jason was an only child whose mommy was rich and his daddy good-looking. My grandmother was distantly related to the Chicago McCormicks and inherited a comfortable amount of stock in International Harvester, which her husband, a dabbler in women, liquor, and public relations, kept whittling away in various star-crossed ventures until finally there was only the hundred and sixty-some thousand dollars left to pass on to Jason. In the meantime, though, he had managed to live reasonably high on the hog, getting his bachelor's degree from Northwestern and doing graduate study in philosophy at Yale and at the Sorbonne. He toured Europe and the Middle East and later tried his hand at being a playboy and then a businessman (a travel agent) but ultimately gave them both up in favor of farming. And I never really have understood this either: why a rich, well-educated young man would freely elect to retreat to the country and start a cattle farm, unless of course he happened to like animals, the out-of-doors, and manual labor, none of which Jason ever demonstrated the slightest affection for. That paradox has been scratching away at my brain stem for longer than I care to remember. My guess is that somewhere along the way—in the Yale library perhaps or sitting on a quay next to the Seine—he got this vision of himself as Squire Kendall strolling over his fields while thinking deep thoughts about Jefferson and agrarian democracy and a Return to the Land. I imagine that he saw himself as a kind of practical Thoreau, a *pater familias* living out his belief in the philosophic line running from Rousseau on down through Jefferson and Warren and all the other bucolic crackpots since. (Jefferson a *crackpot?*)

In any event, he bought this place and moved here with Cliff and my mother (then pregnant with Kate and me) when he was only twenty-six. And here he has stayed ever since, living off his modest inheritance and overseeing the operation of the farm and—except for his brief flyer at politics—somehow filling his time with random reading, cranky causes, and the care and feeding and intimidation of his offspring. Especially Cliff. Poor Cliff.

From what you've read so far, I imagine you have formed the notion that Cliff was something of a prig, not wanting to kill sparrows and all that. If you have, then the fault is mine and I will try to correct it as I go along, for in reality Cliff was nothing like that. He was prudent, yes, but never prudish. And I guess you might say that he was *other-directed,* in that once modish phrase, a boy who all his life wanted desperately to please grown-ups. Especially Jason. And I can't see that there was anything unusual in that. I myself, like most children, had a strong desire to please my parents, and I don't doubt that I would have gone even further in that direction if Kate had not always been at my ear, whispering contrariness and mischief. But the real problem for Cliff wasn't so much in his constant need to please Jason as it was in the standards that Jason set for him. All his young life Cliff was like a high-jumper continually setting records, only to have his coach grumpily move the bar yet another notch higher.

I remember the time that Mother, Kate, and I went to see Cliff's investiture as a First Class Boy Scout, a rank he had attained as quickly as the rules allowed. On the way home Mother suggested that we stop at the Eskimo and celebrate over some ice-cream sundaes, but Cliff begged to go straight on home so he could show Jason his First Class medal. And Mother of course relented, with the result that all of us were soon trekking into the library, acutely aware that we were interrupting Jason in some vital musing or other. In his spiffy khakis, Cliff shyly stepped forward, his eyes shining as brightly as the new medal pinned to his shirt. But Jason did not bother to get up, merely swiveled sideways in his desk chair and gave the medal a cursory examination before looking up at Cliff with an almost bored expression on his face.

"Yes, that's fine," he said. "But of course it's only a beginning. You've still got a long way to go to become an Eagle Scout, haven't you?"

Cliff gulped and nodded. And he went right back and jumped a little higher. He became a Star Scout and finally an Eagle Scout. He also was valedictorian in grade school and in high school he maintained a three-point-nine grade average while joining numerous clubs and earning yearly letters in track and basketball, all in addition to a part-time job he held at the Eskimo and an almost full-time job at home, helping me and Stinking Joe keep the farm and the cattle in that state of high gloss Jason deemed appropriate for a true country gentleman. And what sort of reaction did all this industry elicit from Jason? Mostly silence, a kind of glum acceptance of it as only his due, what every father had a right to expect. In fact, I don't think he ever spoke to Cliff about his accomplishments except in a negative way, as when he would point out an occasional local newspaper article about this or that high school star in track or basketball, someone who was doing better than Cliff. Why did Cliff think that was, Jason would ask him. Was it because the boy had more natural talent? Or was it because he had "worked harder than my son"?

Though Cliff never seemed to have an answer, Kate usually did.

"It's because he's a Negro, Jason. Didn't you notice?"

Toni has long since left her bed of nails (I'm a sucker for that kind of pun) and now she has returned from downstairs and the afternoon television soaps, still wearing the white pajamas and her hurricane hairdo. She hovers behind my chair—pouting, I have no doubt—occasionally brushing my shoulder with a glossy hip.

"What are you gonna call it?" she asks.

"Call what?"

"This phone book you're writing."

"I'm not sure. How about *Me and My Diary?*"

"How about *Killing Toni?*"

"That's good too."

"Well, that's what you're doing, you know."

"Is that a fact?"

"Yes, it's a fact!" she snaps. "Outside it's all ice and spades. You can't lay out in the sun. You can't swim. And inside there ain't a damn thing but TV and Junior. And he's really beginning to bore me, you know that?"

"I wasn't sure."

"I'm going crazy here, Greg. I really am. I'm flipping out. So please. *Please.* Let's leave. Okay?"

"Sure. You got any money?"

"You could call your friends, couldn't you? All those high and mighty Malibu friends of yours. A couple of thousand, they wouldn't even miss it."

"The police would beat the money here."

"Then you've got some real neat friends, mister." She sags onto the edge of the bed. "So that's it, then? Here we stay. In this ugly old icebox, and with nothing to do but sit here and watch you scratching away? That's it, huh? That's my fate?"

"That's it, all right. For now anyway."

"Greg, I'm serious."

"Go wash your hair," I tell her. "Go take a bath."

On her way past, she slugs me in the arm, hard enough to make me drop my Bic. But the important thing is that she is gone and I am free again. In my mind I try to pick up the thread, some raveling line leading back to where I left off, but all I hear is the water running into the tub beyond the door, and now her body, sloshing, making more noise than she normally does. The Bic becomes like a bird in my fingers, drifting here and there, refusing to light upon the paper. And I wait—no more than a dozen seconds.

"Honey," she calls. "Come here, will you?"

I stand in the doorway. "What's the trouble?"

Her smile is a work of art, coquettish and rueful. "I'm so dirty. I doubt if I could ever get myself clean."

In the water she is a beguiling archipelago, her breasts a pair of perfect little islands, her hip and right thigh a steeply plunging peninsula.

"You're interrupting my work," I say, my father's son.

She sticks out her lower lip à la Shirley Temple. "Don't you want me to be clean?"

I don't answer her because by then I'm already rolling up my sleeve. I take the bar of Dove and begin to soap her, giving special attention to her breasts and groin. And she just lies there soaking up her pleasure like a sponge, not closing her eyes or even averting them as any other woman would do. Even as my fingers enter her she does not look away. Her mouth peels back in an expression of raw animal gratification that is, I know, a thing of fearsome beauty. Yet, flaming phony that I am, I feel not just sexual excitement but also a slight touch of revulsion, wondering why she can't experience at least an occasional moment of shame amidst all the throes of her raging natu-ralness. I realize that this thought never crosses my mind when I am similarly engaged with her, or when she is ministering to my own specific needs, but then I never professed to be overly fair-minded. All I know is that if I had been in her position and she in mine, I would have had a hard time not looking away from her at least, if for no other reason than out of simple loyalty to the family name. I am sure Jason would never have lain back in the tub with bared teeth and open eyes while Mother stroked him home. We Kendalls are a proud, if fraudulent, people.

In any case, my lovely Toni does not close her eyes until she is coming, and then only because her paroxysms probably leave her no choice in the matter. As she lies back finally, stretching and smiling, I resist an impulse to push her head under the water and hold it there, for never in my life have I had an orgasm even half as long as this marathon one of hers. Nor, I don't doubt, has any other man. I feel cheated for all of us.

"Feel clean now?" I ask.

"Some," she admits. "But I could be cleaner."

"Really?"

"Well, sure. It'd be better than scribbling, wouldn't it?" To set the hook deeper she rolls onto her tummy, thrusting her enthralling bum up out of the water. "I might even let you do it your way."

By then of course there is no hope for me. I lock the door and begin to shuck off my clothes.

"You don't play fair, baby," I croak. "But, Jesus, I do love you for it."

four

We were in the third grade at the time, which meant that Miss Josephson was our teacher, just as she had been for a generation of third-graders before us. A short, sturdy, gray-haired woman, she seemed to know all there was to know about everything and had no compunction about sharing it with us. Whenever the male principal visited our class she treated him with great deference and rigorously put us through our paces, accepting his authority as naturally as she did her own spinsterhood and a salary that prevented her from even owning a car. She was, in short, a thoroughly exploited woman—and thoroughly indifferent to that fact.

If she had any weakness, it lay in her love for sing-along songs such as "Row, Row, Row Your Boat" and "She'll Be Coming Around the Mountain." Every afternoon for thirty minutes she would sit down at the corner upright piano and begin to bang out the song for the day, lifting her right hand from the keyboard every now and then to direct us as we sat at our scarred little desks, most of us barely mumbling the words to the song, leaving the real singing to three or four gung-ho girls and Miss Josephson herself. Spitballs and paper clips would begin to fly and the comedians among us would do brief clandestine parodies of Miss Josephson thumping away at the keyboard, bounding up and down on her generous hams.

One exception to this general anarchy was on the day she had us sing "Katy." Then even the boys joined in, loudly, happily mangling the tune in their eagerness to embarrass my twin.

K-K-K-Katy, beautiful Katy
You're the only g-g-g-girl that I adore.

Kate meanwhile sat at her desk with her arms folded and her eyes raking the songsters, promising them mayhem on the playground after school. I of course had joined in too, unable to pass up an opportunity to torment a female, even if she was my sister. And even now I can hear the piano and that unharmonious squall of voices. I remember looking over at Kate and trying to smile, but giving it up as she glared back at me.

When the song was finished, some of the boys continued to tease her. "Beautiful K-K-K-Katy," they giggled. "That's you, K-K-K-Katy."

Miss Josephson clapped her hands for silence and asked what the problem was, but all she heard was more giggling and the same gleeful taunt: "Beautiful K-K-K-Katy! Beautiful K-K-K-Katy!"

And it was then that Kate stood up, her pigtails whipping and her eyes flashing.

"I'm beautiful *Kate!*" she yelled. "Not *Katy!*"

The class immediately collapsed in laughter and I even saw a slight smile trace across Miss Josephson's otherwise great stone face. And for the next week or so, Kate was "*Beautiful* Kate" on the playground, at least to the reckless few. Surprisingly, some of the boys even won a smile calling her that, but most of those who tried — including a couple of foolhardy girls — only got sore arms for their trouble. Mine, I think, was sorest of all.

It has been three days since Sarah left, by bus, in the first real snowstorm of the year. I used Junior's four-wheeler to get us to the station and stood with her in the squalid little waiting room as if we were sending her off to prison instead of to Miami

Beach. When the bus finally came, I carried her bags outside and kissed her goodbye and then I watched as she left in a cloud of diesel exhaust and swirling snow, sitting alone at one of the rear windows with her eyes a glaze of tears and self-pity. And I don't knock her for that. These days I think we've all got a little pity coming, even if only from ourselves. Junior, however, is much amused by the fact and the style of her departure. "Bugout," he calls her, saying she just couldn't take the competition.

"Toni was too much for her, that's all," he says. "And Sis wanted you all to herself. Ain't it just too, too sad? Poor little Electra."

I told him that he had his goddesses mixed up, but he said it was no matter, finishing with his usual panache:

"It's all Greek to me."

"I'll bet it is."

"But then I'm not a writer. Not even a failed writer."

"You're too kind."

"A family trait."

"So I've noticed."

Toni wisely told us both to shut up, and we did. But other than such sweet exchanges as that, silence is pretty much the rule here now. We are like four very disparate species immured by chance in the same zoo house, each carefully going out of its way not to cross paths with the others. And when we are forced together, as we were yesterday, to dine on a Thanksgiving dinner of cold and greasy Kentucky Fried Chicken, we seem to outdo each other in unsociability. Wonder of wonders, Toni has even taken to the vice of book-reading, and with such avidity that quite often I don't see her for hours on end. Admittedly, the books are only Harlequin Romances — from Sarah's room, a whole shelfful of them — but it is a beginning. And who's to say? In time the girl might even graduate to reading such splendid stuff as this.

Meanwhile Junior, in a display of hitherto unknown talent, is spending most of his waking hours out in the garage tinkering with his jeep and my TR-6, tuning them for the Indy Five

Hundred it would seem. He still visits the barn on occasion, for a little socializing with the Congo Lords, or at least with certain ones of them anyway. And once, through my trusty window, I saw him a few blocks away pull up to the curb in his jeep and throw open the door for a slender black youth, who hesitated for a few seconds before climbing in. None of this new industry keeps him from getting on my case more and more, however. Almost every day he asks me about my plans: How long will I be staying? Do I have any blockbuster movies about to premiere? Do I have any prospects at all?

Naturally I try to paint the picture even gloomier than it is.

"No, nothing. No prospects of any kind."

"You mean you're just gonna stay here for good?"

"Could be. But then it's no skin off your nose, is it? It's Jason we're living off, not you."

I see his enormous itch to tell me the truth—that he's the one with the money, the one who will be feeding us now that Sarah is gone. But each time he elects for prudence. Better to be thought poor than rich by one's own poor brother. So much simpler anyway.

And then there is Jason. As before, he stays in bed most of the time, with his door closed, listening by the hour to radio call-in talk shows, whose endless democratic babble stirs him to frequent outbursts of vituperative response, harangues of right-thinking lucidity lost on the four walls of his room. Occasionally he will struggle into his ratty old robe and slippers and trek downstairs to watch television or to eat something, usually just a bowl of cornflakes and a cup of coffee, both inundated with enough sugar for a dozen diabetics. His color is fish-belly gray and after any exertion at all he is so short of breath he can barely speak. I raise the subject with Junior, saying that we should get the old man to a doctor and find out what's wrong with him, but my little brother only makes a face and dismisses the idea.

"He's getting old, that's all. He's been this way for years."

And when I try with Jason himself, suggesting that he have a checkup, I get even less.

"What if they said I was dying? What would you do then—

run? Take off for Hollywood? Send us postcards?"

"You look terrible, Jason. And you shouldn't be so short of breath, not even at your age."

"So sue me. And you don't look so hot yourself, you know. You look soft. You, with the physique you had."

"We're talking about you."

"And I say no doctors. I've been getting along fine without them all these years, and I can do it for a few more."

"I hope you're right."

"Sure you do," he says. "A loving son like you."

Thus I am able to sit here at my desk more freely now, knowing that no one wants me elsewhere. I work for a while, writing and rewriting such lines as these, and then I light up a cigarette or pace the room or look out the window at the snow and the cold, sometimes staring so raptly that the stumps in the yard magically begin to climb upward as though in time-lapse photography, becoming again the giants of old. And as clearly as I see the blacks walking to and from the barn, I watch her playing with Cliff and me in the snow, making angels or building a snowman or having a running snowball fight with us, her laughter ringing like cymbals in the brittle air. Like some old actor, some inveterate lachrymist, I feel my eyes growing moist and I sink helplessly into great warm pools of nostalgia and amniotic sentimentality. The self-mockery stops the tears, you see. But it also stops the truth. For if I know anything about myself and about this life I've lived, it is that the love I had for Kate and Cliff was real, even before that last summer, a love so natural and constant that I never even knew of it until they were gone, just as I now prize the California sun.

So I sit here and I remember. I remember a Sadie Hawkins Day dance when Kate and I were high school freshmen and Cliff a sophomore. For some reason this turnabout—girls asking boys—drove Kate high up the wall, especially when she learned that Cliff and I had been invited by the Mandelbaum sisters, Judy and Joan, a pair of very dark, very well-developed Jewish mercantile princesses. Since I was just then beginning to push into puberty, with a cracking voice and a furze of hair sprouting above my perpetually tumid little dick, I was overjoyed at such good fortune, having a date with a girl like Joan, whose "jugs" dated back to the fifth grade at least, making her not just a woman of the world in my eyes but virtually a woman of the streets as well. I looked forward to a truly crushing "stone-ache," our word for the testicle pain resulting from unrelieved evening-long erections, and about all I could realistically hope for. Cliff as usual played it cool, not admitting to any of the lascivious dreams of glory that were already seriously cutting into my study time. Whenever I saw Joan at school, and especially during the one class we shared, I seemed incapable of a sustained thought that did not relate in some way to her wondrous breasts, which were huge and conical, and about as firm as kneecaps, I imagined. Occasionally my gaze would stray to her thick black hair and her pert smile and nice dark eyes, but never for very long. And I ignored entirely the fact that she was somewhat short in the leg. At fourteen, I was definitely not a leg man.

Sometimes we spoke, not unlike boys who would be playing against each other soon in football. How could I admit to my lust? I would have been straitjacketed and put away somewhere, force-fed on vast quantities of saltpeter. At home, I spent most of my time pumping Cliff about The Great Night: What did he think would happen? Would the voluptuous pair put out? Would I get bare jug? Would the two of us finally lose our accursed virginity? Not unexpectedly, Cliff had no answers for me. Mostly he just shook his head, as though in sad recognition of the fact that his little brother finally had gone over the edge. And since I was never one to press, I simply carted all my queries over to Kate, who after all was as much my buddy as Cliff ever was, and in addition had a far dirtier mind, in fact almost as dirty as my own. So I was blithely unprepared for the storm my little litany of questions stirred in her. Her eyes blazed and her mouth curled in revulsion as she shoved me back against the wall.

"*Bare jug?*" she yelled. "*Bare jug!* What are you talking about?

You twerp! You snotnose! You haven't even kissed a girl! You—"

But suddenly she was crying, tears of rage, I realize now. Then, however, I was totally baffled, and somewhat thunderstruck too, as she tore up the stairs and slammed the door so hard even Jason came out of his study to ask what the trouble was. I did not tell him, nor did Kate. But from that moment on, until weeks after the dance, she was not herself. Suddenly she would have almost nothing to do with either Cliff or me, unless Mother or Jason was within earshot, and then she would begin on us. *Hymie* and *Abe,* we were, the newest Hebes in Woodglen High. Had we been circumcised yet? Was she invited to our bar mitzvah? Had our noses always been so long?

Jason, who was never bashful about expressing his own anti-Semitism, took all that in stride. But when she began to refer to us as the tape-measure twins and to our dates as the Jewish squaws, Big Big Tit and Little Big Tit, Jason finally put his foot down, going so far as to send her up to her room.

For weeks he and Mother had been after her to ask some boy to the dance herself, but without success. Kate simply would not hear of it.

"I may have to go to school with the pimply freaks," she said. "But that doesn't mean I have to dance with them."

By then, Kate was already known as a "character" around town and especially at school. Students both male and female had learned early on that it was best not to mess with the pretty Kendall girl because she was as quick now with her tongue as she once had been with her fists. But where, in grade school, she had been content to bloody noses, now she went straight for the jugular, often marking her antagonists with a sobriquet so apt and cutting it would stick with the victim like a wound all through school, and maybe all through life, for all I know. Boys knew better than to ask her for dates and girls knew better than to laugh at her except behind her back. And laugh they did, because she wore no makeup and let her hair hang loose, a decade before it became the fashion.

Nevertheless, one day out of the blue Kate announced that

she too had a date for the dance, a senior named Waldo Fixx, whom Cliff and I would have figured just about the last person on earth Kate would invite even to a dog fight. He was stupid and greasy and had a vague reputation for minor criminality, things like stealing hubcaps and selling condoms on the school grounds. And worst of all, as far as Cliff and I were concerned, he drove a low-slung black hotrod that he himself had labeled— on the door, in gilt script—*The Baby Factory*. Angry and puzzled, the two of us tried to talk her into disinviting the creep, but all she did was smile sweetly and ask us if we didn't want to triple-date.

"We could all go in The Baby Factory," she said. "Or don't the Tit Sisters associate with gentiles?"

Anyway, to shorten this particular story, Kate had Mother cut one her best dresses down to provocative proportions. And she had her hair done and put on lipstick and went to the affair, where she proceeded to draw all the attention she could, not only dancing "fast" but letting Waldo dip her to the floor over and over, with her skirt riding up to her garter belt. Cliff and I might as well have been dating each other for all the attention we paid the Mandelbaum girls, so mesmerized were we by our sister's performance. During slow numbers, she kept steering Waldo toward us like a bumper car at a carnival.

"Oh, I'm so sorry," she said, after one collision. "I guess it's all the booze we had earlier—right, Waldo? A whole *jug* of it. Tell me, twin, are you interested in *jugs*?"

By then I was already spinning my startled date away from her, slamming into other couples in my haste to be free. But minutes later I would see her going through the same routine with Cliff and *his* Mandelbaum, saying something that turned my fair-skinned brother's face crimson as he too wheeled his date to safer ground. Once she and Waldo came upon the four of us between dances, as we stood under the gym backboard daintily drinking punch.

"My, what a good-looking foursome y'all make," she bubbled, suddenly a southern belle. "Why don't we all do something together afterwards? Waldo and I are thinking of the Bide-a-Wee Motel. Y'all want to join us there?"

By then her date had the look of a smiling ox, even when I told Kate to shut up and get lost.

"Well, I declare!" she said, smiling brightly. "If that isn't the meanest thing you ever said to me—you adolescent, perverted little shit."

She gave us a smart bow of the head and walked off, leading Waldo as if by a nose-ring.

Joan Mandelbaum shook her head. "My, your sister's different," she said.

"Yeah, isn't she?" A slow dance had begun and I took her in my strong right arm again, holding her just close enough so I could feel her glorious jugs rubbing against my chest, even through my suit jacket. I was still surprised that they weren't at all like kneecaps.

"It's an act," I reassured her. "Kate didn't mean that about the motel. Because she's a virgin. In fact, she's just about as virgin as you can get."

Joan put her face against mine and whispered silkily. "You shouldn't talk like that. It's embarrassing."

"Well, we're not little kids anymore," I intoned—just as Kate and Waldo blindsided us again.

"Careful," Kate advised my partner. "You might get terminal acne."

And so it went. Cliff and I and the Tit Sisters drove to the Eskimo for sundaes after the dance. And later, try as I might, all I got were a few kisses, a slapped hand, and the expected colossal stone-ache. Kate was already home and in bed by the time we came in, so we could only assume that she'd had no trouble handling the redoubtable Waldo, which he confirmed the following Monday at school, black eye and all, complaining to Cliff that our sister ought to be committed.

"Look at this eye," he whined. "And all I tried for was a kiss. What a jerk that girl is. What a pricktease."

Normally Cliff would have taken a poke at anybody who called Kate such a name. But I guess he felt that Waldo had some justice on his side, so he did nothing. And the Sadie Hawkins Day dance faded into memory.

I realize that I have treated it here like some typical anecdote in a casual comic memoir. And I really don't know why I've done this, since I do recognize, as surely as you must, the fanatic character of Kate's possessiveness. I know now that her problem wasn't any simple case of jealousy, for she had to know even then that the Tit Sisters were not in her long-legged All-American league. No, I'm afraid that, once I had mentioned my quest for "bare jug," she would have gone on the same sort of rampage no matter whom Cliff or I invited to the dance.

In any case, she did not come down off her high horse for at least two weeks after the dance. And I think she did then only because Waldo's black eye had become something of a family joke. Jason kept calling her his little Rocky (for Marciano, not Balboa) and I guess she took sufficient pride in the appellation to allow her to forgive her twin brother for his grossness. And finally she even deigned to speak with me again, one late afternoon as we finished feeding the Holsteins' milk to our pampered Angus calves. Once fed, the little buggers could not stop gamboling about and butting their mothers' inadequate udders to bring down even more milk. Leaning on the corral fence, Kate and I were watching the show.

"It's not fair," she said. "Something so cute shouldn't grow up into just another ugly old cow."

"Bulls don't think they're ugly."

"But they're still ugly. Old is ugly."

I looked at her. "You getting old, Kate?"

She didn't even smile. "We all are. Every day we get older."

"Yeah, and ain't it great?"

She reached out to pet one of the calves, but it jumped back from her. "What's so great about it? I liked it before. The way it used to be."

Genius that I am, I had no idea what she was talking about; and I said so. But she did not explain. Instead she looked over at me—down at me actually—with flecks of mica in her fine green eyes.

"Tell me, Greg—did it work out for you? Did you get your precious *bare jug*?"

"Naaw. Just a kiss or two. That Joan's a real nun."

"Oh really? I didn't know the chosen people went in for nuns."

"You know what I mean."

She looked back at the calves. "Yeah, I guess I do. But that doesn't mean I understand. I can't figure why you're *all* like that. Like my pal Waldo. You'd have thought he needed it to live, like food or water. Me, I wouldn't care if I never kissed a boy. And I'd rather die than have one of the creeps touch me."

"We used to touch," I said.

For a few moments she looked as if she didn't understand what I meant, or maybe didn't even remember. Then she made a face.

"Oh, *that*. That doesn't count. We were just little kids."

It was then I asked her something I always had wanted to, but for some reason never had. "Did you and Cliff ever—you know?"

She gave me a look of withering disgust and turned away, heading for the house.

"Of course not, stupid," I heard.

Since there are no cooks among us, we don't have meals anymore, only snacks, most of which we prepare for ourselves. This evening, however, I thought I would try to set an example for Toni and Junior by whipping up a repast consisting of hamburgers, potato chips, and canned peaches, none of which elicited the slightest word of praise from anybody. Jason took only a bite or two out of his burger and barely touched the rest, turning instead to a bowl of cornflakes, which he got for himself, shuffling about the kitchen, banging doors and muttering. Toni sighed and looked to the ceiling for sustenance.

"What's the matter, young lady?" Jason asked. "You aren't enjoying yourself here?"

"You could say that."

The old man wagged his head in mock consternation. "Well, I can't figure that. You'd think being the mistress of a rich and successful playwright would satisy you. Travel and good food like this and lots of clothes—I thought that's what every woman wanted."

Wheezing and choking and slurping, he barely got through the speech, and I imagine it was this that Toni found offensive, the style more than the content. Just by the way she looked at me, I had a pretty good idea what was coming.

"If I were you, I'd tell the old fart to stick it up his ass," she said.

While Junior whooped with laughter, Jason began to choke in earnest, coughing and sputtering and spraying the table with soggy cornflakes. I patted him on the back and helped him over to the sink, where he slowly rattled down to silence, to the point finally where I was able to get a glass of water down him. Unexpectedly, he returned to the table instead of shuffling off to his room, muttering and pouting. And once again he started on his cornflakes. Finding them insufficiently sweet, he sprinkled on a few more tablespoons of sugar. Then he was ready again for Toni.

"Never thought the day would come when I'd be abused at my own table by a trollop."

Not quite sure of the word, Toni gave me a quizzical look. But before I could say anything, Junior jumped in, the soul of helpfulness.

"Trollop as in whore," he said. "A woman who sells herself."

Toni was still confused. "Well, what's that got to do with me? Who the hell's paying me for anything?"

"What do you do for your keep?" Jason asked. "Besides sleep with a man?"

Again Toni turned to me. "Do we have to take this kind of crap? Aren't you gonna say anything?"

Jason laughed contentedly, rattling his phlegm. "What can he say? He's being kept too. Which means you're a kept man's kept woman."

In a quarrel Toni is like a ten-year-old boy, all fight and no style. So I was not surprised as she leaned across the table now, practically snarling at the old man.

"Yeah, well at least we don't stink! And we don't spit all over everybody else!"

Chuckling and winking at me, Junior was having a fine time. But he apparently felt that my discomfort was not sufficiently acute.

"This reminds me a little of Mama's funeral, when Greg came back here with his heiress wife. You two didn't exactly hit it off either, did you, Jason?"

The old man made a face. "What a pretentious woman that one was!" he snorted. "They fly here in a chartered jet and rent a limousine. And no room in this house was good enough for her, no sir. She and her kept man here had to stay in that new motel near Aurora."

"My kind of woman," Toni said.

But Jason was not listening. "Why, every little thing she did, she had to have a special outfit for. When I chided her about it, she said it was her duty, that it was the duty of the rich to spend a lot of money to keep the peasants employed."

"You don't think she was kidding you?" I asked.

"*Kidding!* That woman didn't have any sense of humor at all. If she did, she wouldn't have married you, a penniless 'writer' of movies."

And so on, *ad nauseam*. I really don't know why I bother to record these pleasant little family gatherings, since they are all so much alike. By now I imagine you are only too well aware what meager love and understanding are lost between Jason and me. And I see no prospect of it ever changing. I do find it interesting, though, how hung up he still remains on the subject of Ellen Brubaker, my "Santa Barbara millionairess." One would think that my first wife, Janet, and our two daughters, Susan and Tracy — Jason's own grandkids — did not even exist for all the interest he shows in them, and this despite the tale I told him about my being sued for their nonsupport. In point of fact, Janet remarried almost a decade ago, bagging a prosperous Orange County realtor, and the girls have grown up secure and comfortable, happy with their lot as future USC coeds and Young Republican homemakers. For all that, they are truly lovely and I miss them more than I care to admit. But let me just mention them to Jason and a few seconds later he is off and running on the subject of my "millionairess." I guess it's simply the idea of all that money that fascinates him, money I married and shared for almost five years — and money very like that which he himself grew up with in Chicago, and then lost, thanks to my grandfather's improvidence.

For the most part, though, all he can do is speculate on the character of my marriage to Ellen, probably because I never have told him much about that relationship, figuring that his dour imagination already gave him enough ammunition without my giving him any more. But I do wonder how he would react if he knew that in the last years of our marriage I received an allowance from Ellen; or that I once fell fully dressed into the Biltmore pool while taking a drunken poke at her; or that she was forever kicking me out and changing all the door locks, only to come traipsing down to Hollywood later, checkbook in hand. And especially I wonder how the old man would take the news that this least favorite son not only received a forty-two-foot Chris-Craft as part of the divorce settlement, but compounded his guilt by failing to keep up the insurance on the thing, and finally by renting it (dearly) to a Malibu coke dealer who thought to expand his operation by importing a few tons of Colombian marijuana, and then who was so foolish as to keep running while under fire from the U.S. Coast Guard, which had been tipped off to the whole enterprise. My boat, the dealer, his crew of three, and probably a ton of grass all went up in a horrendous explosion of gasoline, leaving the authorities with nothing except me, the yacht owner of record, who fortunately happened to be listening to the radio in his girl friend's Venice apartment on the night of the explosion.

And so we came here, as I guess I've already said. Let me say further, then, that if the insurance still had been in effect, and collectible, I probably would have stayed and faced the music, *that* music instead of Jason's. But then, just imagine, these pages and these words most likely would not exist, except perhaps as some dormant electrochemical potential slumbering inside this suddenly aching head. Enough.

five

I am not sure just how old we were that summer: nine or ten, I would imagine, which means Cliff would have been about eleven. It was during the dog days of August, when even swimming had begun to pall for us and it seemed there was nothing to do except work and loaf and sweat through the few remaining weeks till school and football came to our rescue. Much like Stinking Joe and Jason himself, the three of us became solitary and petulant, even with each other—until Kate pushed upon us the idea of the treehouse. Now, we had never done much in the way of building forts or treehouses, probably because we had always had the barn and especially the loft with all its haybales, which were easy to fashion into cubbyholes and bunkers that required only our imagination to transform them into fortresses and clubhouses and the like.

But this time Kate insisted that we go back to the far northwest corner of the farm, to a remote wooded area covered with oak and hickory as well as a scattering of pines. There she had found the "perfect spot," she said. And it turned out to be just that: an oak tree with a stout, three-limbed fork specifically designed, it appeared, to cradle the floor of a treehouse. In addition it offered a perfect vantage point from which to spy on the Regan place, a run-down little farmette bordering our land,

and the home not only of a dozen junked cars and twice that many dogs and cats and squalling geese, but also of Little Tim and Joey, who were schoolmates of ours, a pair of big, dirty, ignorant Irish kids: the bugger-eaters, as Kate called them.

What little enthusiasm Cliff and I had for the project, Kate more than made up for. She scrounged up most of the wood we needed, got the ladder and tools and nails, and carried more than her share out to the site. From that point on, though, it was Cliff who took over and did most of the building, since he was the only one of us who could pound a nail in straight. And by the time we were finished there were hundreds to pound. First, we had to secure two-by-four steps to the tree's main branch, between the top of the ladder and the floor of the treehouse, which we fashioned out of a dissimilar assortment of boards nailed onto a triangular two-by-four frame, itself anchored to the three main branches of the tree. Kate then came up with an unusual idea for the walls of the fort: a latticework of evergreen boughs woven through a framework of uprights, connected at the top with another triangle of boards.

Finished, we had to stock our fortress with provisions, including bread and peanut butter, a canteen, binoculars, blankets, an air rifle and a couple of slingshots. I can remember even now how it felt to be up in that piney aerie, just the three of us, with no grown-ups anywhere around and a whole world out there to be spied upon. And if it excited me, it did even more for Kate, who went off into a high fine state of fantasy that Cliff and I quickly accepted as simply a newer and better reality. Suddenly we were Greek partisans, freedom fighters holed up behind the Nazi lines and spying on them, trying to find out if and when they would attack our main column moving up from the south. Kate and I were lieutenants and Cliff our commander — all appointed by Kate herself of course. She wrote up the laws and by-laws of the outfit and kept an hour-by-hour log of our tour of duty. She distributed cyanide pills to each of us (jujubes actually) and we all took an oath to die before betraying our cause. But this soon struck her as insufficient and she insisted we change it into a blood oath, even after Cliff had

67

pointed out to her that it was a redundant gesture because we already had the same blood flowing in us. She overrode his objections, however, and we went ahead and nicked our fingers and joined hands, happily bleeding all over the treehouse floor.

She also decided that it was not soldierly to have tools and a ladder lying about, so we took them back to the barn. Returning, we climbed up to the fort like proper partisans, rappeling up the treetrunk with a rope till we reached the built-in ladder, which took us the rest of the way. And there we commenced our tireless scrutiny of the Nazi camp—the Regans, going about their slovenly lives.

I realize that the names of Little Tim and Joey sound as if they belonged to a pair of benign elves. But that definitely was not the case. Joey was Cliff's age and Little Tim was a year older, and they were both bigger than Cliff. Yet they were behind Kate and me in school by a full grade, due to such misfortunes as stupidity and measles and a predilection for beating up on other students and sometimes teachers, which naturally had resulted in their being expelled now and then. Consequently we did not take them lightly. We knew they were worthy adversaries, Nazis of the first rank.

So we watched them and their two younger sisters and their parents. Kate kept a careful record of their comings and goings, detailing the time and character of their various missions, such as: *Joey to barn 7:15—chores—takes a leak—returns to house* 8:29. And there were juicier entries too, some covering the old man's penchant for getting drunk and pounding on his wife and kiddies, others covering the myriad atrocities the two little girls inflicted on their many pets. We were not conned by any of this, however. We knew a smoke screen when we saw one and were constantly on the alert for those inevitable signs that would betray the garrison's true intentions.

There were periods, however, when nothing was happening at the Regans', and those were good times too. The three of us would talk and laugh about Stinking Joe and Mama's kids and the Regans, as well as other characters we knew in school. Kate, who had a gift for mimicry, did hilarious impressions of

Reverend Sunbeam and a number of our teachers. And of course we reminisced, we ten- and eleven-year-olds. We looked back fondly upon our lives as we dined on peanut butter sandwiches washed down with warm Dr Pepper. And best of all, we often stayed in the treehouse overnight, like chicks in a nest, lying there looking up at the moon and the clouds and listening to the night sounds as well as the comforting music of our own voices. Kate said it was all very "neat." It was "better than freaking home, any day." And Cliff and I did not disagree.

On occasion we did have to go home, though, for chores and supper if for nothing else. And during those hours our fortress was left unguarded, naked to our enemies in the valley below. So in time the inevitable happened. On the fourth or fifth night we came back from supper—which Jason insisted that we eat at home—and found the treehouse a shambles, with the evergreen walls knocked down and our binoculars broken and Kate's logbook torn into little pieces and the floorboards covered with chalk graffiti, including a number of crude drawings illustrating such lines as *the Kendals suck* and *Kaits a hore* and the ubiquitous *fuck you* scrawled in a half-dozen different places.

We stayed on through the night anyway, honing our anger and making plans for the coming days of sweet revenge. In the morning we went home and did our chores and then we returned to repair the treehouse, bringing it back as closely as we could to its original state, which meant scrubbing the floor as well as having Kate make up a new logbook from memory. That night and the next morning, despite Jason's orders, only one of us at a time left the treehouse for home.

It was a full two days later before we made our move against the Regans (who somehow weren't Nazis anymore—the designation just didn't seem pejorative enough). Cliff had led us around to the other side of the farmyard, to a position that placed the Regans' barn between us and their house, which allowed us to sneak up on Joey without him or anyone else in the family seeing us. There was a moment when he could have yelled, but he apparently felt that he did not have much to fear from us and even got halfway through a greeting of sorts before Cliff and I jumped him. I put a neck hold on him to keep him from calling for help and we wrestled him down onto the slimy floor of the milking shed, where Cliff and Kate proceeded to tie him up with baling twine.

Our original plan had been to kidnap him for ransom (the logistics of which we hadn't worked out yet) but there in the barn, already panting and filthy, we realized that there had to be an easier way. And Kate quickly came up with it. She stuffed Joey's mouth with an old grease rag and then had us drag him into the "slop trench" behind the cows. And there we held him—until one of the Regans' Holsteins did its inevitable thing, all over poor writhing Joey. Thereupon we fled, giggling and jumping and slapping each other like Rose Bowl victors— Kate and I anyway. As for Cliff, even before we reached the treehouse he was beginning to feel bad about what we had done.

"We went too far," he said. "Now there's gonna be war."

Kate looked at him as if he had lost his sense. "Well of course, dummy—that's the whole idea. What good is a fort without a war?"

I don't think Cliff ever did see the logic in that, but at the same time he was not about to run out on us, for that would have been even more alien to his nature than the attack on Joey Regan had been. Now though we had to worry not only about Joey but Little Tim and possibly the mother and father as well, for even Kate and I were not unaware how far we had gone, how grossly we had overstepped the bounds of normal kid warfare. To my surprise I soon learned that Kate was planning yet another giant leap in the same direction. While Cliff glumly sat looking out toward the Regan place, waiting for their attack, Kate whispered to me to run to the barn and get a saw and hammer, but not to let Cliff know I had them when I returned.

"Hide them in the bushes," she said. "They're our secret weapon."

As was my custom, I did what she said and when I climbed back into the treehouse later, winded and sweating, Cliff gave me a searching look.

"I thought you went home for chores," he said.

I looked to Kate for an answer.

"That ain't why he left," she offered. "He chickened out. But then he changed his mind and came back—right, Greg?"

I was nodding.

Cliff looked disgusted. "You really did? You really chickened out?"

"For just a minute or so."

"God almighty." He seemed more puzzled than disgusted. "Least you could've done the chores while you were home. You know what time it is?"

"No."

"Well, one of us has to go," he said. "Jason'll hit the roof if the cows aren't milked—you know that."

"You go," Kate said to him. "We'll be all right here."

But Cliff would not hear of it. How were the two of us going to stand up to Little Tim *and* Joey, he wanted to know. Tim was bigger than both of us put together, and Joey was going to be so mad he would probably kill the two of us alone, without his big brother's help. So Cliff had to stay. He had no choice.

Kate gave him an indulgent smile. "Well, we're not going to stay up here in the freaking fort, you know. You don't think we're that dumb, do you? We'll just lay back in the trees and watch the house. If they head this way, we'll scram for home. I just want to see what they do."

Cliff was able to accept that. Warning us to stay out of sight, he finally climbed down and headed for home. And Kate gleefully laid out her plan, which was simplicity itself. All it required was that we pull a few nails and saw through the two-by-fours supporting the platform—saw through them *except* for about a quarter of an inch—which in effect turned the treehouse into a huge trap door. Whichever Regan climbed onto it first would most likely be the first to hit the ground—an

71

eventuality that excited Kate and me so much that it seemed one of us or the other was always crawling away to pee.

Our vantage point was from behind some evergreens on a rocky ridge about fifty yards from the treehouse, and there we stayed through the rest of that morning and on into the afternoon, waiting for the Regans to show. When Cliff came back after chores, we told him to stay with us on the ground, away from the treehouse, just in case old man Regan decided to accompany his boys on their inevitable quest for Kendall blood. And ironically that is exactly what happened, at about three in the afternoon, with the air so still and hot that even the flies were not budging from the shade. Little Tim was leading the way and looking very eager to beat up on someone and reclaim the family's honor. Next in line came Joey, with a reluctant, hang-dog look, as if he had been marked forever by the moist olive splatter of the cows. The old man (who was probably only thirty at the time) brought up the rear, carrying nothing less than a double-barrel twelve-gauge shotgun, which had the immediate effect of drying my mouth at the same time it dampened my jockey shorts.

"Don't move," Kate whispered to us. "Wait till the crash. Then we run."

"What crash?" Cliff looked from Kate to me.

I shrugged. "Don't ask me."

As the Regans reached the tree, the old man gestured with his gun and Little Tim started up, using the rope to reach the first rungs of the ladder. Then he scrambled up into the treehouse and stood there peering down over the top of the evergreen walls at his father and little brother.

"They ain't here, them bastids!" he said, as he began to kick at the walls, knocking down the uprights and spilling evergreen boughs. And it was then one of the two-by-fours gave way, with a sound like the bark of a starter pistol. And indeed the sound did signal the beginning of a race of sorts—floorboards and braces and Little Tim all speeding toward the ground thirty feet below. Admirably, Tim did not even yell as he plummeted down upon his father and Joey, who stood covering their heads against this sudden rain of boards and boughs and family. That was enough even for Kate.

"Now!" she said, jumping up and scampering off through the woods toward our house.

Cliff and I were behind her when we heard the blast of the shotgun and saw a flock of birds explode from the top of a tree off to our right. And abruptly we were out in front of her and pulling away. But then we had an advantage. We were not laughing.

I recount this escapade only because I think it is a fair example of what Kate probably had in mind later, in high school, when she lamented our lost past, saying that *I liked it before, the way it used to be.* At the time I did not understand her at all, filled as I was with the lunatic juices of adolescence, looking forward to such impending glories as growing tall and driving cars and having sex. The irony is that now that I have grown up, I have no trouble seeing it all exactly as she did then, as the passing of something finer than anything that was to come after, for her and Cliff in their few remaining years just as for me, in all of mine.

As it turned out, the incident closed on a happy or at least a satisfying note, with Jason surprisingly standing up for us like a real trooper. Little Tim had broken an arm and lost a tooth in the fall and his father had come over to our house in a high purple-faced dudgeon, threatening mayhem and lawsuits if Jason didn't beat us there and then, with him as a witness. Instead Jason told him to get the hell off his porch and off his property or he would throw him off, and in the bargain would have him clapped into jail for trespassing and destruction of property and the reckless use of a firearm. Regan blustered and swore and promised revenge—all the way out to his battered pickup, which he drove off in such a heavy-footed fury that the engine kept flooding out on him. It was the most ignominious retreat I have ever seen and it promptly made Jason a great hero to the three of us, which is probably why he neglected to punish us, unaccustomed as he was to seeing such shining admiration in our eyes.

So, for Kate and me, the treehouse incident was a thing of beauty from start to finish. As for Cliff, he never said much about it, evidently feeling that it was not one of our finer moments. And, oddly, this too was something I think that Kate and I relied upon in our young lives: the leavening effect of Cliff's unflagging decency and good sense. Without it, as a counter force, she and I might have had to develop scruples of our own, which surely would have tamed to a degree the considerable joy we found in mischief.

But as I've already said (at least a dozen times, I'm afraid) those innocent days finally came to an end, in the sea change of puberty. And it was really only then, during the transition years, that the going was particularly rough. Later on, such debacles as the Sadie Hawkins Day dance simply did not occur, probably not because Kate had changed so much as that she had learned to adjust, or at least to dissemble. To all appearances, she became virtually a different person, cool and quiet and uninvolved. She did her homework and got good grades, better even than Cliff's, but she never went out for any sports or joined any clubs, nor did she ever date or encourage the friendship of other girls. For the most part, she just went through the motions at school and then came home to her real life, which was the farm. Over the years Cliff and I had become so involved in sports and other affairs (such as his assistant manager job at the Eskimo) that we had less and less to do with the farm. But whatever slack we created, Kate was more than able to take up. In fact, I think she eventually contributed more than Stinking Joe to keeping the place in running order: brushhogging the fields and mending the fences and caring for what cattle we had left after Jason sold off the milk cows and those Angus that couldn't nurture their own young. Her one true passion, though, was an Appaloosa mare and its colt, which she herself broke and then proceeded to ride over our fields by the hour almost every afternoon, often not coming home until dark and missing supper altogether.

It was also during those years that Kate developed into a real beauty, to my mind the most beautiful girl in school, though I'm not sure everyone saw her that way, blinded as they had to be by the carapace she had built around herself, that hauteur which scared off boys and girls alike, just as it did her teachers. Yet she was never the kind of girl anyone would have felt sorry for, and not because of her looks so much as her air of total self-confidence and contentment. If anyone worried about her (other than Mother) it was probably Cliff, who was forever asking me about her. Was she happy? Did she still like us? What did I think she would become? A movie star? A tragic dramatic actress on Broadway? Just what did I think?

Actually very little, for the change in Kate somehow did not bother me anywhere near as much as it did Cliff. For one thing, I still had more important matters on my mind, like getting an actual, legitimate, certifiable piece of ass instead of the measly bare jug and hand-jobs which by my junior year were still the zenith of my sexual experience. Back then, most of the girls I dated—the girls from "good families"—simply were not as generous as I understand they are now. Consequently I made desperate pilgrimages to the east side of Woodglen, hoping to score with the Italian and Mexican girls there. But they invariably turned into little nuns for the occasion, evidently feeling that a date with a west-side Wasp (even country variety) was a social opportunity. (And, believe me, I am not unaware how obscenely smug that sounds. But it's the way we were back then. And I didn't invent the world, not even this one.)

So, for me, Kate was simply *there*, in the background, somewhat like an eccentric and beautiful cousin who I was sure didn't really like me all that much anymore, doubtless because of my commonness, my disinclination to share her enthusiasms for horses and chastity and solitude. At the same time I can remember feeling a certain rueful disappointment that none of my dates looked at all like Kate or had that special quality of hers, that thing that made her stand out in a crowd like a leopard strolling through a herd of sheep. Very distinctly I remember entering the Eskimo with a date one night and thinking, as the other kids all looked up at us from their tables, how much better it would have been, how much more flattering, to have had someone like Kate on my arm.

Yesterday afternoon Junior came in from the barn with a broken nose and a swelling eye and a bad cut across his cheekbone. He knocked over a chair and punched the wall and almost kicked the downstairs bathroom door off its hinges before he finally made it to the sink and began to bathe his wounds. Toni started to enter the bathroom to help him, but he growled at her at leave him alone and she obeyed.

"What do you think happened?" she asked me.

"I can't imagine."

Junior heard me. "Don't be cute, all right? Just bring the jeep around. I'll be out in a minute."

Toni asked if she shouldn't go too, and I told her to save her mothering instincts for me. I put on a coat and brought the jeep around from the garage, revving its cold engine for minutes before Junior finally came out, wearing sunglasses and holding an already bloody towel to his face. We drove to Saint Helen's Hospital and went to the emergency room, where a Chicano doctor had Junior X-rayed and then pushed his nose back into place and packed it. He stitched up his cheek and bandaged it. But there was not much he could do for his eye, he said. The damage there was only superficial, but it was already too late to control the swelling and the discoloration, which would just have to run their course. He gave Junior some antibiotic salve and told him to see his own doctor in a few days, or sooner, if there were complications.

I went out to the jeep and waited while Junior stopped at the desk to pay, an operation that took him a good twenty minutes and had him kicking the banked snow when he came out. Getting into the jeep, he angrily pulled the door shut.

"A fucking hundred and twelve goddamn dollars!" he bawled. "Can you believe that?"

"Sure."

"Too bad I ain't a pauper like you," he said. "Then the stinking government would pay for it."

"Yeah, that is a shame."

For the next couple of minutes, as I drove toward home, he sat there in the bucket seat cracking his knuckles and fuming. Finally he turned to me again.

"Well, ain't you curious how it happened?"

"I got a pretty good idea."

"Oh yeah? Then tell me."

"I figure it was one of your little chocolate fruits. What'd he do, turn straight on you?"

It was impossible to read his reaction, what with all the bandages and swelling. Finally he laughed. "So you've been on to me. Big deal. What you gonna do now, run to Jason and tell him all about it?"

"I figure he probably already knows. You aren't exactly a tower of discretion, you know."

"Jason don't know nothing that ain't on the radio."

"So what if he did find out—what difference would it make? I understand you've already milked him for all he had."

"Now, who could've told you a story like that?"

"I just guessed."

"Sure you did with sister Sarah's help."

"Could've been a little birdie."

"And you believed her?"

"What difference does it make?"

"None. I ain't ashamed of anything I ever did. And least of all, I ain't ashamed of who I happen to like sex with."

"Good for you."

He laughed again, or tried to anyway. "But then in that department, we Kendalls are all a little kinky—isn't that right, brother?"

I felt like a woods creature suddenly hearing the heavy step of man. And it was not Junior's words so much as the tone that alerted me, that oozing burden of informed malice. My hand involuntarily tightened on the steering wheel.

"You trying to say something?" I asked.

"Don't be coy."

"Was I?"

"You're forgetting that old Stinking Joe worked for us a few more summers after you left."

"So?"

Junior wagged his head in mock wonderment. "Ah, such innocence. Such a look of downy innocence."

"You're boring me," I said.

"Sure, I am." He settled back in his seat and crossed his arms, a raconteur about to perform. "Yeah, old Stinking Joe, he really had some stories to tell. Loved to tease me, that dirty old man. Just loved to say such awful things about you and Kate and Cliff, like how you used to swim naked together and play grab-ass — claimed he saw it too, the lying old bastard."

"That's what he was, all right."

"Old fart even claimed he overheard things. And then when Cliff crashed the car like that — well, old Joe he just put two and two together."

"And what did he get?"

Junior looked over at me again, his good eye twinkling merrily. Like an elocutionist, he elaborately formed his answer: "*Incest.*"

And that was as long as I could last. Braking the jeep in the snow, I reached over and slammed my little brother back against the hardtop door, making it pop open.

"That's all," I told him. "Don't you ever open your filthy mouth about Kate or Cliff again. You do and you're gonna wish you were back with your spade boy friends. You got that?"

He did not answer, but I got the impression that he understood. So I drove us on home, getting out and leaving it up to him, in his shape, to put the jeep away in the garage. Inside, Toni started to pump me about how he was and why I had left him outside, but I walked past her and came up here to my room. I slammed the door shut and went over to the window, trying to get control of myself. I pressed my hands together to stop their trembling and I closed my eyes against the tears welling in them. But I could not stop the sound of my little brother's voice, which went on shaking me like a leaf in the wind.

In the three days since Junior was beaten up, Toni has spent much of her waking time with him, changing his bandages, bringing him food, talking with him. And at first I welcomed the change, in that it gave me more writing time than I would otherwise have had, now that she has run out of Harlequin Romances. But then I began to wonder if my little brother, gradually forgetting the warning I gave him, might not be filling her ear with mischief. Which is exactly what happened, as I learned last night.

In her inimitable way, Toni tried to be super subtle in broaching the subject, waiting until after we'd had sex and were lying quietly in bed, smoking what I thought would be the last cigarettes of the day.

"How come you didn't tell me Junior's a homo?" she asked.

"True confessions today?"

"How come?"

"I didn't know he was, not for sure. So I saw no reason to prejudice you against him."

"*Me* prejudiced?" she laughed. "You know I've always liked gays. They're so much more fun than you straights."

"Yeah, they're a neat bunch of fellows."

She dug her toes into my legs. "Don't be so sarcastic and superior. Listen, if I could find a guy who was like you in the one department and like them in every other, I'd jump at him."

"I bet you would."

"Well, I would. And we'd have fun together too. Jabber like a couple of girls. You macho types have got a lot to learn, you know that?"

"Maybe if I went back to school. Say, a Hollywood barber college."

Having put out her cigarette, she nuzzled in close, hugging me with her right arm and leg. And I could tell by her breathing and the tautness in her limbs that she was working up to the big question, having fortified herself with intimacy.

"You know what?" she asked.

"No, what?"

"He told me something else — something I don't believe."

"What was that?"

"It was about you. You and Kate and Cliff."

"What about us?"

She burrowed in tighter and kissed my neck and my ear. "Well, you know. That you and Cliff — you know — *did it* with her."

I kept my voice level, betraying as little reaction as I could. "And where did he get this idea? Did he say?"

"I guess from some old hired man here. Years after you'd left. I forget his name. Smelly somebody."

"Stinking Joe. A very reliable source."

"It isn't true, then?"

"What do you think?"

"Well, according to Junior — or I should say according to this hired man — that's why your brother Cliff drove the car into a tree that night, to kill them both. But he didn't die, so he came back here and finished the job."

"Is that a fact?"

"That's what Junior said."

"Well then, it must be true."

She looked at me. "Well, is it?"

There in the darkness I laughed with soft contempt, hoping she could not feel the angry pounding of my heart. "Maybe Stinking Joe should have written Harlequin Romances — that's what I think."

"There's no truth to it, then?"

I did hear this conversation, but I still find it hard to believe, especially that part rendered by my own voice. "We were all at this stupid dance," I heard. "And we'd been drinking. Kate got sick and Cliff decided to drive her home. On the way, they crashed. He tried to make it home on foot, but he bled to death. Kate was in a coma and died later. Weeks later."

"And that's why you left here?"

Pretending casualness, I hugged her to me and kissed her hair and her forehead. "I don't want to talk about it anymore, honey. Not tonight, okay?"

"I just wanted to be sure about it, that's all. That it wasn't true."

"Well, now you know."

"Yes."

We kissed goodnight and she rolled away from me, pulling my arm across her breasts, making sure that I would be there, embracing her, as she fell asleep. It was a ritual.

Hours later I lie beside her smoking at least my sixth cigarette since she dropped off. I study the stains on the ceiling and I feel time begin to slacken its pace and finally falter and stop altogether, forming a narrow crack in the world through which I try to squeeze my bloody little person so I can escape forever into a field of high soft grass, there to run in the wind with Kate and Cliff, our hard stubby little hands locked tightly together. That, you see, is my earliest memory: a hot summer day on a hillside somewhere near the barn, the three of us not even in kindergarten yet, and we are running downhill through waist-high grass hand in hand, our legs churning and our voices bubbling in laughter and finally shrieking with a fearsome joy as we tumble in a heap at the bottom of the hill. Getting up immediately, Kate again takes our hands and pulls us along after her.

"Come on," she says. "Let's do it again."

But I catch myself now. The hell with them, I growl. They are dead and I am alive and time marches on. Oh, you bet it does.

Slowly I become aware of a sound somewhere in the night, a sound like that of a distant pump throbbing in futility, drawing dryness. Then I begin to realize that it is an animal sound, some creature moaning or fighting for breath and I get up and put on my robe and go across the hall to his room, which is lit dimly by a mercury vapor streetlight on the corner, a light of death, blue and cold. I sit down on his bed and touch him, just his shoulder, lightly, as though I feared for my own life.

"Jason," I say. "What is it? What's the matter?"

The keening diminishes and he seems puzzled now, not quite sure who or what has come to him at this hour. An angel of death, in a torn terry-cloth robe?

"What's the matter?" I repeat. "Can't you breathe?"

"What? Who?"

"It's Greg. I was awake and I heard you."

He stares at me, a death's head in cerulean light. His hands writhe on the blanket. He echoes me. "What's the matter?"

"You, Jason. You were moaning or crying."

"You lie."

"I thought you might need help."

"For what?"

"I just wondered what was wrong."

"Wrong?"

"Yes. Is it your breathing?"

He lies there in the gloom, gathering himself now, catching hold. Long seconds pass, and he repeats my words once again.

"Is it my breathing?"

"Yes, tell me. Let me help."

"You think you can?"

"I can try."

His chest rattles with congestion as he laughs at me. "All right, then. My trouble is I've come to the end of my breathing. It's about over now. Can you help me there?"

"I want you to see a doctor."

"A doctor? They can cure death now, can they?"

It is late and I am cold and he has begun to exasperate me, as always. "Jason—you were moaning."

"And why not?" He looks at me, saying nothing more for a time, his breathing the only sound in the world. Then he starts again, speaking slowly and carefully, wheezing and coughing and pausing for breath as he goes on. "Just think of it, what it is like to lie here in bed in the dark in the winter at seventy, with your body dying and no one to talk to, no one you care about or who cares about you in the whole wide world. You're all alone and you don't believe in religion or afterlife or any of that nonsense. There's just you and your dying body and the cold and the dark. So what if I moan? So what if I cry? What would you do—get on a bus for Hollywood?"

I am on my feet by then, standing there shaking my head as he rattles on. When he is finished, I smile and go to the door, pausing for just a moment as I leave.

"Well, have fun," I say.

six

I have always contended that if you are looking for a dazzling and definitive analysis of almost any subject at all, just turn to the Encyclopedia Britannica. For instance, Sarah's 1970 set has this to say on the subject at hand: *Incest prohibitions are found in all cultures, primitive and civilized.* How about that? Why, it doesn't matter who you are—a Hollywood screenwriter or a visitor from outer space—you learn something from a line like that. Or consider this: *[In the United States] intercourse between father and daughter, mother and son, and brother and sister are [sic] universally forbidden.* Case closed. After that, just what else is there left to say on the subject? What else but a lot of whining words of explanation and self-justification, as if by some sorcery of language one could hope to turn his dirty little pile of linen into the vestments of normality if not sainthood. So consider yourself forewarned, which as we know is forearmed. I am at your mercy.

The first instances of sexual activity between Kate and me happened when we were quite young, only seven or eight; and I understand that the phenomenon is not particularly rare among brothers and sisters at that age. Some experts describe the aberration as a common outgrowth of normal sexual curiosity, though in my case I must admit to motives based less on inquisitiveness than on the simple but exquisite pleasure I felt each time we "touched" each other, as we called our little explorations. During the course of that one summer I don't imagine we did it over a half-dozen times in all, and then only because Kate wanted something from me—a favor or possession—and would give in to my entreaties, submitting to my busy little fingers while she impatiently squeezed and tickled my "bone."

On weekend mornings, when the two of us and Cliff usually wound up in bed together, gabbing like churchwomen, I sometimes tried to pull down her pajama bottoms and press myself against her buttocks. Most of the time she would just push me away under the covers, but once she got angry and yelled at me, which made Cliff realize what I was doing. He promptly tossed me out of bed and punched me on the arm and threatened to kill me if I ever did such a thing again.

"She's your sister, you dumb ass!" he remonstrated. "Your twin! You can't do that! It's not *right!*"

Behind him, on the bed, Kate gave me a look of contented mockery. Cliff may have been shocked, but she most definitely was not.

That was about the extent of our sexual misadventures as children together, a deviancy that I never expected to recur any more than I believe Kate did. And I don't think it would have either, if even one link in the tenuous chain of cause and effect had been different from what it was.

That chain took form on a Sunday morning in May, a month before the two of us were to graduate from high school and join Cliff in proud attendance at the Woodglen Community Junior College, an economy which our Yale- and Sorbonne-educated father deemed necessary and even desirable, in that it would weaken an elitist bent he detected in our attitudes. I can remember lying there in bed alone—no, lying *here,* in this very room—and looking over at Cliff's Big Ben, which gave the time as eleven o'clock, almost three hours since I first had gotten out of bed to relieve my bladder of its beery burden from the night before. I remember being vaguely aware of Cliff getting up and dressing, preparing to escort Mother and the kids to church, as he often did, knowing how much it meant to her in the absence of Jason, who preferred to spend his Sunday mornings with the *Tribune* and in long solitary walks over his fields, undoubtedly thinking deep agrarian thoughts while he inspected his cattle and his fences and his grass. Stinking Joe was off for the day. And Kate — if she was not out riding her pony, she was probably still in her room, I judged, reading a book or sharpening her tongue.

The one thing I was certain she was not doing was contemplating a second act of Sabbath masturbation, as I was, basically because it seemed about the only chance I had of losing my erection before dinner that afternoon or maybe even before graduation in June. I gave continence one more chance, however, picturing in my mind the naked bodies of old men and women. I thought of chickens and cows and finally I concentrated on Jason, a mental *coup de grâce* that seldom failed me in my occasional quests for sexual calm. It did not work for me this time, though, so I slipped on my jockey shorts, arranging them in such a way as to force the damned thing down. At the same time I began to feel a powerful morning-after thirst and I started into the bathroom to get a drink of water — only to stop dead in the open doorway, for in front of me stood Kate, naked, cupping her breasts, studying herself in the full-length mirror on the wall next to the tub. She looked only puzzled at first, as if she could not figure out how I had come to be where I was, evidently believing that she had locked both doors. But almost immediately this other thing hit her, this fit of sudden mindless rage, and she turned on me in a snarl of flailing arms and clawing fingers. I tried to get out of there, bending and retreating under her senseless assault, but she kept coming, hitting and slashing and screaming at me. So I seized her wrists and spun her down onto my bed, trying to hold her there, trying to calm her.

"Kate!" I tried. "Please! I'm sorry! I didn't know you were there!"

But she kept struggling against me, writhing under me, trying to break my grip on her wrists. And she went on trying— for minutes, it seemed—until finally I began to feel the rage draining from her. I let go of her wrists then and she rolled onto her side, under me, giving me her back and pulling up her legs as she covered her face with her hands. And slowly, helplessly, she began to sob, a sobbing like no other I had ever heard, as if some alien force were tearing at her from the inside, shaking both of us as we lay there on the small twin bed. I stroked her head and patted her shoulder. And I pleaded with her.

"Don't, Kate. Please, honey. Please."

But she could not stop, no matter how much I begged. I tried to tell her that everything was all right now and that I had not meant to hurt her. I hugged her and I buried my face in her hair and I may even have kissed her too, but only as a brother trying to get his twin to stop that piteous sobbing.

And then abruptly it happened, the stuff spurting onto both of us, all over her buttocks and back and even up onto my chest. Until that moment I had not even been aware that I still had an erection, and especially not that my shorts had slipped down off it. But there the evidence was, as hot and sticky and shocking to me as it was to Kate. Immediately her crying ended. She turned on the bed and looked up at me, her expression bruised again with puzzlement and disbelief as her hand reached behind her and touched the semen and brought it around, viscous and dangling, for her eyes to see. Then she got up, slowly and carefully, as though she had been lying with a wild beast and feared to rouse it again.

"I didn't know, Kate!" I pleaded. "It was an accident!"

She drew her hand across the sheet, wiping it as she backed toward the door. Unable to meet her eyes, I looked down at her body, at her beautiful breasts and pubis and legs, catching myself only when it was too late.

"I'm sorry, Kate! Oh Christ, I'm sorry."

But she was already gone, running for her room. I heard the door slam and the lock crash into place. And then there was silence. Only silence. Hours of it.

For the rest of that morning and on into the afternoon I felt as if I had forgotten how to breathe, such was my sense of dread. And it was not that I was afraid Kate would tell Jason or Mother what I had done; she would never do that, I knew. Rather it was Kate herself I feared, the prospect of facing her across the Sunday dinner table and falling again within the firing range of her eyes, their cool green ignited now with feelings of disgust and disbelief and what other terrors I could only guess at, and dread.

So I stayed by myself. I showered for a good quarter of an hour, scrubbing my loathsome body until it stung. I put on clean clothes and I even straightened up the room and made my bed, an act of stunning irregularity for me. But finally there was nothing more to do and I left the room, hurrying past Kate's still-locked door and going down the back stairs to the kitchen, where I gulped some orange juice and took two breakfast rolls with me out to the barn. There I climbed into the haymow and made my way up over the mountains of bales to the open doors under the roof beam, almost to the spot where Kate and I had slaughtered the sparrows four years before. And there I stayed, sweating and chewing on hay stems and staring down at the house and farmyard, waiting for Mother and Cliff and the kids to return from church, and then the inevitable call for dinner, which I knew I would have to show up for, much like one's own execution.

So when the call finally came, delivered by little Sarah running about the farmyard, I reluctantly responded. Ironically, the occasion turned out to be an ordeal not for me but for Cliff. From the beginning Kate acted as if everything were the same as always, just another Sunday dinner in our lives. If anything, she seemed in a better mood than she normally was, smiling often and even laughing at Junior's bitter complaints about the hardness of the church seats. And when our eyes met

88

there was absolutely nothing in them to suggest that anything unusual had happened between us. But when it came to Cliff, that was another matter. Looking at him, her face would lighten with sardonic amusement, as if she were grateful that he was there and able to afford her so much fun.

"So how was Reverend Sunbeam today?" she asked. "Did he inspire you to new heights of Christian charity?"

Cliff was used to her taunting him about going to church. "As a matter of fact, he gave a good sermon," he told her. "Reverend Sonnenberg has his moments, you know."

"And it wouldn't hurt you or Greg to hear him either," Mother put in. "The two of you could use a little more Christian charity."

"Oh, don't I know it?" Kate said. "Poor Sunbeam must hate to waste his eloquence on such a paragon as Cliff when there are real lost souls like me and Greg around. But then that's the way it goes, isn't it? The bad just keep getting 'badder' and righteous keep getting 'righteouser.' The Lord's will, I guess."

Jason did not like contention at mealtime, unless he happened to be the cause of it. So he firmly suggested that Kate say nothing more until she had something good to say.

"But what I said *was* good," she protested. "How can one talk about Cliff and Reverend Sunbeam without saying something good?"

"You're trying our patience," Jason told her.

"I know it, I know it," she confessed. "Which just illustrates what I'm getting at. It's sinners like me old Sunbeam should be working on—not Cliff and Mother. Why it's like throwing pearls before Yasseen the jeweler. What Sunbeam should do instead is leave his pulpit and come out here Sunday mornings. That way, he could work on all *three* of us."

She smiled impishly at Jason and he surprised us all by laughing—at himself—something only Kate could bring about, and then only rarely. But he quickly recovered and soon was staring gravely down the table at my mother.

"Isn't it time for dessert?" he asked.

Though he could not afford servants, Jason never lacked for

service. Mother and Sarah quickly leaped up to clear the table, followed by Kate at her languid best.

"And will you be having dessert too?" she asked Cliff. "Or are you already too sweet?"

Afterwards Cliff came to me about Kate's performance at the dinner table.

"Why is she so hostile to me?" he asked. "What have I done? What have I said?"

"Nothing," I told him. "You know how she is lately. She just gets on her high horse and you can't get her off. Today was your turn, that's all. Tomorrow it'll be me."

He was dubious. "I don't know. It seems lately like I'm her target all the time. Jesus, you know as well as I do that I don't give a damn about Sunbeam. I go so Mother won't have to go alone with the kids, that's all."

"I know that. And so does Kate."

"So why all the heat, then? Can you explain it?"

I told him that I could not, and he shook his head wonderingly.

"God, she looks great, though, doesn't she? I wish she *would* go to church. She'd light up that place like a million candles." But even that thought had its dark side for Cliff. "It seems the better looking she gets, the harder she is to know. I really don't know her anymore. I honestly don't."

I mumbled a few words to the effect that she had become something of a stranger to me too. But even then, even after what had happened that morning, I still had only an embryonic understanding of what I meant by that. To me, she was still the same Kate as always, albeit a Kate with growing problems, not the least of which was a twin brother who was sexually out of control.

Later that afternoon, unbidden by Jason, I set out and walked the fence rows, ostensibly to check them for any breaks in the wire, when in reality all I did was mull over the problem of what had happened between Kate and me. And it did not take long for me to realize that the only way I could make sure such a thing never happened again was by changing *myself*. So I vowed to do just that. I vowed to give up masturbating and to throw away all my *Playboys*. I vowed not to think about girls and sex almost every waking minute of every day. And especially I vowed never again to think of Kate in sexual terms, even if I were to see her naked again. And I do believe—I *still* believe—that if it had been up to me alone, the thing with Kate would never have gone past that first strange encounter in my room. Unfortunately it was not up to me, at least not in the main.

When I got back that afternoon I came upon her in the barn, brushing her mare. I tried to talk to her about what had happened, hoping to explain to her the physiology of it, that she had caught me at a time when I had already been hard for hours and that it wasn't she—wasn't her body—so much as the simple *contact,* the pressure, that had caused the thing to happen. But she would not let me speak. She did not want to hear anything about it, she said, not ever again. It had been her fault, not mine. We were to forget it ever happened.

So I left the barn, already beginning to feel as if some great stone had been rolled off my chest. We would forget about the incident. It would never happen again and in time it would be as if it had never happened in the first place, much like the "touching" we had done as children. Within a few months, I told myself, the thing would probably seem unreal, an aberration we would remember only hazily, with a sense of puzzlement and even disbelief.

Thus did I resume the normal cadences of my life. I sailed through the rest of that day and the next two armored with a fool's innocence, trying not to think about the incident at all. I studied hard for my exams and on Tuesday I ran third in the four-forty in a track meet against Joliet—the only white boy in the event—which left me feeling voluptuously weary and contented when I went to bed that night, alone again, since Tuesday was one of three nights that Cliff worked late at the Eskimo.

It was after eleven o'clock, Jason and Mother and the kids were already in bed asleep, and I was just lying there studying the ceiling shapes and contemplating masturbation—for the second time since my Sunday vows—when I heard Kate come upstairs. She was in her room for a short time and then the light went on in the bathroom and I lay there listening while she used the toilet and bathed and toweled herself. I heard her brush her teeth and then her hair. And finally the light went off and the door opened again—only this time it was the door to my room.

In the glow from the polelight, I watched as she came to my bed and sat down on the edge of it, so close to me I already had stopped breathing. She was wearing her yellow robe and she was trembling. And to this day I don't know if I told her that she had to leave, that we could not do this thing, that it was wrong—I don't know if I actually said any of that or if it was all only words uttered in the safe and soundless chambers of my mind. I do know, however, that in the long moments before she spoke, I made no move to get out of there, I made no move to save her life. I watched as she untied her robe and let it fall from her. And I listened.

"Please, Greg. Just hold me. Like Sunday."

She was already slipping under the covers and her hand had found me by then, a touch I can feel even to this day, as if she had reconnected us in a way we had not known since birth, only now in a womb of fire. From the moment of that first touch, on through the whole long terrible summer, I was without will.

"Just hold me," she said. "Hold me tight."

The writing of this chapter has not come easy for me. My Bic is like a baseball bat in my fingers and I am forever getting up and walking over to the window as if I expected to find something outside that could distract me from this masochist's debauch. And, shades of Santa Barbara, I have even begun to drink again (with a manly dedication, that is) in the beginning hitting Junior's beer often enough to cause him to whine like an unemployed actor, and finally by pawning my Omega quartz (another of Ellen's gifts) in order to buy scotch in the quantities I now require. The booze of course has made me a real sweetheart to live with, as Toni would tell you at the drop of a bottle.

Just yesterday she came waltzing in here in the afternoon, evidently tired of playing nursemaid to the still-mending Junior. I told her to get out because I was working, when in fact I was only drinking, as she could plainly see. And since alcohol to this point in our relationship has usually meant playtime, she was ready to play. All she had on was her bathrobe.

"Come on, give it up," she advised me. "You're no book writer, you're a film writer. All you'll wind up with is a stack of tablets that no one will even look at. No one reads anymore."

"Is that so?"

She lay back on the bed, stretching, taunting me. "Yes, that's so. We do more interesting things now. We don't read about it—we *do* it."

It was like red-flagging a bull, for throughout these last ragged days of writing, the one thing I have truly come to despise in me is my ancient and well-documented slavery to cunt in all its lovely shapes and sizes. I put down my glass.

"Get out of here, Toni."

She looked up at the ceiling and shook her head. "No, I don't think so. You're the one who dragged me here to Siberia. So you've got to entertain me."

I told her to go down and play with Junior.

Making a face, she got up. "He stinks—have you noticed that? His breath *and* his body. Almost as bad as your old man." She smiled now. "Your family stinks, Greg. You come from a stinking family."

"I'm warning you." Yes, I'm afraid I actually said that, old screenwriter that I am.

But all it elicited from Toni was a casual shaking of her head. "First, you've got to read some of it to me—say, the last two pages you've written."

"I don't have to read anything to anybody."

"Why—you ashamed of it?"

I refilled my glass. "You could say that."

"Of what? The writing or the story?"

I didn't answer.

"What's it about? Tell me. Your brother and sister?"

I told her that I was waiting for her to leave, and she smiled.

"Well, that's just T.S. then, isn't it? At least you could tell me the title. That's it—you tell me the title and I'll go."

"Is that a promise?"

"Sure." She playfully crossed her left breast.

"How about *Remembrance of Things Past?*"

She gave me a pitying look. "Sounds dull. Real dull."

"*Sparrows,* then. How about that?"

"It's about *birds?*"

"Of a feather."

"No one will read it."

"Well, I'm at a loss then. I don't have any other title."

She was becoming impatient. "Come on. I won't leave until I know."

"Why don't you help me? You give me one."

"I don't know what it's about, remember?"

"Well, what kind of titles do you like?"

"Something snappy. Something that promises dirt. That's what people like. That's what they buy."

"You could be right."

"Of course I am."

I poured myself another drink, making a great show of concentration as I tried to come up with something both snappy and dirty.

"How about this?" I asked. "*My Sister, My Love.* How do you like that?"

Toni considered it. She cocked her head and her mouth rounded into a pensive pout. She repeated the words, and suddenly there was light.

"*Whose* sister?" she asked. "*Whose* love?"

I gave her a bored look. "I'm putting you on, baby. I'm making fun of you—with all your fantastic tales of incest from Junior."

Not unexpectedly, I had made her angry. She stood there for a moment, one hand on her hip, the other working her earlobe.

And then she lunged past me, knocking over my glass and snatching up the legal pad I had been writing on. She turned and almost made it out the door before I caught her by the arm, whipping her back into the room and making her drop the pad. In a rage now, she slapped my face, hard enough to cause me to swing back at her in mindless alcoholic reaction, smacking her on the side of the head and knocking her onto the bed. I immediately put out my hands to her, hoping somehow to absolve myself, to undo what I had done. But all I got was a snarl.

"You get away! Hear me? Get away from me!"

I put the tablet in the desk drawer with the others and locked the drawer. Then I picked up my bottle and my glass and I left the room. Surprisingly I was beginning to feel almost good about having hit her. She shouldn't have pressed me about the book, I told myself. She shouldn't have teased me. It was not a laughing matter.

After leaving Toni, I went down to Jason's library and locked the door. Increasingly in recent weeks I have begun to use the room as a place to get away from the others, a place to drink alone. I love the old black leather furniture and the walls of books, the bay window looking out upon the suburban blight. And best of all, with the door closed, I can't hear the television blaring in the kitchen, where Jason and Toni and Junior usually stay on and watch after supper. (It is warmer there, and they have moved a sofa and a La-Z-Boy in from the living room.)

On one occasion I tried to write in the library but soon gave it up, possibly because I felt Jason's frosty spirit peering over my shoulder and I sensed that I couldn't dredge all this out of me in there, that I'd dissemble and fudge and put a nice warm gloss on it, make it a piece for *McCalls* or the *Ladies' Home Journal*. So, besides drinking, I don't do much of anything when I'm there. I just sit with my feet up on the desk or I stretch out on the sofa, and that's about it. Oddly, this is something of a discovery for me, the considerable pleasures one can derive from total indolence. I don't write, I don't read, I don't listen to the radio,

I don't feel the need for talk or any other form of human intercourse. I have no desire to swim or play tennis or work out. And for that matter, I don't even do much in the way of thinking, except in a rambling, woolgathering sort of way.

As for what I'll be writing in these tablets the next day, I give the matter no thought at all, because of course it requires none. I lived through these heroic events, so I don't have to make them up. I don't have to organize them. I don't have to cheat and lie. No, about all I have to do is endure them in memory, as they track through my head, much like random particles of radioactivity. One barely feels himself dying.

Sarah has called twice from Florida in the last ten days, the first time to whine about the weather and the Cubans and the second time to inform us with a bubbling, breathless joy that she had a new friend, one Hector Ortega, who came over with the boat people in 1980 and now has his own taxicab as well as a luxury apartment. He is "so chivalrous," she said, "so gallant." She had never before met a man like him, and because of him she was thinking of staying on in Miami at least another week or two. (Phoning a fellow teacher, she had learned that the strike was still on, with no prospect of early settlement.)

Jason's only reaction to all this was to repeat the man's name in a scornful snort, as if it were a profanity. "*Ortega!*" he swore. "*Ortega!*" What could she be thinking? *Ortega!*"

Junior, however, seemed to consider it just about the funniest story he had ever heard. "Little Sarah's got a boy friend!" he howled. "A spic! Oh Jesus, I'd love to see them in bed! Can you picture it? Can you believe it? Sarah and Hector!"

Toni said that it was about time, that even if the man dumped Sarah, it would be a good thing. "At least she'll know she's been alive. Not just passing through this messed-up world."

"But *Hector!*" Junior roared. "Sarah and Hector!"

For myself, slurping up scotch in the library, I didn't give the matter much thought at all. If anything, I probably agreed with Toni that the affair would be good for Sarah, no matter how it came out. Better to have loved and lost, and all that. But I didn't

really care. I almost forgot what my little sister looked like—
and the others too, for that matter—Toni and Junior and
Jason. Or at least I wanted to, wanted to forget about them
altogether, for as the days of this chapter have dragged on, the
reality of Kate and Cliff, the *vividness* of my remembering of
them, has become such that I feel almost as if I had stepped over
the edge of this boring dimension of ours into something totally
beyond my experience. I have become an addict of recollection.
I write with a trembling pen. Tears glaze my eyes. My cock fills
and drains. I am living *then,* not now.

The day I hit Toni had been a particularly difficult one for
me, because it was on that day that I had begun to write about
Kate coming to my room. And it seemed there was no way I
could open the doors to that memory without seeing myself all
over again, in all my banal guilt. I was young, yes, but not so
young I should not have recognized the element of emotional
illness in Kate's behavior. The trouble is that it has always been
so easy for me to rationalize what I did—and did not do, to stop
her—on the basis of Kate's then long-standing history of
eccentricity and willfulness. If her coming to me was but
another example of that willfulness, though admittedly an
extreme one, still what was I to do? Chase her off? Run to
Mother and Jason with the problem and risk destroying not only
our own lives but those of everyone in the family?
  Oh, it can be rationalized, all right. There's no end to the
cologne and makeup I can dump on this venal face of mine. But
what I cannot change is the acuity of memory, the killing detail
with which I recall my feelings as she slipped under the covers
and took hold of me: confusion, yes, and panic too. But mostly I
remember the cool and stabbing joy of sexual gratification. And
to sustain that gratification I did just as she told me: I lay in the
resounding silence of this house and this room and let her bring
me to orgasm, without kissing her or fondling her or in fact
doing anything except hold her in my arms, as she instructed.
That, she said, was all she wanted: to be held and to give me
pleasure—why, I didn't know or even care at that point. Much

later—years later—I would begin to realize that it was probably only normality that she sought in my bed, the proof that she was not the cold and loveless loner everyone thought her to be, including herself—that, and her pathetic need to recover the lost intimacies of our childhood together.

Whatever her reasons, I went along with her, went along in precisely the sense that a dog accedes to the wishes of a bone. And that is why the writing of this temporarily at least has turned me into the same foul breast-thumping souse that Ellen dumped in Santa Barbara. It is why I stayed down in the library drinking all night after finishing those pages—and after hitting Toni. And it is why I've managed to darken this old doorstep only on four brief occasions over the past quarter century— because I knew that all I had to do was settle back just once, put up my feet and close my eyes, and I would be *gone*, just as I am now, lost somewhere in the past, hemorrhaging from my guts instead of tending tidily to that small open wound I've carried next to my heart all these years, my own little red badge of guilt.

I sat at Jason's desk and let the scotch do its curious work, until in time the victim was not Kate but Cliff, and the villain not me but Jason. I kept thinking of Cliff dragging himself home, probably not even aware of the pain and the bleeding in his great hunger to get here and put an end to his sister's murderer before Jason did it for him, with his killing eyes and his killing words—a death worse than dying, it must have seemed to Cliff. And I kept telling myself that the whole thing would never have ended that way if it had not been for Jason and the brutal stringency with which he treated his oldest son.

I walked the room and I drank and I sat again at the dinner table with the rest of the family, listening as Jason interrogated Cliff about his responsibilities.

"Did you give the Eskimo notice yet?"

"Not exactly."

"And what does that mean—not exactly?"

"I just haven't put a date on it yet, that's all. I told them I'd be leaving when they—"

"When they what?"

"When they don't need me so much. Right now they're pretty short-handed."

Jason's eyes blazed with pleasure. "I see. The fact that I want you to quit the job and go to work at the bank — in a position that I personally went out of my way to get for you — that doesn't cut any ice. But now, that bunch of dagos at the Eskimo — what they want — that *is* important, eh?"

"No, Father. It's just that I've worked there for so long. All through high school. And it's hard to just up and quit."

"Not if you're a man, it isn't."

Kate started to say something, but Jason quelled her with a look. Then he returned to the culprit.

"You hear me, Clifford? It isn't hard if you're a man. If you've got some fiber in your guts. You just tell yourself, *This is what my father wants. This is what is good for me and my family.* And you do it. And the hell with other considerations."

"I said I'd do it," Cliff mumbled. "And I will."

Jason snorted with contempt. "Sure you will — after fretting and fussing over it like some pathetic old woman."

And that finally was enough even for Cliff, who rebelled in the only way he ever did. He got up and left the table, tossing down his napkin with a modest show of anger. And when Kate and I both immediately got up and followed him outside, ignoring Jason's shouted orders for us to stay seated, Cliff only fled all the faster, apparently needing our sympathies no more than he did his father's constant derogation.

I sat at Jason's desk with my disappearing bottle of scotch and went through the breakfasts and dinners of our young lives, the imperial summonings into that selfsame room, and I became drunk, I became stoned on rage and loathing, to the point finally where the bottle was empty and I could barely stand. Nevertheless I managed somehow to make it out of the library and through the living room and up the undulating stairway to the old man's door, which I kicked open, splintering wood and breaking the jamb, even though the door had not been locked. And I saw him in the scarlet glow of his clock radio, a cadaver propped up on pillows, robed and muffled under a pile of blankets, his black eyes widening in fear and surprise as I crossed to his bed. I distinctly remember the numerals 3:09 burning in the darkness and I remember the droning sound of a man's voice, some anonymous caller-in to the talk show playing on the radio, a southern male softly explaining why a sawed-off four-ten shotgun was his weapon of choice for the coming race riots and social upheaval. *You won't have to shoot twice't,* he said. *Once't will do jist fine.*

As I took hold of Jason's robe, bunching the lapels and pulling him up out of the bed, the talk-show host was answering his caller. But I did not hear him, for I was talking now too. I was shaking my father and cursing him and laying upon his head the deaths of my brother and my sister. I called him a monster and a liar and a leech, and I told him that if he didn't hurry up and die soon I would kill him myself, just for the pleasure of it. By then, Junior and Toni had come in from their rooms and they tried to pull me off him but got nowhere until I decided to throw the old man back down onto the bed. And then I turned, charging out of the room and down the stairs and outside, slipping on the porch ice and falling onto the walk. I picked myself up and stumbled out to the street and headed north, not even feeling the cold as I lurched along, slipping and sliding on the icy, week-old snow.

I vaguely remember going along for miles that way, seeing no one except an occasional car and driver moving past. I even remember crawling along at times, mushing through the December snow like a malemute. And most of all, I remember calling out for Kate and Cliff.

"I'm here!" I cried. "I'm here! I can't help it—but I'm still here!"

seven

Somehow I managed to get through the weeks of exams and graduation without advertising the fact that I had become a mental case. When I was alone and thus free to brood on what had happened between Kate and me, I often became so tense that my hands would shake. Sometimes I could not eat and at other times I would feast ravenously, only to throw it all up later. I dutifully went to every senior beer party and swim party I could, both because I knew Kate would not be there and because it afforded me a good excuse to get drunk. Girls who had been valiantly defending their cherries against me for years were suddenly confronted with this morosely inebriated eunuch, and I am not sure which they felt more keenly: disappointment or relief.

Because I had asked one of them to the prom a month earlier, I stood by the commitment and double-dated with her and Cliff, who had been invited by the elder Tit Sister, over the years probably his most dogged admirer. I was politely civil to my date and in the car later I did not touch her at all, which was such heretical behavior for me that Cliff kept asking if I was sick, which of course I was—sick of thinking of Kate, who had turned down the three seniors foolhardy enough to have invited her to the dance. Her rejection of them was only a matter of habit, though, not of any new melancholia brought about by what we had done. If anything, she seemed happier and more carefree than she had for years. Every now and then I would hear her singing in her room or in the kitchen as she helped Mother with the dishes. Once I saw her skipping like a nine-year-old out to the barn, there to saddle up her colt for a sunny canter over our fields. She began to spend a lot of time on her hair and she even went so far as to wear dresses to school, which caused a number of our classmates to turn and look at her as if they were seeing her for the first time. She also began to smile more often, often without the taint of that old superiority, that air which said she was privy to things that you were not.

Despite all this cosmetology, though, at heart she was the same Kate as before, just as willful as always. She even took it upon herself to refuse to give the valedictory despite her having the highest grade average in our graduating class. Shrugging off cries of outrage from Jason as well as from the school administrators, she went her own singular way.

"I don't believe in all that upbeat patriotic junk," she said at dinner. "And if I told them what I did believe, they'd hang me."

Jason was apoplectic. "And just what beliefs are those, young lady?"

"Well, let me think," she said, with a show frown. "How about this? The race is to the swift. And the rest might as well not even bother."

"Oh, that's so cynical," Mother remonstrated.

But Jason thought it worse. "Cynical? It's downright disgusting, that's what it is! And from a girl like you, Kate. You ought to be ashamed."

She smiled sweetly. "You see why I don't want to give the speech? Think how ashamed I'd make you all."

She gave me a look of private amusement, stopping just short of a wink, and I looked away in stunned confusion. I still could not believe her reaction to what had happened between us, that she could accept it all so easily, as if it were nothing unusual or wrong. One would have thought the two of us accidentally had seen each other naked, something no more serious than that.

"Maybe I could let Greg give the speech for me," she said. "He made a B average without trying and we all know what a paragon of virtue he is."

The family got a good laugh out of that, even though the real joke was meant only for me. I had the feeling that Cliff, sitting next to us, sensed the current of cryptic irony flowing at the table. But he said nothing, perhaps out of fear of Kate, who had continued all through this period to shower him with her usual gifts of reckless invective.

In any case, she did not give the valedictory and by the second week in June the two of us were high school graduates still living at home, with nothing much ahead except the long hot summer and the dreary prospect of matriculating at Woodglen Junior College in the fall. I had not been able to find a summer job and had no real alternative except to slip into the routine of helping Stinking Joe around the farm. As for Kate, she never even looked for summer work, evidently feeling that she was contributing enough to the family finances by not going on to a legitimate college or university, which realistically should have been her lot, considering her splendid scholastic record.

Throughout that period I wanted desperately not to be alone with her, but everyone seemed joined in a conspiracy against me. Cliff was almost always at the Eskimo; Mother took the kids to Daily Vacation Bible School, where she taught a class; Stinking Joe could usually be found bogged down in some minor job conveniently located in the shade somewhere; and Jason of course confined himself to his library more and more as the days grew hotter. So I felt I had no choice except to make myself just as scarce as everyone else was doing. When Cliff got up early to go to work, I often got up too and had breakfast with him. Then I would rush through the farm chores and take the pickup into town for a long day of time-killing at the municipal swimming pool and at Ellie's Billiards as well as at the Eskimo, where I began what was to become a lifelong addiction to strong black coffee, over a dozen cups a day, probably because that was the only kind of freebie that my straight-arrow brother would allow me.

In the evenings I would go out drinking beer with Tim Regan or the Camelli brothers, hoping to find in oblivion a workable substitute for a clean conscience. And on more than one occasion during those weeks I stayed in the truck and slept it off rather than try to negotiate the tricky doors and stairways of our house. My problem, you see, was not only what I had done, but what I *wanted*. I don't think a full minute passed during those days that I didn't think of Kate and the last time she had come to my room. I kept seeing the tears in her eyes and her slight rueful helpless smile. Over and over I saw her breasts, her high firm beautiful breasts, as she opened her robe and let it slip from her. I remembered the feel of her body, the long silken hardness of her legs and trunk pressed against mine as my hands timidly brushed over her back and buttocks. And above all, I remembered the feel of her hand on me, as if it were not made of flesh and bone like mine but of something altogether different and altogether wondrous.

Even though I avoided her like the plague, hers seemed to be the only face I saw. Her hair and eyes, her lips and the white blaze of her teeth—they were all somehow new to me and beautiful beyond description. The fact that this creature had been mine, that she had lain naked in my bed and made if not love to me then something dazzlingly similar to love—I found it almost impossible to believe, let alone understand.

The one thing I did understand, however, was that it was morally wrong, all of it, not only what had happened but what I secretly longed to have happen over and over again. It is a terrible admission, I know, and one I never wanted to make. Yet in my heart I knew it to be the truth, and it was a truth that condemned me to even deeper feelings of guilt and responsibility. I was convinced that it was *my* duty, not Kate's, to make sure that the thing never happened again. So I felt I had every reason to stay away from home, and I thought I had reason to drink too.

Mornings when I was too hung over to get up with Cliff, I would manage to get out of bed and lock the door to the bathroom so she could not repeat her performance. And on one occasion she did tap on the door and ask me to unlock it.

"All I want to do it talk," she whispered. "What are you afraid of?"

I growled something about still being asleep when in fact I was wide awake, lying there in my sweat and anguish.

Later that same day she came upon Stinking Joe and me replacing fence posts in the south pasture. Joe promptly opined that a girl could do what he was doing—essentially just handing me tools—and that since he had more pressing work waiting for him in the implement shed, he would be generous and let Kate take his place. As he walked off, carrying his lunch bucket, she shook her head in mock admiration.

"Don't you just love him?" she said. "Isn't he just too cute for words?"

"That's our Joe, all right."

In the distance, the old man had turned to wave, and Kate now waved back at him. "Bye, you old mountebank!" she called.

I laughed with her, trying hard not to let on how uneasy I was at being alone with her again, even out there in the sweltering sun. To cover my anxiety, I worked furiously, tamping the ground in rock-hard around the three new posts we had sunk. Kate meanwhile crimped the loose barbed wire tight and I finished by stapling ("steepling," Joe called it) the wire to the posts. Finished, we picked up the tools and started back. For fifty yards or so the silence between us grew. Then Kate broke it.

"How come you didn't let me in this morning?"

"You know why."

"No, I don't. That's why I'm asking. I just wanted to talk."

"About what?"

"Oh, I don't know. Nothing in particular. Just talk. Like always."

I took a deep breath and somehow choked out the words.

"That one night, Kate—that night you came to my room—aren't we ever gonna talk about *that?*"

"What is there to say?"

I looked at her in disbelief. "For God's sake! You think it's normal, what we did? You think it's natural?"

"Was it so bad?"

"Jesus Christ!" I turned away from her, shaking my head and looking to the blazing sky for commiseration or at least comprehension. My twin was lost. We were both lost.

And as if to prove we were, she laughed at me. "Oh come on now, Greg, don't be so damned dramatic. It wasn't that big a thing. I don't know why it happened—it just did, that's all. I guess sometimes I'm like a sleepwalker. Like someone in a trance. I guess I don't always know what I'm doing."

"Don't give me that, Kate. Come on, we've got to face this thing. We've got to overcome it."

"Overcome what?" She shook her head. "Boy, I sure don't know what the big deal is. We're both still in one piece, you know. Nothing really happened."

"Nothing?!"

"Nothing to speak of. And even that won't happen again—I can promise you that."

She turned away from me and started to walk on, but I quickly caught her by the arm and roughly spun her around, so filled with rage and anguish I could barely speak.

"Jesus, Kate—don't you think I've got feelings? Do you think you can just—" But I could not finish.

"Can just what? What did I do?"

By then I was looking at her through tears, and I still could not believe her attitude of blithe innocence. I shoved her away from me so forcefully that she tripped and fell.

"Get away from me," I got out. "Get away and stay away."

She scrambled to her feet with a very different expression now, shock and anger taking the place of that maddening insouciance. Then she turned and ran off through the field toward the house in the distance. I watched as her figure grew smaller and finally disappeared beyond the barn. Then I sat down in the long buzzing grass and cried, helplessly, like the child I still was.

In the days after that I became something of a "case" both at home and in Woodglen. No longer caring enough even to do chores on the farm, each morning I went straight into town as fast as I could to begin a long day of drinking and fighting and getting into whatever other trouble I could find. When Jason confiscated the keys to the pickup, I either hitchhiked or went over to Tim Regan's and drove in with him. Never much of a friend in high school, he became my inseparable buddy, mostly because we now shared the same passions for indolence, pugnacity, and alcohol. When we could not afford the hard stuff, which was most of the time, we settled for beer and spent endless hours at Ellie's Billiards or at any bars that would let us in. We terrorized the high schoolers at the swimming pool and tried to get into at least one good fight a day, a regimen that finally not only got us kicked out of Ellie's but also landed us in jail overnight, for resisting the efforts of three middle-aged steelworkers to run us out of an east-side bar. The result was that old screenwriter's staple: broken chairs and bottles and windows as well as a few fearsome bruises. At the police station a friend of Cliff's had the good sense to call him instead of Jason, which meant that on the way home I had to endure only earnest concern and advice instead of moral outrage.

"I just don't know what the devil's going on anymore," Cliff lamented. "First, Kate changes into somebody I don't even know. And now you suddenly become some kind of half-assed town drunk. I just don't get it. We're all going to hell in a handbasket."

"What other way is there? You gotta take the old handbasket."

"This isn't funny, Greg."

"Yeah, I know."

"So get ahold of yourself, okay? You got your whole life ahead of you. If you have to fall apart sometime, why not do it in your forties? You got a lot of time."

"Okay, I'll try to wait."

But I did not. The next day I was back at the same stand, borrowing money for beer from friends and sweet-talking ancient Ellie into letting Tim and me back into her estimable establishment. And by twelve or one that night I once again made it home, stumbling out of Tim's pickup with an offhand wave and weaving my way on up the drive, deciding as I went that it was not sleep I needed but a good cold swim. So I went on past the barn and down the path to the pond, where I did a little jig on the swimming dock, trying to get out of my clothes. Making it finally, I dove into the water and swam slowly through the dark silence to the center of the pool before coming up. And I was amazed at the racket I suddenly heard, the frogs and crickets and cicadas all joining in a mighty chorus of disquiet. For some reason, it irritated me, all that noise, and I dove again and again to get away from it, staying longer each time in that black and soundless haven until I finally had no choice except to come up or drown.

Breaking the surface, I sucked in the sweet if raucous air, gasping, laughing at my own stupidity. And then I saw her. She was just standing there on the dock in her bathrobe, with her arms folded and her head cocked, in playful derision.

"Ah, there you are," she said. "I thought you'd drowned."

The cold water and her sudden appearance had left me feeling almost sober as I treaded water in the center of the pond.

"What're you doing here?" I asked.

"I heard Tim's truck. Then I saw you out the window. I saw you coming here."

"You go on home," I told her. "I'm drunk. I don't want you here."

In the faint light from the farmyard, I saw her smile flash. "Well, that's just too bad. I happen to live here, dear brother. It's my pond too, you know."

"Please, Kate. Don't—"

But I was already too late. With a twist of her shoulders she had shed her robe, and now she stepped to the edge of the platform, her body limned by the distant light.

"Don't be frightened," she mocked. "I just want to take a dip. I won't come near you."

With that, she dove into the water and came up about five feet in front of me, laughing, tossing her head to get the hair out of her face.

"Oh, this is great!" she cried. "This is the only time to swim!"

I quickly swam around her, back to the dock. But because I was naked, I did not climb out of the water, not yet. I just wanted to be able to leave quickly if I had to. But she made no move to come toward me. Instead she made a surface dive, which alternately put on display her buttocks and then her breasts as she broke the surface, smiling now, having a great time. Treading water, she came closer.

"I wanted to tell you," she said. "I think I've figured it out — what happened that night."

I said nothing.

"Don't you want to know?" She had reached a point where she could stand on the bottom with her head above water. I still did not answer, and she went on.

"Well, I figure it's because I'm queer and normal both. Queer in that I seem to dislike other people so much. The idea of having some boy at school touch me — it makes my flesh crawl. And yet the sex itself — that I'm not against. It's just that you and Cliff are the only boys — the only males — I can stand."

She said all this as if she were discussing muscles and tendons, a recent limp she had acquired. Somehow her inclusion of Cliff went right past my head, to be recalled only later, much later.

"It's still wrong, Kate," I told her. "And it's illegal too."

"The pharaohs didn't think so. Or the Romans. It was common then."

"But we're living now. In the twentieth century."

"Well, it doesn't matter. It's all past now, isn't it? It'll never happen again, will it?"

"No, it won't."

"Just that once."

"Yes."

She gradually had come closer, until finally she was standing only hip deep in the water, her arms crossed over her breasts, whether in sudden modesty or for warmth I could not tell. And only then did I see the tears brim her eyes and begin to spill over. And somehow they ran not just down her face but through my heart as well and I could not find the will to move as she continued toward me. At the end she unfolded her arms and reached out for me and I gathered her in. I crushed her glistening body to mine as we stood there in the waist-deep water. Her arms and legs curled wetly around me and locked, and I carried her that way to the grassy bank, already in her, already plunging. She pulled her mouth from mine just long enough to cry out.

"Oh love me. Please love me."

I have been on the wagon the last few days, with Toni cheering me every miserable step of the way. Since she herself has just about kicked the marijuana habit, albeit involuntarily (Junior's stash having finally run dry), the two of us have become a regular Mr. and Mrs. Clean. The opiate industry need not panic, however, for Junior magnanimously has rushed into the breach, expanding his daily six-pack of Bud habit into two and three packs, to the point now where some of the younger Congo Lords are scrounging his empty cans and selling them. Ironically, I get the feeling from things Junior has let slip that it is the Lords themselves who are contributing to this big new thirst of his, possibly in that there has been some sort of change in the protection agreement he had with them — the use of the barn in return for our not being burned out. Whatever the change, I gather that it doesn't enhance our security, though I can't be sure of this, since my little brother will not talk about the matter, evidently feeling that his dealings with the Lords are his business and his alone. But of course it *is* our business too, especially if this old tinderbox of a house happens to go up in flames one of these nights.

Now, you may wonder why we simply don't call the police

and have the Lords tossed out and put on warning against any acts of retaliation. If you do, then I can only surmise that you dwell in Butte or Fargo or some other quaint place like that, for here the police are powerless against the gangs. The Congo Lords, as I understand it, have protection arrangements of one kind or another with virtually every business in the area, as well as with many families—especially white families—that might conceivably have something of value to exchange for the privilege of not being burned out or worse. Such is the lovely state of affairs in the good old U.S. of A. in this ninth decade of the twentieth century.

By now, one would think that a man would have adapted to this sorry state. But not old Jason Kendall's boy Greg. No sir, no way. He was born free, white, and entitled, and that's the way he's going to stay if he has any say in the matter. So yesterday— a Saturday—I put on my coat and went out to the barn and into the lower-level room that once had served as a shop for repairing and servicing everything from tractors to birdhouses but which now was a clubroom, a large garishly painted affair crowded with two pool tables, a Foos Ball game, a number of pinball machines, and a classic Wurlitzer jukebox from whose neon splendor roared a soul number with indecipherable lyrics. The walls were covered with posters, many of them pornographic blow-ups (no pun intended) of black men being fellated by white girls, while others were handlettered recitations of what the Congo Lords were all about, pleasant little messages such as THE LORDS KILL. . . THE LORDS BURN . . . and the ever-popular THE LORDS RULE.

The Lords themselves—the half-dozen I could see—were spread out over an orange velvet pit group, some smoking grass, others fondling a couple of black girls who appeared to be about ten years old. Seeing me, most of the boys reacted as if a police raid were in progress. One of them even pulled a knife as he came toward me.

"Who you, motherfucker?" he demanded. "What you want here?"

I raised my hands in a gesture of peace and tried to ease into the argot. "Hey, cool it, man — I'm from the house. Kendall's brother. I want to see the man in charge."

"Charge of what?"

I shrugged. "In charge of you, I guess. Your boss. Your leader."

"How you know I ain't the boss?"

"Well, are you?"

He sniffed with contempt and pointed beyond me with his knife. Turning, I saw the youth Junior had described as "Sandman" emerging from the room that once had been a storage place for grain and feed. Despite the cold weather he was barechested except for an open sheepskin vest and a necklace of what appeared to be dog fangs. As before, his head was shaved.

"You the man to see?" I asked.

A thespian, he took his time answering, first picking up a pool cue and chalking it. He began to rack the balls.

"Didn't your brother tell you this place off-limits?"

"It's him I wanted to talk about."

Sandman slammed the cue ball into the rack so hard the six ball leaped the cushion and fell to the floor. "So talk," he said.

I took my time lighting a cigarette, figuring I knew as much about dramatic pauses as he did. "You two have some sort of protection arrangement, as I understand it. You get the use of the barn and we don't burn — something like that."

He stroked in the two ball, but scratched in the process. Shaking his head in disbelief, he took out the cue ball and started over. "Yeah," he said finally. "Something like that."

"Well, I was just wondering — he's acting kind of strange lately. Like maybe the deal between you two has changed. And he's worried about it."

Sandman looked at the others and laughed. They immediately laughed too. "That ain't what got you brother shook," he told me. "That ain't his problem."

"What is, then?"

He stroked again, and missed. "Motherfuckin' pole! It's bent!" He angrily exchanged the cue for another one.

I repeated my question.

"His problem," he said, "is Willy's old man."

"Who's Willy?"

Again Sandman laughed. "Sheeit, man—you don't know Willy? Willy's the little kid you brother fuck, that's who. Which is why Willy's mama kick you brother's ass." He glanced at the other Lords and they promptly joined again in the laughter.

"But now," he went on, "now the old man—the old nigger— he come home from somewheres and find out about it and he say he ain't just gonna kick ass—he gonna *kill* someone. And that someone is you brother. You dig?"

I nodded stupidly. "I dig, yeah. But is he serious? The old man, I mean."

Sandman was still trying to get a ball in clean. He gave me a pitying look. "Serious? Well sheeit yes, he serious. All us niggers is serious, man—didn't you know that?"

I mumbled my thanks and started for the door.

"But if I was you brother," Sandman said, "I wouldn't sweat too much. Willy's old man's a fuckin' wino. He ain't got half the balls the old lady got. Week from now he won't even remember who *Willy* is."

"Okay, I'll tell him. Thanks again."

But Sandman had more for me. "One other thing, man—this place, it *is* off-limits. You dig?"

I nodded as if I were grateful for the information. "Sure, I'll remember that."

Outside, the sky was whiter than the snow. The old house looked cold and uninhabited. Yet I returned to it with a lighter step than when I had left twenty minutes before, thanks to Sandman, for now at least I felt that we could all go to bed at night with some reasonable expectation of not being incinerated before morning. At the same time, I recognized that I was the only one who had gained any sense of reprieve, since I hadn't shared my recent concerns about the matter with Jason and

Toni, and since Junior naturally would have been only too keenly aware of the source of his anxiety—the danger not of fire but of being shot, by his youthful sex victim's wino daddy. So, having no one to share the good news with, I simply trudged back into the house and made a cup of instant coffee. Turning on the kitchen TV, I got a rerun of *The Rockford Files,* which as usual had my psyche zipping back to the Coast within seconds, overdosing on Malibu and sunshine and acres of tanned female flesh. What in the name of pathological nostalgia was I doing here, I wondered, immured in snow and useless memories when I could have been out there in the sun breathing fresh smog instead of the stale air of a Midwestern past?

I got the bottle out and laced the coffee just as Junior came down the stairs.

"Caught you," he said. "At it again, huh?"

"Yeah. Just can't help myself."

"Sometimes it's only in jest that we speak the truth."

"Is that a fact?"

He got a beer out of the refrigerator and joined me at the table. "That's a fact. And you want to know another fact?"

"Sure."

"Your Toni. She's leaving you."

"Really?"

"Yep. She's fleeing the coop. She's absconding."

I affected an indifference I did not feel. "Is she now?"

"So I'm told."

"By the lady herself?"

"You could say that."

"What did you do—give her a stake?"

"*Me?* What the hell kind of stake could I give anybody? No— she called her agent in Hollywood. What's his name—Dandy? Something like that."

By now my indifference was such that I could feel my face flushing and I had to resist a powerful urge to sweep my coffee cup off the table and go raging up the stairs to find Toni, for I knew what a bloodsucking lowlife her agent was, knew that the man would call the police and give them my whereabouts just for the pleasure of it, as well as to get me out of Toni's life. If he could not have her for himself, at least without me around he might be able to slip her into a few more porno flicks, out of spite as much as for the few bucks involved.

"She called him from here?" I said.

"Yessir. Called him collect, she did. And the gent's wiring her the air fare. She asked me to take her down to Western Union."

"Beautiful," I said. "Ain't that just beautiful."

"Well, it isn't my goddamn fault, you know. I don't want her to leave either. She livens up this tomb."

"Yeah, doesn't she." I finished my coffee and went on upstairs, warning myself every step of the way not to lose my temper and especially not to hit her again. That had never been my style.

I found her packing in our room, already dressed in her favorite traveling outfit, a Calvin Klein ranch-hand ensemble with every accoutrement except spurs.

"Don't try to stop me," she advised. "I've made up my mind."

I made a gesture of helplessness. "So be it. But *Dandy?* Can't you do better than that?"

"To get out of here I'd take money from the devil."

"Obviously."

She angrily closed and locked one bag and started on the other. "I kept begging you to go. For over a month now I've been begging you."

"And I explained why we couldn't."

She turned on me. "Oh, that's a lot of bullshit and you know it. You could've got money from somewhere. One of your wives or your rich Malibu buddies—they would've come through for you in a minute. But no—you're so far into this weird game of making like a penniless fugitive that you don't even know what's real anymore. Why, they would've had you out of jail in an hour and you never would've served five minutes more—you know that as well as I do."

I was almost struck dumb, as much by her uncharacteristic trenchancy as by her anger. "Do I?" I managed.

"Yes, you do. Your kind just doesn't rot in jails. It's like a law."

"I see. So all this is a game, then?"

"That's right. Some weird kind of *Roots* thing, that's about all I can figure. You're here because you want to be and because of what you're writing, whatever the hell *that* is. All I know is it's not for me — none of it."

"So you're running out."

"That's right. I'm running."

"Back to Venice and crawl into the sewer with Dandy."

"Sunshine and crowds, that's all I ask."

"Some standard."

"Better than this iceberg."

"And what about *us*?"

She laughed at me. "*Us*? What *us*? As if you gave a flying fuck about anyone except your dead brother and sister. And incidentally, isn't there a word for that? For someone who likes to hump dead bodies?"

That was the one thing she should not have said, the one button she should not have pushed. Going over to the bed, I picked up her two vinyl suitcases and tossed them out into the hall, where one of them broke open, spilling its contents as it tumbled down the stairs. Toni started to yell at me but I grabbed her too — by the collar of her wrangler's jacket — and gave her the bum's rush out of the room. I slammed the door behind her and locked it. And then I got a bottle of Red Label out of my desk and took a thirsty pull on it. I filled a glass and took it into the bathroom, where I proceeded to work on it while I soaked in a tub of hot water.

In time I heard the jeep leave and after that I heard Jason making his way down the stairs and interminably banging around in the kitchen, hoping to rouse someone to wait on him. But I stayed right where I was, adding hot water every so often, as the tub cooled in the wintry upstairs air. I kept sipping at my tumbler of scotch, hoping to warm the spirit as well as the flesh. And I thought about Toni and what an unlikely couple we made, not really lovers so much as participants in a one-night stand that we just didn't know how to fold. Or at least so I characterized the two of us to myself there in my cups in the tub. How in the world could we ever have had anything real together, I asked, a middle-aged pseudo-intellectual screenwriter and a high school dropout beach-girl and one-time porn bit-player? What possibly could we have had in common except sex? Which in this case just happened to be the whole ball game, though I didn't feel like admitting it just yet, soaking myself as I was, inside and out. But of course it was the good sex that made for the good quiet meals together (in California anyway) and the good long walks on the beach in the dying light. Admittedly, we seldom got around to discussing *auteur* theory or the symbolism in Bergman, but in extreme cases one just has to make do. In the absence of chicken soup, chateaubriand will suffice.

Before Toni, most of my women fell loosely into two categories epitomized by my two wives: either tough, smart, ballbreaking maneaters like Ellen Brubaker or soft, smothering, empathy-ridden soul-mates like Janet. Each in her own way was informed and stylish and intuitive and at times good company and fine in bed. But they also seemed to feel that the going rate for pussy was full and unencumbered title to a man's mind, body, and soul through all eternity. Not as beautiful as Toni, not as sexy, each of them nevertheless put a far higher price upon herself. And when each in time discovered my tendency to commit occasional adultery, one would have thought they had uncovered a mass rapist-murderer under their roofs, whereas Toni tends to view the weakness as only human, possibly because she herself shares it. And in California at least she had a considerable talent for helping a man relax, letting him just kick back and grow moss on his ass for weeks on end, with interruptions for only the big-ticket items like food and drink and sex. Now and then she might toss a dish or take a poke at you, but at least you never had to worry about those little showers of poisoned verbal darts unhappy feminists are forever launching your way. And the fact that Toni has been a royal pain in the ass of late doesn't really count, you see, because she is such a total and unreconstructable California Girl. Unable to roast in the sun, she naturally has begun to spoil.

So it was not some casual pickup who had just walked out on me, though at the moment I tried to pretend otherwise. I drained the glass and got out of the tub and toweled off. Going back to the bedroom, I wandered over to the mirror and stood there for a time—why, I don't know—perhaps just to get off a nifty thought or two about the mulish durability of our bodies, in that they could reveal such infinitesimal differences between youth and middle age, when in fact the essential self had undergone a journey so unremittingly arduous and harrowing that one would not have been surprised to see in the mirror a wizened and crippled grotesque. Or perhaps I just wanted to look at *it* yet again, the old one, my lord and master, agent of my Thirty Years' War, or rather my thirty years of peonage. Such a homely thing, so limp and harmless and somehow even obsequious, it seemed—how could it have reigned over my life as it has, pushing me this way and that way, demanding, possessing, ruling, this comic appendage, this *tissue*. It was an Augustinian plaint, I knew, and perhaps it merited an Augustinian solution. But of course we are not so simple anymore as to think that we could actually whip the old fellow, flagellate him into submission as it were. Polymorphous perverse creature that he is, he would only enjoy it and probably ask for more.

So I stood there as helpless as ever, not particularly impressed by my emperor but not cowed by him either. Rather, I merely accepted the reality of him—and his dominion—and the necessity of keeping him as quiet as possible. So I slipped into pajamas and a robe and settled in at the desk, confident that the feelings of Olympian eloquence induced in me by the alcohol would easily translate onto the page. But the minutes drained into hours and almost nothing came. So I drank more. I sat here at this desk over this very legal pad and the words became like dollars to a bankrupt. I was beginning to feel the loss of Toni more severely than I would have imagined I could. Suddenly I did not feel whole anymore. It was as if, in leaving, she had packed my guts in with her other belongings. I tried to think of what I was writing, but even there all I came up with was a feeling of loss, a vast blubbering alcoholic sense of deprivation and abandonment. I tried to convince myself that it was only Kate and Cliff I bled for, that all my bleary grief was due to what I was writing, a typical example of the artist so lost in his work that he finally becomes a part of it, a victim of it.

When I heard the jeep pull into the farmyard, I almost did not bother to get up and look, since the comings and goings of my little brother are not exactly of great moment in my life. But when the words are coming hard, any excuse to leave the desk will serve, and I went over to the window and looked down upon the darkened driveway—and saw not only Junior heading toward the house *but Toni too!* My heart, as they say, leaped. My guts were back in place. And, yes, even the old fellow stirred. Though I might not have known what I wanted, he did. He always does.

It was not an easy rapprochement. At first, Toni would not even talk to me and I had to make do with Junior's explanations. It seemed that reliable old Dandy had failed to put his money where his mouth was, with the result that Toni and Junior had waited in vain at Western Union for the telegraphed funds and finally had to leave when the place closed for the day. Junior then treated Toni to dinner and cocktails at a nearby Ramada Inn, where both of them concluded that I was a boiler-plated jerk and a rip-off artist and that if she returned to the house it would be simply as a family guest and not as my personal possession, to be abused in whatever tyrannical way I chose. She would be staying in Sarah's room from now on, I was informed, and that if I "tried any more funny stuff" with her, I would be out on my ear.

As I learned all this, Toni stood across the kitchen table glaring at me in sullen triumph, obviously quite pleased that she did not have to explain Dandy's failure to me or in fact even speak to me. You may remember that I was not totally sober at this time, which meant that I had resources of wit and daring not always available to me. So I just stood there smiling and nodding until Junior—the great beer drinker—made his inevitable pilgrimage to the bathroom. Then I vaulted over the kitchen table and, literally sweeping Toni off her feet, carried her upstairs with all the panache of a Rhett Butler. Our back staircase, however, is not quite as grand as the one at Tara and Toni's head kept banging against the wall on the way up. Screaming, she pounded me on the neck and shoulder, but I still managed to get her into our room and to lock the door behind us. I sat down on the bed with her on my lap and pinned her arms. I kissed her on the neck and ears and spoke softly to her, all the while trying not to let her bite me.

"Baby, I missed you so. I really did. And I love you. I really do. I didn't know how much until you left me. Please stay, okay? I do love you, baby. I really do."

By then Junior was pounding on the door and yelling a lot of nonsense about calling the police and having me committed. But Toni gave him the score.

"It's all right, Junior. I'm okay. I've decided to stay."

And that was that. I loosened my grip and she turned on my lap, smiling through her tears.

"Did you mean all that?" she asked.

"Of course."

"Then I'll stay."

We lay back on the bed and kissed and made up. We gradually got out of our clothes and we made long and passionate love. In time we went into the bathroom and bathed together, and then I went downstairs and got a tray of food for us. We ate and drank and afterwards we made love again. And finally, in each other's arms, we fell asleep.

Later, at close to three in the morning, I woke and put on pajamas and a robe and came here to my desk to work. I was feeling pretty good by then, sated and rested and ready. And I wondered as I sat here, gathering myself, how many men before me had recited those same hackneyed promises of love and devotion that I just had, and for the same inglorious reason—to assure himself such necessities as sex and comfort and human companionship so he could then get on with what was important in his life. Somehow I did not feel at all alone. I figured there had never been a dearth of bastards.

eight

Elsewhere in the world I believe it is Christmas week, that best of times for children and drunks and retailers. I am afraid, though, that the blessed season is going to pass almost unnoticed here at 101 Woodglen Road. No one has bothered to put up stockings or a tree; outside the snow is gone except for a grimy patch here and there; and we are all quite adept now at leaping upon the television or radio to change stations the moment a Christmas show or carol comes on, threatening to corrupt the almost religious mood of hopelessness that permeates the house. My reconciliation with Toni is fading with the snow and she has once again taken to flouncing about the house in her kimono, kicking furniture and breaking heirlooms. Yesterday in a fit of unspecified pique she took one of my mother's old Wedgwood plates and sent it sailing like a Frisbee the length of the living room and on into the library, where it smashed against the wall above my head. I pointed out to her that she had just destroyed a couple of hundred dollars, but she was not impressed.

"There's plenty more where that came from," she said, eyeing the rest of my mother's china cabinet.

She has left the cooking and housekeeping (what little gets done) to me and Junior, who lately has seemed almost as reluctant as Jason to leave the security of these four walls. Occasionally I will hear my little brother on the phone with someone, trying to score pot or coke, and other times just making gossip, bemoaning his outcast state with a fellow gay. The great rapport that once seemed to be building between him and Toni is now a shambles, I gather, possibly because she found him insufficiently swishy for a male friend in a nonsexual relationship. (Sounds like an Emmy-award category, doesn't it?)

Whatever, I go my own way, and increasingly that way leads me into the leathery ambience of Jason's library. Wonder of wonders, I am now even able to write there (witness these very words), which means that I can insulate myself from Toni's restless petulance for hours on end—except of course for those times when the door opens suddenly and I find myself dodging Wedgwood Frisbees. For the most part, though, I am quite alone, just me and my legal pads and my ghosts. And when the words are coming like kidney stones, I am able to get up from the desk and wander over to the bay window, there to look out upon the dazzling squalor of Woodglen Estates. "My town," I say to myself, like the comedian Jackie Gleason standing on his Fifth Avenue terrace. Or I can lie down on the sofa and put my hands behind my head, as though to support the great weight of cerebration going on inside it.

That happened to be my position when Jason wandered in yesterday, wheezing laboriously as he closed the door behind him and shuffled over to sag into one of the leather chairs.

"To what do I owe the honor?" I asked, ever the smartass.

"It's my house," he told me. "I go where I want."

I sat up and lit a cigarette. "So you do."

The man's color seemed to be getting worse, seemed more gray now that white. And he continued to breathe as if he had just run a mile.

"Jason—can you hear yourself?" I asked.

As expected, he dismissed the problem with a wave of his hand. "We've been through that," he got out.

"I guess we have."

"I came to talk about Sarah. What should we do?"

"What *can* we do?"

"Well, we have to do something!"

Not having heard from her for over a week, Jason had me call her motel in Miami yesterday morning, only to discover that she had checked out three days before without leaving a forwarding address. My opinion on the matter had not changed appreciably, and I repeated it for him now.

"She's a grown woman, Jason. She can take care of herself. Chances are, she and Hector just took off for the Keys for a week — something like that."

Jason shook his head in sorrow. "She's got no experience. That man could rob her. He could kill her and rob her."

"Not likely. They've already been together for weeks."

"It could *still* happen."

"The most he'll do is spend her money and then dump her. Which is bad enough, I guess."

"I don't know why she just left here like that. One minute she's here, and the next minute she's gone."

"Maybe because Toni and I were here. She knew we could fill in for her."

"Toni!" he snorted. "What could that tart do? What *does* she do? Only one thing in this world, as far as I can see."

"She ain't exactly overjoyed at being here herself," I told him.

"So why doesn't she leave? In fact, why don't you both leave?"

"I've already told you, Jason. If you could lend me a thousand or so, we'd be on our way."

"A thousand *what*?" he scoffed. "What money have I got? Keeping this place going and paying Junior all these years to stay on — what have I got left? *Nothing!* You know I don't get any social security. I never paid a penny into it."

"Well, it's bankrupt now anyway."

"People still get their checks!"

His anger had left him even more breathless and he went into a prolonged spasm of coughing and choking. I gave him a glass of water and patted him on the back, and he slowly came around.

"I wonder if I'll make it to the new year," he said.

"If you feel that way about yourself, you should see a doctor."

This time he didn't even bother to dismiss the idea. He just sat there watching me as I sat back on the sofa.

"I'm glad you came home, son," he told me. "I'm glad I saw you once more in my life."

"Well, I'm glad I came home too," I managed.

He continued to look at me, a ghastly smile pulling at his mouth. "What you said to me the other night—all those terrible things—did you mean them?"

"No, Jason. I was drunk."

"*In vino veritas.*" Unlike my fellow Hollywood illiterates, he pronounced the V's as W's.

"Not always."

His fingers began to drum on the arms of the leather chair. "How could I have had anything to do with Cliff's death? Why, I never even knew why he did it. How could a boy like that, with everything to live for—"

It was like telling a story to a child, only to have to tell it over and over again. "It was the car crash, Jason. Nothing else. He undoubtedly thought Kate was dead, and he blamed himself."

"So he punished himself. In that terrible way."

"Yes."

The black eyes fixed on me. "And I'm somehow responsible for that—it's what you said that night. Why, you even said I did it. You said I killed *both* of them."

I got up and went over to the bay window. "I've already explained that," I told him. "I was drunk. I could barely stand up."

He made a snorting sound again. "Just how does it feel to be that drunk? Can you tell me?"

"Liberating."

"I've never been drunk in my whole life. In Paris I got tipsy a few times. But that was all. I never liked the feeling."

"I seem to."

"Yes, you always did."

He was silent for a while and I finally moved away from the window, sitting down at the desk in a hopeful gesture of dismissal. But he ignored it, possibly because the desk was his.

"I never did understand that summer," he said. "Never understood any of it—the way you started drinking, and then running off to St. Louis like you did. And fighting with Cliff when you got back. Why, you two hadn't fought since you were kids. I couldn't figure it out. And then the night of the accident—Kate and Cliff being alone like that. What happened to their dates? Where were they? I never could figure it out."

When he looked at me for an answer all I gave him was a shrug.

"It was a strange time," I said. "Things just came undone."

He was shaking his head again. "And then Kate in the hospital the way she was, so terribly hurt and all covered with bandages. Not a day goes by I don't see her that way. And I *hear* her too—did you know that? In my mind, I *hear* her. And it's you she's asking for. You, and sometimes Cliff. Never me or Mother." He looked up at me now. "Tell me—do you ever hear her? Do you ever hear her asking for you?"

I was almost to the door by then. "It's about time for the news," I said. "Let's go see who got it today."

Even before Kate left me there on the bank of the pond, I had begun to feel a wholly new kind of desolation, a despair that I knew a man ultimately would not be able to live with. I lay face-down in the dew-drenched grass like some poor wounded animal too weak to get up and crawl away, and I listened as Kate slipped back into the water to clean herself, softly humming "Wake up, little Susie." When she came out again she put on her robe and knelt down next to me and kissed me on the head and shoulder.

"Don't worry about it," she said. "It'll be all right. Just think of me as someone else."

I did not answer.

"Just think how beautiful it was."

She kissed me on the head again and said that we were truly

lovers now and then she got up and ran towards home, humming again, a lover leaving her tryst. For a time, I still did not move, could not find the will or the energy for such a travail. And when I finally stirred, it was only to slip back into the water, a pathetic inverse of that creature purported to have crawled out of the primeval slime. I stretched out my arms and floated for a while, knowing that it would do no good to try to wash myself, that the mark was on me for good now, a scar for life. I could almost understand what had happened in the water with her and carrying her to the bank as I had. I had been without will then, really no more than an extension of her, an appendage. But that had ended with orgasm, in a brief cold hiatus of reality that I was only too willing to ignore there in the cradle of her thighs, ignore it over and over as it died in the mindless surge of our passion. I had, in short, known what we were doing, what *I* was doing. But I had done it anyway. I had done it over and over again.

So all I could do now was hang there in the dark water like a drowned man, a dead animal. And I have no idea how long I stayed in that position, whether it was only minutes or hours before I climbed onto the dock and got back into my clothes. I walked up the lane to the farmyard and went on into the house and up to my room, where I packed a toothbrush and razor and a few changes of clothes into an army surplus duffelbag. I kept expecting Cliff to wake up and start asking questions, but all he did was stir and hug his pillow.

In the kitchen, I left a note for my mother, saying that I had left for parts unknown and would probably be back in a few weeks. I told her not to worry about me and closed the note: *Love, Greg.* I got a paper bag and stuffed it with cold meat and bread and apples. And then I left, walking the three miles to the Route Sixty-six cloverleaf, where I had to thumb for only a few minutes before getting a ride with a sleepy cattle-truck driver who kept eyeing my duffelbag as if he suspected that it contained booty of one sort or another. He went only as far as Bloomington, though, so I had to get out there, alighting on the gravel shoulder of the road just as dawn began to spread above the flat fields of corn on the other side. But again I scored fairly quickly, this time picking up a ride with a heavy balding thirtyish salesman who was already nipping—or more likely, *still* nipping—at a fifth of P.M. bourbon as he pushed his late-model Cadillac along the freeway at a steady ninety miles an hour. In truth, it seemed an almost conservative speed, given the ease and comfort with which the huge car handled it. The salesman in any case thought it safe enough as he lounged back in the capacious front seat, driving with one hand and sometimes none as he lit one cigarette after another or punched in a new station on the car radio, all the while looking over at me with considerably more interest than he showed in the road.

His name was Comfort, he said, Dolan A. Comfort, and his game was restaurant supplies—"everything from Tums to toilet paper." It was a dog-eat-dog business and the bastards he dealt with would switch suppliers at the drop of a dime. But he was doing just fine, thank you, and when the boys at the warehouse in St. Louis saw his latest stack of orders they were gonna know once and for all just who *numero uno* was—not Mister College-Educated Watson after all, but rough old Dolan Comfort, that's who.

"How come you're so quiet, boy?" he asked finally.

"I'm tired, that's all."

"Didn't sleep last night?"

"Not a wink."

"How come?"

"I've been on the road."

"How come?"

"I had a fight at home," I said. "My old man tried to stab me, so I broke his arm with a baseball bat. Felt I'd better leave after that."

Dolan Comfort surveyed me again, grinning now. He took another pull on the bottle.

"You're bullshittin' me, boy," he said.

"Could be."

"Come on, admit it."

I shrugged in defeat. "Okay. Actually it was one of those toy bats. And it was his wrist that broke, not his arm. His wrist— and a couple of ribs."

Comfort laughed uneasily, apparently not quite sure what to make of his new rider. "Well, you sure got some tall tales to tell," he said.

But they were not tall enough, for he quickly veered the conversation back onto his favorite subject. Did I think I'd own a Cadillac by the time I was twenty-eight, he wanted to know. Well, that was how old he was when he bought his first Caddie four years before. This was his second, and he planned to go on buying new ones every two or three years for the rest of his life, and what did I think of that? The secret, he said, was simple. You just had to want the damned car so bad you'd go out and do *anything* to get it, which in his case meant selling the balls off the competition.

"You got to live to sell," he said. "You got to eat sell and breathe sell and sleep sell. So when you come marchin' in with your order book, them poor bastards know they ain't got no more chance than a snowball in hell of not givin' you an order. A *big* order. And you know why? 'Cause you drove up in a Cadillac, that's why. With a Caddie, you got 'em beat down and ass-whipped before the game even starts. Yessir. And what do you think of that?"

I was thinking that I wanted to sleep and Dolan A. Comfort's big voice was keeping me from it. "I don't know," I mumbled finally. "It seems to me that if you sold less, then you couldn't afford a Cadillac. And without a Cadillac, you wouldn't have any reason to sell anything. You could quit. You could retire."

My tale of arm-breaking may not have impressed him, but this observation definitely did. He made a sound of total disgust, a kind of bark that sprayed P.M. all over the dashboard. And immediately brakes were squealing and tires were smoking as the big car fishtailed to a stop on the shoulder of the road.

"Get out, asshole," I was told. "Get out or I throw you out."

My next ride was with a quiet old trucker who was content to let me sleep the rest of the way to St. Louis. When he let me out, on the riverfront, he asked me who Kate was and I told him that I didn't know anyone by that name.

"Is that a fact?" he said. "You could've fooled me."

I thanked him for the ride and pushed the door shut, wondering what I had said in my sleep. But it was a concern that the riverfront, with its air of violent bustle, quickly swallowed up. I had never been in St. Louis before and have never gone there since, so my memory of it is a vague jumble of street scenes and interiors of hotel and bar rooms that I can't place in any meaningful framework. I do remember that on getting out of the truck I found myself in an area of warehouses and working-stiff bars that held little attraction for me despite my thirst. So I shouldered my duffelbag and kept walking until I found an area that could boast a few run-down hotels as well as a string of strip joints in addition to the usual bars and warehouses.

I had seventy-six dollars on me, all that was left of my farm earnings. And it would go rapidly in a big city, I knew, so I chose a hotel that appeared to be only a step above a flophouse, getting a tiny room with a down-the-hall bath for four dollars a day. The room's one window opened on a brick wall, and the hammocklike bed reeked of mildew and worse. But I did not plan to be there very much, for that would have meant being alone and having time to think about my problems, when what I wanted was to forget them. Even more, I wanted to establish my sexual independence of Kate. I wanted to prove at least to myself that I was not some kind of incestuous pervert incapable of consummating the act except with his own twin sister. So it was the street I was interested in, getting drunk and finding girls and having sex—and never thinking about Kate, never thinking about what had happened at the pond.

But over the course of the next few days I found that getting drunk was the sole part of the regimen I seemed able to carry out. The only young and attractive women in the area were whores and strippers, and they were not particularly drawn to an eighteen-year-old who kept most of his money in his shoe. And as for never thinking about Kate, I seemed incapable of doing so for even two minutes in a row. It made no difference whether I was sober and wandering the riverfront or swilling beer in some filthy bar or falling asleep drunk on my hammock bed, Kate remained the empress of my mind. By day it was a thralldom I could handle, but at night, in dreams, it became increasingly terrifying, largely because my unconscious insisted on dragging not only my family onto the scene of our coupling but also the whole frightening menagerie of my childhood nightmares. Great black trampling bulls and mounds of dying birds and wolf-fanged dogs slashing at my feet—all figured in the dreams, right along with my mother, who at one moment would be pounding on my back and pulling at my hair as I continued to thrust into Kate, and at the next moment, despite all my pleas, would slowly and maddeningly *take her place*—this while Jason and Cliff sat watching or finally joined in themselves, dragging a shrieking Kate off through the sopping pondside grass. Sometimes the scene would shift and Kate and I would be copulating under water or in the center of a burning chicken house or as we tumbled downhill in deep grass, with the dogs steadily ripping at my feet.

I would wake whimpering and sweating in the tiny room, my heart racing as if I had just run the four-forty. Usually I would get up and stagger over to the canted sink to splash cold water on my face, hoping to wake myself, not just for the moment but for the rest of the night if I could manage it. Inevitably, though, I would find my way back to bed and the moment my head hit the pillow again I would be gone, sinking helplessly into the same old abyss of beasts and lust and violence. To sleep was to die a little. And all that week I kept on dying.

By day, I felt more hung over from the dreams than I did from alcohol. And it must have shown in my eyes, for on my second afternoon in town, in a place with sawdust on the floor, a tough-looking river worker came swaying down the bar and propositioned me in a voice loud enough for everyone there to hear. I told him that he had the wrong boy and he called me a liar, saying he knew I was "gay" (a new word to me then) just by the look in my eyes.

"You got pain, cocksucker!" he yelled. "Don't tell me you ain't got pain! I can see it!"

I got up from the bar, thinking my size might cool him off, but he kept on coming and finally shoved me backwards, shouting for me to admit it, admit I "liked it." I had my fists doubled by then and was getting ready to swing on him when the bartender reached out with a baseball bat and prodded him hard in the ribs.

"Out," the bartender said.

Only that, the one word, but it was enough to send the bastard on his way and to let me get back to my beer. I did so without any sense of relief or pleasure, though, for I was feeling oddly humiliated by then. I wanted desperately to leave the dump and get away from the amused and knowing looks the old-timers were casting my way. But even more, I did not want to leave and have them thinking that I had gone to meet with my propositioner. So I stayed for another hour at least, grimly drinking beer and eating rubbery popcorn and wondering what the hell the homo could have seen in my eyes. Was it that indelible, I wondered, the mark of the pervert, the sex criminal? My mark.

By my third or fourth day in St. Louis, I was spending a lot of time in a strip joint named the Lucky-O, much of it waiting for evening and the appearance of "Ginger Baby," a honey blond dancer with long sinuous legs and a perfectly hypnotic ass. A trucker sitting next to me at the bar one night said that her "going rate" was a hundred dollars an hour and that she always had plenty of takers. He himself was trying to lay aside a few bucks every week so he too one day could join that fortunate lineup at her door after hours.

As I sat there sipping Budweiser and watching her on the ramp behind the bar, it began to dawn on me that what had me staring at her with such slackjawed fascination was not her kinetic sexuality so much as the fact that she could have been an

132

incarnation of Kate, only older and coarser, her eyes unlit by a kindred intelligence. Still the physical similarity was enough so that I soon had given up beer alone for the faster oblivion of boilermakers. And when she came on again, hours later, I got up and stumbled out into the reeking riverfront night, for a few panicky moments not sure where I was or even who I was. I remember being crowded off the sidewalk by a pair of hookers and their dates. And I remember climbing the stairs at the hotel and clattering into my room, there to fall face-down on the hammock bed to sleep through the rest of that night and much of the following day.

Hung over and miserable, I treated myself to a late afternoon breakfast of steak and eggs and hash browns, washed down with Jereboams of fresh orange juice and coffee. I overtipped the waitress and walked down to the jetty to watch the great river flowing past, so muddy one would have thought it long ago would have carried the entire Midwest out to sea. I watched the light drain from the sky and then I dutifully marched back to the Lucky-O, this time sitting at a rear table and sticking patiently with mugs of Budweiser all through the evening, even when Ginger Baby finally came out onto the tiny stage and provocatively peeled down to a G-string and pasties. I watched the other strippers and I sat through the dragging intervals between shows. I stayed there until closing time and then I went back to my hotel room and again slept through much of the next day, once more having a huge late breakfast and wandering around the riverfront until night fell and it was time again to return to the Lucky-O and my ardent eyeball affair with my twin's double.

On that night, though, I waited on the sidewalk after closing, and when she finally emerged, with two other strippers, I asked if I could walk her home. It seemed to me a straight enough question, but Ginger Baby found it funny. Laughing, she asked the other girls if they wanted to adopt a baby boy, and they laughed too. Like a perfect jerk, I just stood there for a time with the rest of the sidewalk crowd gazing at the three girls as they piled into a cab and drove off. Then I caught myself and hurried on, having already heard enough jibes and laughter at my expense. Still not wanting to go back to my room, I thought I would try to find an after-hours club somewhere. But I had gone only a short distance when a smiling black woman suddenly reached out and took hold of my arm.

"Fuck them white chicks," she said. "You don't need 'em. You got you mama now."

She asked me how much money I had and I shrewdly told her ten bucks, figuring that what was in my shoe was my own business.

"Sheeit," she said, "that ain't enough to drink on — and forgit the rest."

"Sorry about that." I started to pull my arm free, but she held on tighter.

"Now, don't be in such a hurry, boy," she said. "Where you headed?"

"Home."

Under the streetlight, she gave me a look of extravagant suspicion. "You mean you don't want you mama?"

I tried to smile. "I'm pretty drunk."

"Well, me too, honey!" She laughed and gave my arm a squeeze. "So why don't we just see what we can work out, huh? Together?"

We went down an alley and up another street for a couple of blocks and then she took my hand and guided me through four or five black men sitting on a tenement stoop drinking wine and smoking what I thought were home-made cigarettes. They ignored me totally and I followed the woman into a hallway so foul-smelling that I immediately pulled away from her on the rickety staircase.

"It stinks in here," I said.

"Not in my place it don't, honey. You just come on along."

On the second floor she banged on an apartment door and got a gallon of red unlabeled wine from the man inside. Then she pulled me on up to the third floor and into her own apartment, which smelled only slightly less foul than the stairwell.

"Well, this is it, honey," she said. "This is Mama's paradise."

The only light in the place came from a television set, a black and white test pattern dimly illuminating two little girls sleeping peacefully on the floor. On a nearby cot a smaller boy and girl also lay asleep, tangled and sucking their thumbs. Across the sparsely furnished room an older girl stood rubbing her eyes in the doorway to a bedroom.

"What you got there?" she asked her mother.

"None you damn bidness, chile. You just go back to bed. And you feed the babies in the morning. You hear?"

The girl nodded and retreated into the bedroom and I wondered how many more children were in there with her. Mama meanwhile had picked two glasses out of the sink and rinsed them. And now she shuffled on into a second bedroom, this one lit by a large red Budweiser sign three or four blocks away, standing sentinel over one of the river bridges. She poured us each a drink and then she sat back on the bed, bowing it with her ample hams.

"Well, what do you think of you mama?" she asked. "And what do you think of Mama's place?"

"Fine," I said. "Both fine."

In truth, the woman did have nice warm eyes and a beautiful smile, but she was dark brown and heavy and the grease of her processed hair looked as if it had been troweled on. We could drink together, I thought, but only that. Anything else was out of the question.

"You ever had a Latin lady before?" she asked.

I shook my head.

"Then let's see you money, honey."

"I don't want sex," I stammered. "I've had too much to drink."

She laughed again, the same rich easy laugh. "Baby, nobody ever gits that much."

"I do."

She cocked her head at me. "What you so sad about? Purty young white thing like you."

"I'm not sad."

"Sure you is." She took a drink of the wine and nodded at me.

"Come on, drink up, chile. We got a long ways to go."

As I drank, she kicked off her shoes and slipped out of her dress, which was all she had on except for her brassiere. I watched, mesmerized, as she undid the clasp on the brassiere and let her great fat breasts spill out. Naked, she looked like a mound of basketballs.

"I got to be going," I said.

"Sheeit, you do. You just come here a minute, baby. One little minute and then you still want to go, fine, I let you go. I even wave you bye."

I was drunk enough so that it was not hard to do nothing, let her take me by the shoulders and sit me down onto the bed and then just loll back and watch as she pulled off my pants and shorts. She smiled up at me and then abruptly buried her shining black head in my lap, and immediately I could feel the rush beginning, the blood and heat and joy surging to the touch of her mouth and tongue. She let out a laugh and looked up at me.

"So you gots to be goin', does you?"

From that point on, the night took on the character of what my colleagues and I inevitably call a montage sequence: random frames lifted here and there out of a long reel of time. I remember my black "mama" sitting astride me like a Buddha playing jockey, laughing and whooping and rocking the bed as her older daughter, holding a crying infant, stood watching us in the doorway. In another frame the baby is lying next to us and Mama is cooing to it and tickling it with one hand while with the other she guides me into yet another of her orifices. And then there is the drinking, the taste and smell of too-sweet wine as we sit on the bed in the crimson gloom among dozing children and pass the bottle and laugh and begin again. I remember going to the bathroom a few times, adding to the foul blocked mess already in it, and I remember her taking the money out of my pants, though not out of my shoe — when and how that happened, I still don't know.

But in time even the individual frames began to blur and later I remembered only vaguely a huge black man abruptly appearing on the scene, switching on lights and knocking over chairs and even tipping over the bed—with us in it—flipping it as if it were a mat. I remember the screaming of Mama and the girls and I remember my fear as he came at me. But the fight itself— the beating, that is—I have only glimpses of: the sudden pain and the taste of blood, the sensation of falling and crawling and finally tumbling down the stairs and getting up only to fall again, and finally plunging out into the riverfront night without any clothes on, limping and bleeding my way down the street. I recall the oldest daughter coming out of nowhere and throwing my clothes and shoes at me, then running off. Too drunk to get into them, I carried the clothes down an alley and crawled back behind some garbage cans and empty boxes, and lay down. There I remember hearing a soft moaning sound, my own voice echoing out of one of the cardboard boxes I lay among. And then there was nothing, not even the sensation of falling.

Late the next morning, I woke to find a trio of mangy dogs sniffing at me and licking my feet and hands. I jumped up, scattering them, and hurriedly dressed and left the alley. On the street, people stared openly at me and wagged their heads, and when I got back to my room and looked into the mirror, I learned why: my cheek was swollen and there was dried blood below my nose and on my jaw. Every bone and muscle in my body ached and I could not tell how much of the pain was due to the beating and how much to my hangover, which was prodigious. I checked my pockets and shoes and found the money gone, all of it. Not knowing what else to do, I washed the dried blood off my face and crawled into bed, grateful that the room was paid for until noon of the next day. I dozed off now and then and got up only to drink water and to use the bathroom down the hall. And by early evening I fell asleep again and slept all that night, hardly dreaming at all.

The following morning I went to the diner where I had eaten most of my meals since hitting town and I explained to the owner-cook that I had been mugged and that I was broke and would be willing to wash dishes in exchange for food. In answer, he brought me a glass of milk and two aging breakfast rolls, which he said I could pay for later, after I found a job.

I went back to the hotel and checked out, carrying my duffelbag with me as I looked for work, anything to see me through the next few days. As hungry and beaten-down as I felt, I was tempted to walk over to one of the bridges and hitch a ride home. But the thought of arriving there and limping up onto that wide front porch with Jason contentedly taking in my swollen face and whipped spirit—that, I felt, would have been too steep a price to pay. So I kept looking and finally talked a jolly old cement-block maker named Donato into letting me help unload a freight car of bagged cement that had just come in. A young deaf-mute was already on the job and Donato said that my pay would be the same as his: one dollar an hour ("but fer *woik*, not coffee-breakin'") and that if the two of us got the load off by the end of the next day we would each get a bonus of four dollars.

The job was simple enough. All the deaf-mute and I had to do was pick up the hundred-pound sacks one at a time and carry them to the freight car door and then down a ramp to the ground, where we stacked them on skids, which Donato himself would then pick up with his forklift truck and transfer into the kiln yard. It was simple, much as torture is simple. The temperature inside the car had to be over one hundred degrees and the cement dust made the air all but unbreathable. And the huge freight car held close to fifteen hundred sacks, which meant that the deaf-mute and I each had to heft and carry almost ninety thousand pounds over the two days.

But we did it. I slept there in the kiln yard at night, and I ate at the diner (*after* paying for the milk and buns I owed for). And when the job was finished I continued to sleep out-of-doors for the next two nights, wandering the waterfront through much of the day, doing nothing and drinking nothing, lost in a useless debate with myself. Hour after hour I went over the thing in my mind, what had happened between me and the black woman who called herself "Mama." I still found it incredible that I'd had sex with her, and not just once but *repeatedly*. For in my eighteen-year-old mind, she was as sexually alien as a female could get, being fat and middle-aged and of another race. And yet the fact remained that I had responded to her. I had gone along with her. I even had initiated some of the things we did. I kept seeing myself there with her in bed, red-lit by Budweiser, accepting the smell of the place, the children, the whole squalid ghetto scene. And I began to tell myself that it was all only natural, no more or less than a man obeying his instincts. Reason had not entered in. I had made no choices. I simply had let go, much like letting go of the jetty railing and dropping into the great brown surge of the river. A man could protest and flap his arms or he could screw on a look of noble determination and pretend to the whole wide world that he was swimming, when in fact all he was doing was going with the flow, the irresistible flow of the river, like any other flotsam. And I told myself that if this was true for me and the black woman, then was it not also true—a thousand times truer—for me and Kate? Had I ever really had any choice in what we did? Was I actually at fault? Or was it that the decisions all had been made for me, back at the sources of rivers, in the springs of time?

It was a comforting line of thought and I gave it a good play during those last few days I spent in the city, waiting for my swollen cheek to go down and for the soreness to work its way out of my body. But in truth it was an idea that prospered only in daylight. At night, as my dreams kicked up again and had me lying awake under the stars for hours, I found myself wondering if my experience with Mama could ever be construed as anything except a bizarre and degenerate rutting in the filth, proving only that I was out of control, a sexual outlaw with no more concern for myself than I'd had for my sister. And as for achieving any sexual independence from Kate, had I really managed such a feat in Mama's bed, or was it that in accepting her black and alien embrace I had managed only to brand myself more than ever my twin's slave?

Lying awake in an alley, I grudgingly gave up on the Great Debate. Whatever the truth was, it would make no difference in the end—that much I was sure of anyway. Above me, I could see a patch of night sky and I could smell the river a few blocks away, flowing on, just as it always had flowed. And I realized suddenly that I would be heading home when it was light, if for no other reason than that I had to see Kate again, had to be there with her when it all finally came out, as it inevitably would. And then—that was the part I didn't know. Not then anyway.

nine

When we went to bed last night the rain already had begun, a cold steady drizzle that even then was starting to freeze onto the power lines and the trees. So on rising this morning I was not surprised to find a somewhat seedy version of a Hallmark Christmas card outside my window: the sun glinting coldly off a world immured in ice. Down the street a spindly hickory tree had fallen across a power line and I could see, like a string of exploding ladyfingers, a steady electric discharge onto the ice-covered pavement below. The trees still standing had the look of crystal willows and I did not doubt that a number of them might also take the plunge.

There was not much I could do about it, however, so I padded back to bed and kissed Toni on the ear in the hope of waking her and having some company, but all she did was sigh and pull the covers more tightly around her, which left me with no choice except to go into the bathroom and shave as noisily as I could. I was just finishing when I heard a sharp, cracking sound, followed by the splintering racket of the front porch and the front wall of the house giving way. Toni incredibly went right on sleeping, even as I yelled at her on my way into Jason's room, where I found the old man propped up in bed, his eyes afire with indignation more than shock as he stared out at me from behind a maze of ice-covered oak branches. Beyond him, through a yawning hole in the wall, I saw blue sky where our one surviving oak so recently had stood.

"Get me out of here!" he croaked.

Junior was in the room now too and he pushed back some of the branches while I coaxed Jason free and got him onto his feet. I walked him into Sarah's room and helped him into her bed.

"My home!" he complained. "Even that! They won't even leave me that."

I told him that it was only *part* of the front of the house that had been hit and that it could be repaired, could be made to look like new again, but he was not listening.

"My home!" he said again. "Even that!"

I went back to his room and helped Junior pull the bed away from the tree's invading branches, which were already beginning to rain melting ice onto the furniture and the floor.

"This is all we needed," Junior grumbled.

"Better get in a call to your insurance agent," I told him, only to get a sour laugh in response.

"*What* insurance?"

He had started down the stairs by then and I followed him into the living room, where we found the main part of the tree-trunk braced at one end on the old upright piano and running across the room, down and out through the shattered wall to the point of the break. There a single white spire of oak still stood, as though to mark the spot of the killing. Inside the living room a small forest of ice-coated branches scraped at what was left of the ceiling—and the floor of Jason's bedroom.

"Jesus," Junior said, "the old bastard almost bought it."

"Yeah, he was lucky."

"Wasn't he, though."

"Getting back—what were you saying about insurance?"

He made a face. "Just that we ain't got any, that's all. In an area like this, they really sock it to you. So Jason canceled."

"Beautiful."

"Yeah, ain't it. Especially with the Congo Lords around."

"I get the picture," I said. "But what about this mess? You got a chainsaw?"

That made him laugh. "Oh sure. There's so much for me to cut up around here."

"Then we'll have to buy one."

"And after you cut up the tree, what happens then? Do we rebuild the front of the house? You a carpenter now, as well as a has-been screenwriter?"

"We could board it up anyway. With plywood and two-by-fours."

He was smiling wearily. "I take it you haven't been to a lumberyard lately. You got any idea what plywood costs?"

I asked him what alternatives we had.

"Just close the rooms off. Take what we want out of here and Jason's bedroom, and close them off. It's just a lot of space. Who needs it?"

"Jason, for one. I don't think he'll like being in Sarah's room."

"Then that's kind of his problem, isn't it?"

Hugging herself for warmth, Toni had just come down from upstairs.

"Your old man's crying," she told us. "He wants both of you."

"Yeah," Junior said. "*Now* he does."

As I turned to go, Toni ran her hand through the branches above her head. She pulled an icicle and touched it to her tongue.

"You know, I didn't even hear the damn thing fall," she said. "I must've been dreaming of the beach."

In the hours that followed I learned more about Jason and Junior's finances than I had in all the weeks since my return. As I expected, Jason insisted that he could not stay in any room except his own and that both it and the living room would have to be repaired immediately.

"We're not animals," he proclaimed. "We don't live in the out-of-doors."

Junior patiently heard him out and said, fine, he would do

just what Jason wanted, all he needed was money—a statement that immediately had the old man shaking with frustration. And only slowly did it come out that Jason's checking and savings accounts at the bank were empty. The checks he had written two weeks before to pay utility bills had cleaned him out, he admitted. There was only nine dollars left in the account.

"So it's up to you now," he said to Junior. "All that money I've been paying you all these years to stay on here—it's time you spent some of it. With Sarah gone, it's all we've got."

Junior's reaction to this was, first, to punch the wall upon learning that the kitty was empty and that he would no longer be getting his monthly check, and second, to have a short sour laugh at the idea of his paying for any repairs on the house.

"I'd like to know how the hell I'm supposed to have saved any money on the princely salary of two hundred bucks a month," he said. "These days, that's about enough for cigarettes and beer. But of course you wouldn't know that, holed up here in this house like some kind of mole all these years."

Jason had begun to cough and wheeze. "That's enough!" he got out.

"Not hardly, old man. You should also know that even if I had the bread, none of it would go into this place—unless of course you want to put my name right up there with Sarah's in your goddamn will!"

"You got the allowance!" the old man thundered. "Sarah gets the farm!"

Junior looked at me for commiseration. "Listen to that, will you? *Allowance,* he calls it. And this place is a *farm.* All three acres of it."

He dismissed the matter with a contemptuous wave of his hand and went back downstairs, where I heard him and Toni begin to move some of the furniture out of the living room. Meanwhile I tried as best I could to comfort the old man, which is not saying much, I realize. But he responded well enough and in time I even got him to discuss his finances more calmly, in the hope that we could turn up something somewhere. And sure enough, there it was, just within reach of his senescent memory now that I was prodding him—a safe deposit box. It had been a couple of years since he'd even checked the thing, he said, and though he couldn't be sure of this, he vaguely remembered keeping something in it besides his legal papers.

"It could be cash," he went on. "Yes, I think there could be some cash there. I've been worried about the banks for years, you know. That they'd fail. I didn't want everything in my savings account."

"Well, it's certainly worth looking into," I said, enjoying the pun even if Jason did not.

He was growing more excited. "I'm almost sure there's money in that box. I'm almost positive."

I wanted to ask him how *much*, but bit my tongue, knowing that he immediately would have pointed out that it was none of my business. Then suddenly his excitement evaporated and he sank back onto the pillows.

"But I can't go to the bank," he said.

"The streets ought to be better tomorrow. They're probably salting them already."

"I can't go anywhere."

"Why not?"

He looked at me with narrowing eyes, as if he only now remembered something very important. "You think I've forgotten that night? How you shook me? How you told me to *hurry up and die?*"

I asked him what that had to do with anything, and he gave me a derisive snort.

"I just might have an 'accident' out there, eh?" he said. "A fall on the ice. Something like that."

All I could do was shake my head in amazement. "You are something else, you know that?"

"I'm alive, if that's what you mean."

On my way downstairs, he yelled for me to tell Junior about the safe deposit box, which I did, barely getting the words out before my little brother had run up the stairs to offer the old man any assistance he could. Within minutes Jason was trying to get the bank on the phone, only to discover that the line was dead (as it was to remain for most of that day). Undaunted, Junior got the jeep out of the garage and roared down our ice-covered drive to the ice-covered street, doubtless slipping and sliding all the way to the bank, where he found that he had to bring a new signature card home for himself and Jason to sign. That done, he sped off in the jeep again to check out the safe deposit box, suddenly the most cooperative son a man could have.

While he was gone, Toni decided to have another go at me. Bundled in boots and two pairs of jeans and a hooded winter coat of Sarah's, she kept opening the hitherto seldom used sliding doors to the living room, letting in the bracing January air.

"Come on and enjoy!" she said. "Don't deny yourself like this. Here we have a tree in the living room and blue sky and everything, and what do you do? You try to close it off. You shut it out. And that's just not like you, Greg. Come on, let's get into this thing and really *freeze*. Let's really *suffer*. That's what it's all about, isn't it?"

After patiently closing the doors again, I put my arm around her shoulders and guided her back to the kitchen, which the electric range kept almost toasty. I sat her down at the table.

"You haven't had breakfast yet, as I recall," I said. "Let me make you something."

"How about some gruel? That sounds like something you might be into."

"How about scrambled eggs instead?"

"Or hardtack?" she countered. "Maybe gruel *and* hardtack."

"You're very funny today."

"And why not? Sitting here in a fucking parka at the fucking breakfast table—what else could I be but funny?"

"Be grateful for the parka. It shows what good care I take of you."

She picked up her coffee mug and started to throw it at me, but reconsidered and put it back on the table.

"Jesus, I don't know what's happening to me," she said.

"You've turned me into such a jerk. I think we've already played this scene a hundred times, and here we go again."

I cracked her eggs into a bowl and began to whip them as she went on, sounding reflective now, almost bemused.

"At first, I kept telling myself that it would just be another day or two and I could stick it out till then. I could take almost anything for a couple of days, even this place. But then you changed it to another week and I accepted that too, just so we could be together. *Leave* here together. And now—" She looked up at me. "Just what is the new timetable? Another season? Do we wait till summer now?"

I told her that Junior just might be returning from the bank with some money, possibly enough for Jason to give me a loan.

"Then maybe we could leave in a few days," I said. "When the weather breaks."

She gave me a pitying look. "And you expect me to believe that, don't you? With your old man in the shape he's in, and the great American diary unfinished? You're here for good, buster. And we both know it."

"I don't know any such thing."

"So I've just got to face it, that's all. The only way out of here is by myself. With my thumb. And I'm gonna do it too. I figure a couple of rapes and one or two beatings ought to get me back to California. What do you think?"

I told her that she was breaking my heart.

"Yeah, well, you'll see, buster."

I brought her eggs and toast to the table and she poured herself another cup of coffee. Squatting next to her, with one hand on her bottom, I lifted a forkful of egg to her mouth. She took a bite and then very deliberately relieved me of the fork.

"I'm in no mood for your games," she said.

I nuzzled her breast, lost somewhere under the thick parka. "You wouldn't leave before my birthday, would you?" I asked. "Remember, it's just two days away."

"How could I forget? *Forty-four.* Jesus, it's like living with my own grandfather."

"Grandpa wants a kiss."

But all I got was her cheek and the same rueful look. I kissed her anyway, and stood.

"Well, Junior should be back soon. Maybe he'll have some good news."

Toni went right on eating.

Despite his service's motto, the postman was six hours late that day. But among the usual junk mail was a postcard from Sarah, with a picture of Disneyworld on the front, looking like a kiddieland Kremlin. On the reverse side she sent us greetings and said that she was still having a great time. She was staying at a Holiday Inn. Hector had had to return to Miami on business for a day or two. But he would be back soon, she wrote. She just knew he would. Then it was *Love to All, Sarah,* followed by a postscript saying that she missed us but not the snow and would be coming home soon.

Jason scoffed at the whole thing. "*Disneyland! Hector!* What can she be thinking of?"

Nevertheless he kept the card with him in bed.

I did not make it back to the farm until six in the evening, which in the home of Jason Cutter Kendall meant that everyone was already at the dinner table. Little Sarah, perched on her seat pillows, may not have been the first to see me walking up the road, but she most definitely was the only one to come running out to greet me, undoubtedly over Jason's stern objections. She took the porch stairs in one bound and I had all I could do, still carrying the duffelbag, to catch her in my free arm at the end of the driveway. She hugged me around the neck so tightly I could barely breathe, let alone talk, yet I was quite happy to put up with the discomfort and carried her that way all the way into the house.

My reception in the dining room was much more restrained. Only Mother got up, but as usual she was more mindful of her husband's wishes than her own and she spent more time clucking over my bruised cheek and brushing at my dusty clothes than she did in welcoming me. I felt no such reticence, however, and gave her a hug and kiss.

"You wash up before you sit down at this table," Jason instructed me. "You're not 'on the road' here."

Sarah and Junior were chattering at me, asking where I had been and what I had done and why my face was "all hurt." But Jason silenced them.

"We're not interested in any of that now. This is the dinner table and we'll behave accordingly."

More than once I had glanced at Kate and Cliff at the far end of the table, but they both were strangely intent upon not looking at me. And in Cliff at least this was so uncharacteristic that I immediately sensed the worst. The thought that he might *know*—that Kate might have told him everything—set my heart sprinting right there in the dining room. I looked at my twin, at the way her hair was done just so and at the freshly ironed dress she was wearing instead of her customary jeans and cowboy shirt, and I could almost feel the change in her, the cool malice coming off her like an emanation of dry ice.

Rattled, I laughed and blurted, "Well, what's up, siblings?"

Kate, saying nothing, kept her eyes on Cliff, who seemed to have to force himself finally even to glance my way. But that was enough for me to see his pain.

"Welcome home, Greg! Glad to have you back!" I said, and then promptly answered myself. "Well, glad to be here. Home is where the food is."

Not unexpectedly, the only laugh I got was from Sarah. So I quickly exited to the bathroom to wash up. By the time I returned to the table, Kate and Cliff were both leaving, having been excused by Jason. On the way out Cliff gave me a withering look and said that he would see me later. I nodded indifferently, as if there were nothing unusual in the exchange. But even Jason had caught the difference in Cliff's attitude.

"What is this between you two?" he said. "Did you have a quarrel?"

"Not to my knowledge."

After Mother served my dinner, Jason interrogated me about the trip and my bruises and for the most part I told him the truth: that I had hitchhiked to St. Louis, that I had bummed around there, taking in the night life, and that I had been mugged and robbed. I also volunteered that I had learned a few things while I was gone.

"Such as?" Jason asked.

"Smoking. I learned how to smoke cigarettes."

He solemnly wagged his head. "I've been waiting for that. With all your other vices, I wondered when you'd be getting around to that one."

"I don't run anymore. Might as well enjoy myself."

"You could run in college."

"Woodglen Junior College? You must be thinking of Yale, Father."

Later I sat on the front porch trying to answer the many questions of Sarah and Junior, both of whom wanted a blow-by-blow account of the "mugging"—or how I lost my money but saved my life while fighting off three St. Louis hoodlums. The kids were properly impressed. But for some reason they were just as interested in my hitchhiking, and I had to tell them who picked me up and where and exactly what was said. My tale of the speeding Cadillac unexpectedly elicited a few wows from Junior, who tended even then to be stingy in his enthusiasms. All the while, though, as I responded to their questions, I was watching for Cliff or Kate to come and invite me to the inevitable showdown. And it happened finally around eight o'clock, when there was still over an hour of light left. Kate, appearing at the corner of the porch, asked me to follow her.

"Cliff wants to talk with you," she said.

Telling the kids that I would see them later, I followed her back towards the barn. And as we walked, I still found it odd how she was dressed, as if for church, here in the country, on a weekday. At the same time, watching her lissome body move under the silken material and catching her in profile as she turned to see if I was following, I realized that whatever resemblance I thought the stripper Ginger Baby had borne to her was illusory at best, no more than that of an impressionist to a star. And as I followed her into the barn, so close to her now, I felt it all beginning again, that same shriveling of the will, that death of the spirit that had driven me away ten days before. I longed to reach out and touch her, hold her. At the haymow ladder, she stepped aside, facing me, and I realized that my emotion had been strong enough to bring tears to my eyes.

She pretended not to see them. "He's in the mow, waiting for you."

"You told him!" I got out.

She did not answer.

"Why? Can you tell me that?"

"I said he's waiting for you."

"Let him. I'm asking you why."

She looked at me with a scalding contempt. "You had to run," she said. "Like a dog."

"You don't know *why* I left?" I waited, but again she made no answer. She just stood there staring at me, her eyes almost frightening in their childlike lack of doubt or compassion.

So finally I turned from her and climbed the ladder to the mow, where I found Cliff sitting on a hay bale, holding his head like a man with a hangover. On hearing me, he got to his feet and turned to face me. The plank floor between us was strewn with loose strands and clumps of hay from the hundreds of bales fed out during the winter. Beyond him one of the haymow doors had been hooked open and the light poured into the dusty gloom, framing him, reducing him to a slender silhouette. I watched as his hands curled into fists.

"This is stupid, Cliff," I said. "You'll be fighting over something you don't know anything about."

He started towards me. "Oh, but I do. Because Kate told me. She told me what you tried."

Tried. The word sang in my head, made me want to fall to my knees and bawl with relief. Though what he thought about me now was bad enough, it was not as bad as the truth. And for that I was grateful. Like a plea bargainer, I almost wanted to confess to this lesser crime, as though that might keep Cliff and everyone else from ever knowing what I actually had done.

He was closer to me now and his fists had come up, as if he knew something about boxing, as if it were in him to smash a face, to pummel, to injure.

"And you believed her?" I said. "Kate wouldn't lie, would she?"

"You tried the same thing with her when we were kids."

"That was a little different, wouldn't you say?"

I had started to back up now, because he was still coming at me. As I've said before, he was slightly taller than I was, and he also had a longer reach. But he was lighter and slower and had never been able to dominate me physically except during that year when he was well into puberty and I was still a boy. Even then, however, I think I could have beaten him in a fight simply because he had so little talent for truculence and meanness. In fact, I don't think we'd had a real fight since we were kids and even those altercations had not been fist fights but wrestling free-for-alls that usually ended with me getting on top of him and holding him down until he "gave up."

But I knew instinctively that none of that was relevant now. I could see in his normally warm blue eyes a pallor of rage that no amount of talking or pleading was going to turn. So I had no choice finally but to raise my own fists, and immediately the first blow came, a right hand that I took on my shoulder. Then a left and another right, and he kept on swinging, roundhouses I could see coming a long way off. But he was big enough and fast enough so that I could not block them all, and I took a couple of hard shots to the face.

"*Fight, will you!*" he cried. "*Fight!*"

My nose was bleeding and I could feel my mouth puffing up, and his fists were still whistling at me, so I did as he suggested. Blocking one of his roundhouses, I stepped inside and hooked him twice into the stomach as hard as I could, and he folded, his mouth gasping for air that would not come. Kate evidently had been standing at the top of the ladder watching us, for she rushed past me now and got down in the reedy dust with her new champion. She cradled his head and stroked his face. And she looked up at me with raging eyes.

"You hurt him, you bastard! You hurt him!"

I told her that he had the wind knocked out of him, that was all. But she kept yelling at me anyway, telling me to get out of there, to get out of her sight.

"I hate you!" she cried. "Oh God, I hate you!"

In the remaining hours of that long evening, I got my things out of the bedroom that I shared with Cliff and moved into the empty hired man's room in the basement. (For years, Stinking Joe had been only a day laborer at our place.) But I found it difficult to get anything done, what with all the company I was having: Mother fussing over my wounds and Jason demanding to know why Cliff and I had fought, and Sarah and Junior expecting me to carry on as a kind of living theater for the two of them, topping my mugging and hitchhiking tales with an inside look at the fight game. But it was Jason of course who won out, finally ordering me to follow him upstairs to the library, where he closed the door behind us and had me take a chair facing him at his desk, like a miscreant in the principal's office. And he again demanded to know what was going on, why Cliff and I had fought, and I knew that I had no choice except to give him an answer that he could accept as truth, even over the white lie Cliff ultimately would have to tell him. So I reluctantly admitted that the fault was mine. Cliff had just been trying to straighten me out, I said. He had been worried about me and my behavior since graduation, not doing the farm work and carousing with Tim Regan and running off the way I did. He had tried to talk to me about it, but I had gotten angry and shoved him and he defended himself.

"And the first thing I knew, we were fighting."

"It isn't like Cliff to fight," Jason said. "You two never fight."

"Well, that's the way it was."

He frowned in anger. "And since when is he the father in this family? Does he think I'm unaware of your behavior? Does he think I can't discipline you?"

"I don't know, sir."

"Well, I can. And I will. But not on your first night back—I knew your mother wouldn't want that."

"Before you do, may I say something?"

"Of course."

I am hesitant to detail what I said to Jason then, because I know it will only sound like your typical screenwriter's typical snow job. But I did mean what I told him, and in the six or eight weeks I was to remain at home I somehow managed to live up to my words. I explained to him that I had done a lot of thinking in St. Louis and that I was not proud of my recent behavior. I said that I would not be hanging around with Tim Regan anymore and would not be drinking and getting into trouble. I said that I planned to start cutting our hay the next morning and that I would get it all in, with whatever help Stinking Joe could give me. And I also observed that our fences were getting old and that if Jason wanted to buy the posts and wire, I would put in all new fences for him. I would also repaint the barn and corrals if he wished. I wanted to work hard, I said. I wanted to get in shape and stay in shape.

By then his frown had given way to a look of bemusement. "Well, you must go to St. Louis more often," he said.

"No. I just want to work."

"And so you shall. We'll check the fields in the morning."

"The blossoms are already turning," I said. "The clover's ripe."

"We'll check it in the morning."

"Yes, sir."

With that, I left him and returned to my new room in the basement. I got my things put away and then I took a long hot bath, wishing I could have soaked the pain and the fear out of me as easily as the soreness from the fight. And oddly, I found myself almost looking forward to the days of work ahead. Sweat and dust and insects and straining muscles, surely that would be a world that even Kate would not be able to intrude upon.

As I sit here in the library writing this, I have no idea how I could have been, even at eighteen, so ignorant of the world as to think that all I had to do was work hard and keep to myself that summer and everything would come out all right in the end. I evidently was not overly concerned about the fact that Kate in less than a fortnight had changed from my pond-side lover into an enemy who wanted me hurt, or that she had turned from me to Cliff. Possibly I thought that, given her other recent behavior, this new twist was only to be expected and that in the end it would be for the better anyway, in that I would no longer have to worry about resisting her madness—and mine. I don't imagine it even crossed my mind that she might try the same thing with Cliff, who had told me more than once that he would probably be a virgin until he married, since he could not bring himself to try to seduce a girl he did not love. In my mind, it was preposterous enough that Kate had told him what I had "tried," let alone confronting him with the fact of her own guilt. And if it did cross my mind that she might try such a thing, I must have dismissed it immediately, assuring myself that she had to know Cliff better than that. It would have been like proposing an act of murder to Mohandas Gandhi.

In retrospect, the only way I can explain my behavior that spring and summer—and my state of mind that night as I went to bed in the hired man's room—is to plead ignorance. At eighteen, and even after my St. Louis "adventure," I simply did not understand the full enormity of what had happened between Kate and me, how irredeemable it was, how fatal. I have always told myself that, given the nature of our childhood together, how insular we were, how my best and virtually only friends had always been Kate and Cliff, it was only natural that the three of us in time came to form the matrix of each other's reality. If Kate had become a saint, I would have considered sainthood that much more common, just as I now judged her behavior with me as more a willful aberration than some sort of neurosis.

And then too there was my *own* sickness. To lie in bed was to feel her hand close around me; to shut my eyes was to see her smile and taste her mouth; to sleep was to enter her again and hold her, twined with me as in our mother's womb, for all time. In short, how was I to kill my own dream? How was I to think my lover mad?

Nevertheless I did have the door locked as I lay there in the dark, smoking and listening to the sounds of the night. Somewhere in the distance I could hear the trumpeting of a bull in rut, one of the most fearsomely beautiful sounds in all of nature, yet not fearsome enough that night to prevail against the sound of the township's hotrodders on Reardon Road, measuring each other's manhood in calibrations of squealing rubber and roaring metal. At midnight the grandfather clock in the living room chimed a peaceful and harmonious end to what had been a discordant day, but for me the sounds of the night went on: the scratching of mice in the walls and the sibilant rustle of elm leaves in the wind and then that most mysterious of all sounds, the one that dwells only in silence, that soft rushing beating thing I can only conceive to be the flowing of time or of one's own blood.

It was almost one o'clock when I heard the creaking of the back stairs, followed by the padding of bare feet across the kitchen floor and down the basement stairs. The door handle turned in vain, and finally there was a knock, light and hesitant. By then my heart was punching away at me, because I thought—or was it hoped?—that it was Kate at the door. But it was not.

"Greg, it's Cliff. Let me in."

I took my time getting up and going to the door. After I had unlocked it, I went back to the narrow bed and fell into it, making a show of my indifference. Cliff meanwhile was fretting about the room, unable to decide whether to look out the basement window at the darkness or to sit in the chair or just stand there in front of me, like a supplicant. Not owning pajamas, he had pulled on a pair of jeans for the trek down to my new room.

"How come you had the door locked?" he asked.

I did not answer. "What do you want?"

"Just to talk, that's all."

"About what?"

"*About what?* All of it. This whole mess. None of it makes any sense."

"Out in the barn you seemed pretty sure about everything."

"I know, I know. But I'm not. I'm all mixed up." He sat in front of me now, trying to see into my eyes. "*Why,* Greg? Can you tell me that? Why would you try such a thing?"

"What did she tell you?"

"Well, what do you think? You were there."

"I still want to hear it. In detail."

"Why? Isn't it disgusting enough the way it is? Without raking it all up again?"

"Maybe it's not the same—what you think happened and what I think happened."

"Okay, then. All right." Embarrassed and even stammering, he laid it out for me: how I'd come home drunk that night and how Kate had seen me heading for the pond and had followed me there, wearing her bikini.

"You were skinny-dipping, Kate said. So she'd expected you to stay away from her. But you didn't. She said—"

Cliff had to get up and walk to the window. He leaned against the wall there, as though he were submitting to police search.

"She said what?" I asked.

"That you tried to kiss her. That you tried—" He was strangling on the words, but finally he got them out. "That you tried to feel her up."

I asked him if he believed her.

"Why would she lie?"

"I don't know why. I'm just asking if you believed her."

"Yes."

"Then what are you doing here?"

Shaking his head, he sagged down onto the chair again, straddling it. "I don't know, I don't know. I guess I just can't believe you'd do such a thing. And yet I can't believe she'd lie about it either. I'm caught in the middle."

He had lowered his head onto his crossed arms. "Can't you tell me anything? Can't you give me some help?"

I truly did not know what to say, did not know what I *could* say. So I offered him a piece of advice, without really thinking of its implications.

"Be careful with her, Cliff."

His head came up abruptly. "What do you mean by that?"

"Just that. Be careful with her. She's not like she used to be. She's changed."

"You got something to say, spit it out!"

"Nothing more. Just that."

He stood up so suddenly he knocked over the chair. Without intending it, I had thrown him a lifeline—of righteous indignation.

"You bastard, Greg!" he hissed. "To imply something about your own sister—your own *twin!*—and not have the guts or decency to spell it out! I swear to God, I don't know what's happened to you."

With that, he was gone, slamming the door and running up the stairs and across the kitchen floor like an animal in flight. I locked the door behind him and fell back into bed.

"I don't either," I said aloud.

Junior came home from the bank with considerably less enthusiasm than he had taken to it. The safe deposit box was "pretty much a bust," he said. Aside from a stack of old legal papers, there had been only one small envelope holding four one-hundred-dollar bills, which he had changed into twenties for the sake of convenience. But, other than the loss of enthusiasm, he seemed oddly unruffled by the affair, almost as if his drooling greed of an hour earlier had been only a pose. And when Jason philosophically allowed that we would at least be able to fix the front of the house now, Junior did not even berate him as a senile fool living in a pre-inflation dream-world.

Toni made much of the bonanza, dancing around the house and singing out that we were all rich now and could retire to Malibu.

"For your birthday, J.R.," she said, "how would you like a

nice little pearl gray Mercedes SLR? Or would you prefer a Big Mac?"

In the face of such levity, I retreated to the library to scratch out a few more words. Junior meanwhile had hired a black youth who worked at a nearby service station — and who, unlike us gentry, owned a chainsaw — to come and cut up the tree. The resulting racket drew me from my desk and before I knew what I was doing I was out in the fresh air stacking the cut-up limbs and splitting a few of the massive stumps cut from the trunk. It was hard work for a man in my condition — soft and lazy, that is — and I was soon panting like a longhaired dog in August. At what I hoped were decent intervals I kept taking breaks to go into the kitchen and have coffee and a cigarette, two of the habits that made such breaks necessary in the first place.

Throughout the afternoon I noticed that Junior and Toni had their heads together more than they normally did. For some time I could not imagine what they were discussing so secretively and then it dawned on me that they just might be planning a birthday party for me. Admittedly, neither of them was precisely the type for such a gesture, party-givers usually being an affectionate and sentimental breed. But it was also true that for each of them killing time had become something of an occupation. If the idle rich can try to fill their empty hours by party-throwing, why not the idle poor as well? In any case, for the rest of that day little visions of the party danced in my head: the four of us sitting around the kitchen table the next night, with me the shyly smiling center of attention, blowing out a candle atop a Hostess Twinkie as the warm voices of my family sang a rousing *Happy Birthday, Dear Gregory.*

So I was not at all put off by Toni's show of cool antagonism throughout the evening, taking a shot at me every chance she got. And even that night in bed, as her belligerence gave way not to her usual languorous lovemaking but to an abrupt and desperate passion that ended in tears as she held me tightly and had me tell her over and over that she was mine and that I loved her now and would love her always. And for once I did not remember her falling asleep in my arms — possibly because she did not sleep at all. Sometime during the night she must have edged out from under my arms and crept out of bed and dressed in silence, taking with her the bag that she had packed earlier that day, while I was blissfully stacking firewood. Where she met Junior — downstairs or in the garage or in the driveway — I have no idea. I only know that they left together and that neither Jason nor I heard them go.

Ten

For days after Toni and Junior's departure, Jason would not eat or listen to the radio or in fact do anything but lie there in Sarah's bed like an old Indian waiting for death. Whenever I tried to feed him or talk with him, he would roll away from me and pretend to fall asleep. Finally I brought him some tomato soup and threatened that if he failed to eat it, I was going to pack up and leave within the hour, abandoning him just as Junior had done. And I guess that he believed me, for he finally permitted a few tablespoons of the lukewarm stuff to pass his desiccated lips. But he was not grateful.

"I wouldn't miss you," he said. "Not for a minute."

Like him, I did not lack for self-pity. If ever there was a case of being hoist by one's own petard, I felt that mine qualified. Coming here for asylum (as I prefer to think of it) I now found myself in the dicey predicament of being broke and wanted by the law while taking care of a dying old man in a three-sided house in the middle of winter. And like that man, I had a strong urge simply to crawl under the covers and let nature take its course. The only problem was that I had an even stronger urge to eat and stay warm, with the result that I was soon spending most of my time tending the fire and pottering around the kitchen, cooking up such delicacies as instant oatmeal from packages that were probably as old as Toni. And, speaking of my dear departed, I also spent a fair amount of time pondering her note to me, which I had found on the kitchen table the next morning.

> *Greg honey,*
> *I'm really sorry about this but I just can't take it here anymore. Please don't think I've run off with Jr. I found out he was leaving & threatened to blow the whistle if he didn't take me with. Maybe he can get me to Calif in one piece. Thats all I ask. If you ever leave this hole, look me up. I still love you — Toni*

It was not much, I'll admit, but it was more than Junior had left for Jason. For him, there was nothing, not one word from his youngest son as to where he was going or why or on what. I assumed he had closed out his own account at the bank, figuring that however little it amounted to, it would at least get him to California, where Toni would somehow grease the way for him, perhaps even put him onto a gay black crowd that would abuse only those portions of his anatomy that he wanted abused. Perversely, now that he was gone, Jason began to think of him in terms of saintliness that even poor Cliff could not have equaled. Suddenly Junior was the light of the old man's life, the selfless son who had stayed with him and cared for him and Sarah all these years, protecting them from the "forces of darkness" in a slum community. Junior had been stalwart. Junior had been a joy.

"And now even he's gone," the old man wheezed. "Yes, they've all left me now — except for the one who wants to kill me in my sleep."

I had nothing much to say to all this, being more concerned with the rattling sound of his breathing than with any words he cared to bandy. And, anyway, on the fourth day after his now-favorite son's departure, he had all those sentimental words stuffed rudely, if innocently, down his throat by the local banker, who called to ask if Jason had been able to locate a buyer for the Krugerrands Junior had found in the safe deposit box. If not, the banker himself was now interested in purchasing them, and for cash, as Junior had specified. I learned all this firsthand, from the banker himself, after Jason had weakly thrust the phone at me, shaking his head in confusion. I identified myself and explained the situation here and the man patiently went through his message again. I had only one question for him.

"How many Krugerrands were there?"

"Didn't your brother tell you? He took them with him."

"No, as a matter of fact, he didn't. And he's gone now. My father would like to know how many there were."

The man nervously cleared his throat. "There were twenty, Mister Kendall."

I thanked him for the information and for his offer and asked him to forget about the whole matter, because it was strictly a family affair and that we expected Junior to be returning soon, either with the Krugerrands or with the cash he had gotten for them.

"He also closed out his savings account with us," the banker said.

"A family affair," I repeated.

After hanging up, I explained to Jason that in addition to the cash, Junior evidently had found some gold coins in the box and had taken them with him. The old man looked baffled.

"*Gold coins?*"

"South African Krugerrands. Twenty of them."

"Gold, huh?"

"Yes—twenty ounces. Twenty coins."

He shook his head in bewilderment. "I don't remember. Isn't that funny? I just don't remember buying them."

"Maybe Mother did."

He snorted at the idea. "She never handled any money. I gave her a housekeeping allowance. That was all she ever had."

"Anyway, they were in the box. And now they're gone."

"With Junior."

"Apparently."

Jason nodded stoically. "Well, that completes the picture,

doesn't it? I have five children, and they all fail me or run out on me. And now one even robs me."

He said this to me as if I were a third party, not one of the peccant five myself. And I went along with him, in the same vein.

"Twenty Krugerrands would be worth about eight thousand, the last gold price I heard."

He shook his head in amazement. "And to think, I didn't even know I had them. Oh well, at least *you* can't steal them from me now."

"That's the attitude. No sense letting it shake your faith in human nature."

He looked up at me with those eyes which had seemed so clear and black upon my return, but which now appeared only rheumy and old. "When will you leave?" he asked.

"Not yet. I still haven't finished my story."

"Ah yes. The movie writer's magnum opus."

"Hardly that. Just a record actually."

"Of what?"

"Things that happened."

"A diary?"

"That's what Toni called it."

"That slut," he said. "Junior never would have left if it hadn't been for her."

"Junior was a saint."

He looked away from me, as if he were disappointed by my lack of contentiousness. "How much food is there left? Will we starve?"

"There's some. And you have the four hundred from the bank."

He shook his head. "Just one-seventy now. Groceries and cutting up the tree took the rest."

He coughed feebly, as though to demonstrate the frailty of his lungs. "Not that it matters. Soon I won't be needing food."

That was enough for me. I told him to be of good cheer and that if he wanted me, he could ring his little bell; I would be down in the kitchen. Taking me at my word, he began to rattle the bell before I even reached the stairs. I kept moving, however, telling myself that the exercise would do him good.

In the days and weeks following my return from St. Louis everything changed. I for one became the somber family drudge, working on the farm like an indentured coolie, some days from six in the morning until after nightfall. Cliff and Kate meanwhile had metamorphosed into a pair of cockroaches as far as I was concerned. Cliff seemed more and more like a scared and silly twit when he was around Kate, staring after her and jumping for her at the slightest glance, as if she were some visiting princess, which at times she seemed to believe she was too. Suddenly she was all smiles and sweetness and propriety. She put on makeup and set her hair almost every day and wore dresses except for those increasingly rare occasions when she would take her pony out for a ride. Cliff bought her a small record-player and for the first time in her life she began to share her gender's mysterious passion for the grosser troubadours of the day, papering her room with glossies of Fabian and Frankie Avalon and of course Elvis.

The greatest change, though, was that she had begun to date, thanks to the efforts of her big brother. For some time Cliff had been going out with a girl named Sally Fielding, who was a fair paradigm of everything Kate herself now seemed to want to become. Still a senior in high school, Sally was your typical bright and pretty National Honor Society future coed and Successful Homemaker. As such, she naturally saw in Cliff some inordinately solid husband material and consequently dated him whenever he asked. And best of all, the dear thing also had a brother, Arthur, a sophomore at Urbana now home for the summer and working in his father's hardware store. What could be more natural than that Sally and Cliff fix Arthur up with Kate and all of them go out on a jolly double date? The only problem with it was mine, in that I clearly remembered a younger Kate referring to the Fielding siblings as Spanky and Alfalfa, the latter being the brother. In point of fact, though, she dishonored the memory of the real Alfalfa, who at least was funny and likable, which was not so with Arthur. A slender, humorless fellow with a leg up on middle age, he had always struck me as someone just marking time until he got his big chance—behind the hardware counter. Nevertheless he became, with Cliff and Sally's promotion, the first date Kate had had since her memorable outing with the black-eyed Waldo Fixx.

It was my misfortune to come in early from the fields on the Big Night, having just finished mowing the west hay ground, which, with luck and sunshine, would be ready for baling the next afternoon. At the time, though, the only thing on my mind was getting my tired and filthy body into a shower as fast as I could. So, approaching the house, I was quite unprepared for the vision of splendor that suddenly came towards me around the front corner of the house, heading for our '53 Packard Clipper in the driveway. I immediately jumped off the flagstone walk, bowing and scraping like any other field nigger abruptly confronted with the white folks all gussied up for a social occasion.

"Pardon me, young Massuh!" I cried. "And young Missy! My my, but don't you all look fine!"

In reality, Cliff was wearing nothing grander than a sportcoat and tie, and Kate had on a simple summer dress with white pumps and purse. But they did have that look of terminal spiffiness I had no choice but to mock. Then too I was feeling a touch of jealousy—a touch like that of a tractor rolling over me—at seeing her this way, about to go out on a date *with another man*. And this in turn filled me with anger and guilt. When would I ever see her again as only my sister, my twin?

But my words had no effect on Cliff. He was so obviously happy in the moment, so pleased with this brand-new sister of his—shiny and friendly and *normal*—that he merely smiled at my sarcasm. Kate, however, was not as totally reborn as she looked.

"Talk about Stinking *Joe*," she said, tossing her head.

"Have a good time with Alfalfa," I told her. "I just did."

It was a sorry joke, I know, and she justly ignored it.

As the two of them got into the car and drove off, I went around to the front porch, where Mother and Jason were proudly watching the departure. Mother in particular was ecstatic.

"I'm so happy about her now," she was saying to Jason. "The way she's turning out. She used to be—well, so *different*. I worried about her."

"Yeah, now she's only boring," I said.

"That is not so, young man."

Whenever my mother disapproved of me, even in childhood, I abruptly became a *young man*. It had always mystified me.

Jason asked me if I had finished with the west field and I told him that it was all down, fence post to fence post.

"We'll bale it tomorrow," I added.

"If it doesn't rain."

"Right." I opened the screen door to go inside. But my mother was not finished with me.

"I do wish I knew what's wrong between you three," she said.

"There's nothing wrong."

"There is too. When you just run off the way you did. And when you and Cliff have a fist fight. You must think we're blind, your father and I."

"What could be wrong?" I said.

"That's what I'm asking."

Shrugging, all innocent confusion, I let the door close behind me. "Everything's just fine," I told her.

The next day was hot and sunny, with the result that Jason, on a rare foray out into the fields, pronounced the alfalfa ready for baling by midafternoon. Stinking Joe had the baler greased and ready to go, and normally I would simply have followed along after him with the second tractor and the lowboy wagon, getting down every hundred feet or so to load the bales onto the wagon myself. But because the west field was our largest and Jason did not want to risk leaving any hay on the ground overnight, he pressed Kate into service—over Mother's objections, it should be noted. In former years Kate had always driven the hay-wagon tractor, often jumping down to help with the heavy work when we got behind. But this year Mother evidently was so taken with her daughter's recent plunge into silly, helpless femininity that she tried to put her foot down: Kate was not to do farm work anymore. Apparently my mother feared that even a one-day reversion to the old ways might somehow become permanent and condemn the girl to a lifetime of being "different."

As usual, however, it was Jason who prevailed, with the result that by two in the afternoon Kate was out in the sun with Stinking Joe and me. And though she stayed up on the tractor as it pulled the lowboy slowly through the field, her hair-do of the night before soon was wilting in the sweltering heat and a spine of dark sweat had begun to spread down the back of her chambray workshirt, all of which meant that she was looking better by the minute as far as I was concerned.

I don't want to overdramatize the character of the work I did that day, and had been doing off and on for weeks, but the truth is that it was about as hard as work gets. Normally farmers exchange their labor or hire an entire crew to bring in the hay, with at least three "buckers" on the ground, picking up the bales and loading them onto the lowboy and then unloading them in the barn. But Jason never had much to do with our neighbors, which effectively precluded our exchanging labor with them. He also refused to hire anyone other than Stinking Joe, who resolutely believed that his only job was to *bale* the hay. And while Cliff in previous years had been able to help out, this summer he was simply too busy at the Eskimo to get away. So everything inevitably fell on my weary shoulders—which I could not really bitch about, I guess, since it was precisely what I had wanted and asked for.

Nevertheless the work was rarely easy. The temperature out in the sun often was over one hundred degrees and the air was usually soggy with humidity and full of nasty little bugs and bounding grasshoppers that pelted my bare torso like a biblical rain of toads. In a kind of trance I would hop up onto the tractor and pull the lowboy wagon a short distance ahead and then jump down again and start whipping my hay hook into one eighty-pound bale after another, swinging them up into the air and shoving them into place on the wagon, each time eating a heavy shower of dust and chaff as the stack grew higher. And yet I took a kind of mindless pleasure in it too, sometimes feeling as if I were nothing but muscle and bone, a lifting machine, as insensate and tireless as the tractor itself.

But this day Kate made all the difference, and not only because I no longer had to keep jumping up onto the tractor to move the wagon. More important was the difference she made in my head, in my constant awareness of her sitting up there on the old John Deere, turning every now and then to look back at me, to see whether she should speed up or slow down. I kept wondering what she was thinking, whether it was about me or about her date with Arthur the night before or about something entirely different. Somehow, just because she was working again, and sweating, letting her hair wilt back to its natural long blond straightness, I could not help feeling that her head might be undergoing a similar reversion to normality — or should I say to abnormality? In any case, I preferred to believe that if she was thinking about anybody, it was me, the great haybucker. Callow narcissist that I was, I even speculated on her reaction to the sight of my hard, brown torso shining with sweat in the brutal midday sun.

I realize now, writing these words, that all this must sound like a very strange attitude for one who thought he had put the past behind him and who was going to work hard and keep his nose clean and make sure that nothing ever happened again between him and his twin sister, no matter what she herself might do. And though I really can't explain it, I am led to wonder if it wasn't at times when my guard was down — when I was full of alcohol or half asleep or lost, as on that day, in a trance of physical labor — that I would let that lovely serpent of an idea come coiling out of my heart, to hold me in the sweet death-grip of a desire, a love, I often pretended did not exist.

Whatever the reason, when Mother came out to the field that afternoon with ham sandwiches and a thermos of lemonade, I was more than willing to take a break and sit down with Kate in the grassy shade of one of the fence row trees. Mother left almost immediately, saying that she had some pies in the oven—"And you know how fussy your father is about the crusts." Stinking Joe meanwhile had stretched out under a tree of his own, where he could spit his tobacco juice in peace, away from Kate's customary jibes.

So the two of us sat back alone in the cool shade and ate our sandwiches and drank the lemonade. When I lit a cigarette, she shook her head in mock sorrow.

"I see the track star has passed on. What comes next?"

"The haybucker," I said. "I figure if I work hard, I can be one of the best."

"No doubt."

She had stretched out in the grass, with her eyes closed and a haystem in her mouth. In her jeans and sweaty workshirt and with her hair a golden tangle in the grass, she looked as beautiful as I'd ever seen her. I wanted to take her in my arms. I wanted to hit her with the hay hook.

"Well, how'd it go last night?" I asked. "The big date."

"Boring. We went to the Lincoln and saw some lousy John Wayne western. The popcorn was all right, though."

"How about Arthur?"

She smiled. "He's good at opening doors."

"Well, I'm happy for you both."

She continued to lie there with her eyes closed and her mouth teasing the haystem. And I could see the tension coming into her face. She bit off the stem and blew it away. Finally she spoke.

"Why did you leave?"

"Why do you think, after what happened?"

She said nothing for a few moments. And finally she sat up, squinting as she stared out across the freshly mowed field, which shimmered in the heat.

"I try to understand," she said. "But it isn't easy. It doesn't really make sense. I mean, it seemed so right that night. So easy. So—perfect."

"Kate, we're brother and sister, for God's sake. We're *twins*."

"I know, I know. It's unnatural and it's wrong. I know all that." She looked at me now. "But it didn't *seem* wrong."

"Well, it was. And it can't happen again. Not ever."

"I know that now. I knew it when you ran off." And suddenly there was an edge to her voice. "I guess I thought you were different from the herd. Not so timid and conventional."

All I could do was shake my head in amazement. "Jesus, Kate, don't you have any idea what it would do to Mother and Jason—what it would do to all of us—if people found out? They'd probably put us in a madhouse somewhere."

"Maybe I'm a monster," she said. "Maybe that's the problem."

"I didn't say that."

"No, but you believe it."

"I do not. Don't put words in my mouth."

"Well, if I am a monster, at least you know how it happened. You were there."

"Kate, please. Let's talk about something else. All that's over and done, and the best thing we can do now is forget about it. Forget it ever happened."

But she was not listening. "You were there. So you know."

It was my turn then to lie back in the grass. I covered my eyes with a sweaty forearm and pretended deafness to the seductive drone of her voice. Incest was something she had read about, she said. But that was all. She had never thought of it in terms of the real world and certainly not in relation to me.

"Like I told you before—I knew that I was different and I wondered about it, why I couldn't stand the thought of a boy—" She faltered for only a moment. "I wondered if I'd ever be normal. That's what I was doing at the mirror when you broke in. I was just looking, and wondering."

"The door was unlocked. I didn't *break* in."

"Anyway, when we fell on the bed that way and I was crying, I had no idea—what was—until you—"

"I know, Kate. I was there."

"Well, later it dawned on me what it meant—that I had that kind of appeal for you. And that it was natural—"

"Kate, please." I looked over at Stinking Joe sitting back against his tree, Caterpillar cap down over his eyes, and I wondered if he could hear her.

"It made me feel good," she said. "Can you understand that? For a change, I didn't feel like some kind of freak."

It was then her voice broke, a cracking I felt in my own body, as if I were thin ice that she had stepped through. And when I saw the tears standing in her eyes, I grasped her by the arm. I had to fight to control my voice.

"Stop it, Kate. Don't do this."

But she would not stop. "Come to the pond tonight. Please come."

Abruptly I was on my feet and calling to Stinking Joe.

"Come on, we can't loaf all day!" I snapped. "There's work to do!"

And I started back into the field, without even looking at my twin.

The rest of that afternoon and evening I worked like a Jap on amphetamine. Kate had left after our break, running most of the way back to the house. So it remained for me to get the rest of the hay bales out of the field and into the barn. Normally we would have winched them up into the mow, but that required at least two men, and Stinking Joe remained glued to the baler. So, having no other choice, I temporarily stacked the bales—almost six hundred of them—in the cow's loafing shed, which was closed off for the summer. And when I was finished, I went into the house and wolfed the dinner Mother had waiting for me. I showered and dressed and drove the pickup into town, to Hogan's bar, where I drank boilermakers until closing time at one o'clock. I talked the waitress, a blowzy thirtyish woman named Rita, into getting me a pint of bourbon, and when she hinted that she might want to share the whiskey with me, I invited her along. We parked in the forest preserve and drank and made futile attempts at sex and conversation, but I could sustain neither an erection nor any interest in what she said, and finally she fell asleep, muttering something about my being "a queer or worse." At first light I drove her home and she got out without a word, saving all her resentment for the closing of the truck door, which she effected with such force that I thought the window would break. I went on home then and slunk into the house and down to my room like any other recidivist drunk, except that I quietly locked the door before dropping into bed. And I remember now the feeling of relief I had, lying there looking up at the beautiful dust-swarmed slab of sunlight running horizontally across the tiny room. It meant that I had made it through the night, without going near the pond.

Saying that he was feeling better, Jason got out of bed yesterday and let me help him down the stairs and into the kitchen. But the effort exhausted him and I practically had to carry him back to bed. His weakness alarmed me and as soon as I could, I left him and began making phone calls, trying to find a doctor who would come to the house. But all I got was a series of receptionists, each assuring me that her employer did not make house calls and that if my father was as sick as I said he was, then I should take him to a hospital. This was something I already knew of course, but at least now I felt I had some professional opinion backing me up, something with which to beat down Jason's objections. But when I got back to his room, I found him propped up in bed waiting for me, his arms crossed and his jaw set. Even his breathing seemed stronger.

"So I'm going to the hospital, am I?"

"My, what big ears you have."

"Nothing wrong with my hearing," he assured me. "I asked you a question."

"Yes, you're going to the hospital. And I don't want any argument."

"There won't be any—because I'm not going anywhere."

Straight and reasonable discussion never had worked with him, so I tried a more oblique approach. "That really puts me in a nice position, you know? You get sicker and sicker and finally die, and what do I say to the doctors? To the police even? *Oh yeah, I knew he was dying, but he didn't want to go to a hospital. So I didn't take him.* That's the predicament you want to put me in? Christ's sake, they'll probably charge me with criminal negligence. And when Sarah gets back, she'll blame me. Everyone will."

"What *everyone?*" he scoffed. "I could die tonight and not two people in the whole world would ever know about it or give a damn."

I sighed and sat down in the chair next to his bed. This obviously was going to take a while.

"Jason, do you know what's wrong with you?"

"Of course I do. Congestive heart disease."

"Well, that's treatable, isn't it?"

"By all means. They thin your blood and put you in an oxygen tent, and you live a few months longer. Big deal."

"So what's the alternative? Just lie here and die?"

"Don't we all finally?"

In my frustration, I got up again and went over to Sarah's window, which looked out on a long row of ranch-house roofs, all of them the same shape and set the same distance from the street. They were like stepping stones, a giant's walk into infinity.

"I guess I've got no choice then," I said. "Finally I'm just going to have to pick you up and carry you out to the car and take you to the hospital."

I was not looking at him as I said this and for some time he made no response. But when he did, I could hear the new thing in his voice, the ring of old steel.

"Gregory—we have a few hundred dollars left. Enough for me to lie here in peace a while longer. I will not die in a hospital. Do you understand that? *I will not die in a hospital.*"

174

There was not much I could say to that. To argue the matter any further would only have infuriated him and put an even greater burden on his weakened heart and lungs. When the time was right — and I imagined that would be soon enough — I would simply bundle him up and take him to the hospital, by ambulance if necessary. Ultimately it would have to be done and I did not doubt that he knew this as well as I did. For now, though, I felt an overwhelming need to get away from him and out of the house, so I brought the phone up from downstairs and plugged it in next to his bed. I made sure he was comfortable and then I left him, assuring him that I would be back within an hour.

Walking — and especially walking along the beach — is something I have sorely missed since leaving California. Often, when I was sharing a house at Malibu, I used to walk all the way to Sunset before turning back, a distance of at least six miles, much of it decorated with the most beautiful female bodies in the western world, which may have had something to do with my remarkable stamina. Here, though, one can't help taking into consideration the fact that being alone on foot often means being a lone white man among hostile blacks, usually kids, who just might want something you have, like your life. Which brings to mind as I write this one of Ellen's better lines, tossed off as we drifted down the Harbor Freeway through Watts in the cool hush of her Rolls Silver Cloud: *Cowardice doth made liberals of us all.*

But enough of cynicism. This day I needed fresh air and movement more than I needed security, and I set out walking up the road, past that long row of roofs which had looked so neat and orderly from Sarah's room but which here at street level served only to divide the leaden sky from the ramshackle blight of Woodglen Estates. Most of the houses, the abandoned the same as those in use, had broken windows and boarded-up windows and some were even doorless (though none had any holes quite so grand as ours). The yards were mostly dirt and

175

littered with a decade's accumulation of discarded toys and appliances and other junk, including automobiles, all of it patrolled by packs of skinny, shivering dogs, scouring the debris for scraps of food.

So it was not quite the same as Malibu, except perhaps for the fact that I did not feel any more at home there than I did here. Fortunately it was a cold dismal day and I had the streets pretty much to myself, just me and an occasional crew of winos passing the bottle around a barrel fire in their Goodwill costumes, probably feeling the cold a good deal less than I was. And it crossed my mind that there had been a time — not many years ago, in fact — when my properly liberal Hollywood heart would have bled outrageously at the sight of such social and economic want. But now that I am playing fair to join their impoverished ranks, I find my capacity for moral indignation somewhat diminished, much I suppose as a man in a burning building does not overly concern himself with fire codes. Maybe later on, again, if I am lucky.

In any case, I continued on my way through the Estates, down streets that cut across fields where I once had mended fences and baled hay. And I kept going, on through the Regan place and past it, to what had once been Detweiler and Morgan land, all of it dismally the same now: a grid of identical streets running through a blighted forest of government-subsidized housing. At the west end of the Morgan farm, along a street named Park Place, there was indeed a park: a swimming pool, skating rink, and a half-dozen tennis courts, all radiating from the charred ruin of a central administration building and surrounded by a chain-link fence that for the most part was lying flat on the ground, severed from its posts. Not unexpectedly, the pool and the courts stood empty; but so did the skating rink, the government in its wanton generosity evidently having overlooked the little matter of providing ice skates as well as the rink on which to use them.

It was the area beyond the park, though, that was my real concern, and my goal too, all along, I realized now as it came into view up ahead, like a childhood nightmare flashing back to life. Yet there was beauty in the sight too, the spare old winter trees reigning over the stones and the few faded mini-flags and a single new grave, its flowers already scattered and frozen. Coming upon it in the midst of Woodglen Estates, the cemetery at first glance appeared serene and inviolable, like an artifact from another time, possibly because the fence surrounding it was not chain-link but wrought-iron and would have required a bulldozer to knock it over. But as I entered through the open gate and started up the hill, I saw that I had been wrong, that everything here — the scarred trees and grassless ground as well as the gravestones — was very much a part of the present. Those markers too sturdy to push over had been lavishly spray-painted, to the point where the graffiti on them eerily resembled the work of Jackson Pollock, undecipherable hieroglyphics for some confounded twenty-fifth-century Champolion.

But in truth, I barely saw the other gravestones as I threaded my way back toward a particular one standing on a slight rise near the cemetery's back fence. It was about the size of a gasoline pump, a stout chest-high block of polished gray marble, with a single word cut into it, a word all but invisible under the graffiti. To satisfy myself, I took off my right glove and *felt* it, like a reader of braille. And I was relieved to find that it was all there, nothing chipped away, no letters missing, just that single word, *KENDALL,* as if it said all there was to say about those who lay under it. It crossed my mind that its obscene coating of paint would one day fade away just like that on the Parthenon and human eyes would see it again as it was meant to be seen, by our standards if not by those of the ancient Greeks. Jason had it cut and put in place at the time of my mother's death, as the family stone, with the individual markers arrayed in front of it, each rising only about six inches above the ground.

It took an effort of will for me to look down at them now, my mother's first. Happily I saw that she had survived relatively unscathed, with only an orange squiggle running across her name: *Emily Simpson Kendall 1911–1971.* But Cliff and Kate, not so lucky, had been raked with spray cans of many colors, the topmost one a lavender rendering of the central message of our time: Kate, on the outside, had caught the FUC; Cliff the K–U. And I realized, kneeling there on the ground, that even if I'd had some paint remover, I would not have used it, for fear of what other messages would take this one's place.

By then, I was feeling an enormous sense of regret that I had not brought something with me to place on the graves, even plastic flowers, anything that might have served as a token of what I felt for the three of them, the lifelong sense of loss and deprivation and useless love. But all I had were tears, which felt as if they were beginning to freeze on my face. So I impulsively placed my hand on the sharp corner of Kate's stone and pushed down on it, twisting the heel back and forth until the skin finally broke and blood began to run onto the painted marble. Then I touched the wound to Cliff's stone and to Mother's. And standing, I placed it against the family marker as well, for what reason I really don't know. All I remember is that it felt good. Maybe blood is thicker than tears, too.

I wrapped a handkerchief around the hand and put my glove back on. And as I turned to leave I saw a small old black man watching me from behind a tree. His wiry gray hair exploded out from under a stocking cap topped by a fedora and he was wearing an incredibly ratty fur coat over an odd assortment of sweaters, suitcoats, and sweatpants. At my glance, he gave me a wide toothless grin and nodded vigorously, as if he were in profound agreement with me about something important. Leaving the graves, I had to walk past him, which only seemed to broaden his smile and quicken the pace of his nodding. Though I assumed he was mad, I smiled at him and nodded slightly myself, as if to confirm our accord. Then I went on down the hill and out through the gate of the cemetery. And it was only then that I realized it had begun to snow, light random flakes, confetti for my lonely parade.

eleven

By the time I reached home those random flakes had turned into a snowfall heavy enough to make even Woodglen Estates look soft and lovely. But that evidently was not Mother Nature's ultimate intention, for the snow continued to fall all through that evening and on into the night, increasing in intensity so steadily that I found myself unable to go to bed and instead spent my time checking on Jason and feeding wood into the kitchen stove and staring out the dining room windows at this new white world raging under the streetlamps. By ten o'clock, there were no cars moving on the road, not even snowplows, and at midnight, as I sat watching a television newsman give assurances that the storm was about to end, the electricity abruptly went off—out in the street as well as in the house. When I checked the phone and found it dead too, I felt a cold breath of panic, as if a door suddenly had blown open.

The reason of course was Jason. It had been two days since his ill-fated attempt to get out of bed and I was beginning to wonder if he would ever try again. He ate almost nothing and had not had a bowel movement since before Junior and Toni left. Though his breathing seemed almost normal on occasion, much of the time it was so labored he could barely speak. He no longer listened to the radio and he rarely rang his little bell or did anything else except just lie there in Sarah's bed trying to stay warm under a half-dozen covers. Even during normal weather the gas furnace in the basement failed to heat the upstairs bedrooms adequately, which was why I had kept the kitchen stove going lately, hoping most of the heat would rise through the back stairway and edge into his room. But now, with the electricity off and the furnace inoperable, the problem of keeping the old man warm became critical.

If we had not been snowed in, I would surely have taken him to the hospital that night. As it was, all I could do was try to move him down to the kitchen, near the stove. But he was so opposed to the idea, by turns cussing me out and weeping helplessly, that I relented for the time being and instead tried to fashion by candlelight a giant makeshift heat duct running from the kitchen up into his room. Essentially all this involved was tacking blankets over the doorway to the dining room and across the upstairs hallway so that what little heat there was would more easily find its way into his room. I also tried to get him to drink some blackberry brandy I had found in the pantry, but he refused that too, leaving me with little choice except to knock off a few ounces of the stuff myself.

I then tried to get some sleep, stretching out on the sofa that we had moved into the kitchen earlier. But between keeping the fire going and listening for Jason, I was unable to fall asleep for hours. When I closed my eyes, all I could see was the fire in the stove, its open door a kind of miniature trapdoor to the infernal regions. And all I heard was the wind as it began to pick up outside, moaning and whistling under the eaves and around the corners of the house.

Time after time I got up and went over to the window, hoping to see something outside, especially the lights of a snowplow. But there was nothing save blackness and the soughing wind and I could only wonder if snow was still coming down, driven now by a blizzard wind. By the firelight I saw the porch thermometer standing at eighteen degrees, which should have been too cold for it to continue snowing. But I was not convinced. I drank more brandy and went upstairs to check on Jason again. Finding him peacefully asleep, I returned to the kitchen and put more wood on the fire and again stretched out on the sofa, under an unzipped sleeping bag. And in time I dropped off, sleeping until the morning light woke me in a cold and fireless room. The windows were frosted over and I had to open the door to see out, forcing it against a three-foot snowdrift, even there, on the side porch. Through the opening I saw a world of whiteness in which nothing moved or sounded. The snow was drifted high against the barn, covering the door to the Congo Lords' clubroom as well as the corral running east to the garage, which itself was invisible except for a narrow two-foot strip under the eaves. I closed the kitchen door slowly, telling myself like a budding Pollyanna that at least it wasn't snowing anymore.

Later, after starting the fire and getting some hot tomato soup into Jason I peeked outside again, half expecting to find a Saint Bernard standing there in the snow with a keg of brandy around its neck. But all I saw was the same gorgeously terrifying scene as before, except that the drifts were standing even higher as the wind continued to blow. I had no doubt that elsewhere the snow was probably only a few feet deep—just enough, that is, to immobilize the entire area. But here the house and garage and barn formed a perfect L-shaped snow break, catching almost everything a northerly or easterly wind cared to blow against it. Now, I realize that this sounds like a stupid arrangement, but in point of fact most of the winter storms here come out of the west, putting the driveway and the entrances to the buildings in the lee of the wind. And then too, in all the winters I have spent here, I can't remember a single storm as devastating as this one.

So here I sit at the kitchen table, hunkered over my single remaining tablet, one eye on the fire and my ears cocked for any sound from Jason upstairs. The temperature outside is still in the teens and inside I doubt if we are even thirty degrees warmer. (The thermostat, in the closed-off foyer, is not even registering, fifty-five being its lowest calibration.) The phone remains dead and there is no electricity, and every time I go upstairs I listen to my father's breathing as if I were on a police bomb squad, putting my ear to the ticking of a device that might well blow me to hell. I accept it that he is a sick man and could easily die soon even in a hospital; I accept his truism that we all die finally; but nowhere in me can I find acceptance of the possibility that his life will end like this, lying in a strange bed in a freezing house with no one to look after him but *me,* the prodigal, the bugout. But then, whether or not I accept something really isn't all that crucial, is it? One of life's little lessons.

By now I am beginning to feel the loss of Toni like an amputation. In a way, I know it is fortunate that she is not here, because the storm and the failed electricity would surely have thrown her into such a rage of resentment ("It's fucking *Siberia* in here!") that I doubt if I could have handled her, short of manhandling. But oh God, I do miss the girl, all of her, her person as much as her body. I sit here with the pen almost frozen into my hand and the smell of her suddenly is in my nostrils as much as in my mind, and my arms tense for want of her. I feel hollow and incomplete. I put my hand upon my fly, as though to console my cock or maybe just to trick it. But it is not to be fooled, and stays soft, stays dead.

Upstairs Jason coughs feebly. Outside the wind sings over the snow. And right here, now, at this cold and messy kitchen table, I find there is really nothing else to do except push on, making these strange little scratchings on lined paper, for what purpose I don't quite remember anymore.

By August, all the hay was in and I had begun tearing down the old fences and building new ones, which like haymaking was not an easy job for one man. But Stinking Joe had developed a bad case of hypertension and on doctor's orders was able to do only part-time light work. So I labored alone, pulling the rotted old oak fence posts and replacing them with steel ones that I could drive into the ground instead of "sinking" them, as with the old. Then I would unroll the new wire, anchor it to the corner posts, stretch it tight, and finish by fastening it to the steel posts all along the line. Now and then Mother would come out and watch me, usually with the kids in tow. And once she even helped out for a time, taking a pliers and fastening the four-point line to the steel posts. But Junior promptly got tangled in some of the rusty old wire and cut himself and she had to take him to the doctor for a tetanus shot. Jason too made it out to the fields on occasion, normally after supper, when it was cool. Looking properly solemn, he would check on my progress, making sure he was getting full value for the twenty dollars "allowance" he paid me each week.

For the most part, though, I was alone. Evenings, if Kate was gone, I would go for a swim in the pond and later sit out on the front porch for a while with Jason and Mother, watching Junior and Sarah torment each other in the front yard. Then, downstairs in my room, too distracted to read, I would turn to my trusty yellow legal pads. Having found a whole package of them in Jason's desk in the library (just as I did this last fall) I had begun to use them as a kind of cutrate psychotherapy, doodling out my worries, spilling my guts, making chilling lists of my crimes and their inevitable consequences. I tried again and again to draw a reasonable portrait of Kate, only to give it up finally in favor of words. I described her. I listed her features. I estimated her measurements. Like an eight-year-old, I scrawled over and over the terrible restroom-wall charges: *Greg loves Kate...Kate fucks...Greg and Kate must die.* And finally, hopeless, out of control: *I love you...I love you...I love you.*

Needless to say, each night I destroyed what I had written, burning the pages in an ashtray on the windowsill. Purged then, I would try to sleep. And usually I did—like a drugged man. But some nights I slept hardly at all, especially when Kate was out with her devoted Arthur Fielding. The thought that she could be lying in his arms and kissing him or letting him feel her breasts or going even farther — it all made me feel physically ill with jealousy. I longed to go to his family's hardware store and pull him out from behind the counter and beat him half to death, and in his absence I often took my rage out on the bed, punching it so hard it had grown lumpy in spots.

But most of the time, whether I was lying awake or working in the fields, it was Kate I thought about, and only Kate. I thought about her as I imagine a bull thinks of grass, almost every second of every goddamn day. I saw her in the night light on the pond bank, her eyes a glaze of tears and her mouth pulled back in anguish, crying *Oh love me! Please love me!* And I saw her in the hayfield shade, lying in her jeans and sweaty workshirt, her hair careless in the grass. And I thought — yes, I will admit it now — I thought over and over again: *Why not? Why couldn't we do it?* If it was what we both wanted, why couldn't we be lovers? Why couldn't we run away together and make a life of sorts? Who would have to know that we were brother and sister? Whose business would it be? And as for the family — Jason and Mother had chosen their mates, hadn't they? And wouldn't Cliff eventually do the same? So why then should Kate and I have to forgo a kindred freedom of choice? Why should the two of us be the only ones not allowed to have the lover we wanted?

I knew the answers to these questions, of course. And that was probably the reason I lay awake so often in my locked basement room: because I knew the answers and none of them made any difference. None lessened the jealousy I felt; none enabled me to think of Kate again as only my sister, my twin; none offered me salvation from this bizarre hell of my own devising. So it seemed that I had no choice except to go on as I was, working like a solitary slave by day and spending my nights in either stuporous sleep or endless hours of lacerating introspection. More than once it crossed my mind that one day soon I would have to pack my bags and hit the road again, only this time for good. But I couldn't bring myself to make the move yet — why, I didn't know, not at the time, though I suspect now that I was hanging on in the perverse hope that some miraculous something would step in and shatter my resolve and extinguish my sense of guilt, so I could go to the pond with Kate night after night, all the rest of our lives, if we so chose. I was, in short, becoming as mad as she was. Mad with love, in my case anyway.

On the occasion of one of Kate's dates, I innocently happened to be sitting with Jason and Mother on the front porch, luxuriating with a succession of Pall Malls after a late supper, when the hated Arthur Fielding arrived in his father's new Chrysler Newport. I immediately got up to go inside, having no desire to exchange pleasantries with the wimp. But before I reached the door, Kate came running out, signaling for Arthur to stay where he was, that she would join him there. Mother and Jason protested, saying that they wanted to meet the young man. But Kate skipped on down the stairs, turning at the bottom and walking backwards for a few steps.

"No, you don't," she told them. "He's really such a jerk. But he does get me out of the house, doesn't he?"

Smiling happily, she went on out to Fielding and his car, her long legs giving a touch of splendor to her Penney's dress and high-heel shoes. A perfect footman, Arthur scurried around the car and opened the door for her. Meanwhile Jason and Mother were having an embarrassed laugh about their daughter.

"What a girl," Jason said.

"What an *actress*," Mother amended.

Which left one other still to be heard from. "What a phony," I muttered, and went on inside, looking for something to punch or kick.

On another day, as I was stretching wire at the far north end of the farm, Kate came riding up on her pony, much like the plantation owner's daughter out for a canter in the fresh air. Only this time I forsook my awed slave routine in favor of sarcasm.

"Still haven't mastered sidesaddle, eh?"

"What's that supposed to mean?"

"Or at least get some jodhpurs and riding boots."

Still mounted, she confided to her pony. "The sweaty one is trying to tell us something."

"Only that there's a right way and a wrong way to dress—if you're Princess Grace. Jeans just don't cut it."

"You're right," she said. "I ought to have a pair of jodhpurs."

"Maybe Cliff could buy them for you. Or Arthur."

"Why not? And yes, riding boots too. With real hard toes, for kicking people."

"That's the ticket."

"Especially the hired help. Sweaty fence-makers and the like."

"We've got it coming, all right."

She leaned forward on the pony, so she could peer down the row of new fence posts, which, as I expected, failed to please her.

"There's a squiggle about a hundred yards down. A couple of posts out of line."

"No problem," I said. "You just bring Arthur over and have him pull them out of the ground with his bare hands. Then I'll reset them."

She smiled at that. "You don't like him very much, do you?"

"Not that much, no."

"Well, I don't see why not. I think he's just what I need—now that my twin won't have me."

The remark left me shaking my head. "Jesus, how can you joke about it? Sometimes I think you're from outer space somewhere."

"Well, crying didn't do me much good, did it?"

I turned back to the fence, saying that I had work to do. But she would not leave.

"Cliff gets off tonight," she said.

"Good for him."

"Be a perfect night for a swim. Just the three of us, like old times. You want to come?"

"I don't think so."

"You needn't be frightened," she assured me. "Cliff will be there. He'll protect you."

"I said, I don't know."

"I'll be a perfect lady."

"For Christ's sake, Kate!" I turned on her in a rage, throwing my fence pliers down at the ground so hard that her pony jumped in fright.

She coolly reined him in and calmed him, patting his neck and talking to him. Finally she turned back to me.

"Don't bother to come. You won't be missed."

She rode off then and for a time I just stood there watching her move out of sight. When I turned back to my work I found that I had no stomach for it, nor did I care to sit down in the shade and loaf. So I set out walking, back through the trees onto Regan land. And then I began to run, slowly at first, just jogging along. But my body seemed to have a will of its own and before long I was running over the rough weedy ground as fast as I could go, arms pumping as if I were in a sprint. And I kept on that way, hurtling through the tall grass and bushes and under trees whose branches lashed my face and over hills and down along Thorn Creek until my lungs were sobbing and my heart thumped in my ears and all I could do finally was stumble out into the shallow water and pitch forward into it, stale August creek water almost as warm as the air. But it was water still, that finest of balms, and I lay in it, I rolled in it, I wept in it.

And I think now, sitting here at this freezing kitchen table, how deeply, how acutely, one suffers at eighteen. There in those rocky shallows I lay as broken and bleeding as I thought a man could ever be. But I was wrong. Though I didn't know it at the time, I had not yet begun to hurt.

That evening I stayed at the house with Jason while everyone else went swimming down at the pond. This is not to say that I was *with* Jason, however, for he had retreated after supper to the cool of his library, probably to pore over a new book on Egyptology that he had acquired. So I had the house pretty much to myself, and I used most of it too, roaming around like Little Boy Lost, wondering what kind of mischief Kate had up her sleeve, inviting me to join her and Cliff at the pond. With Mother and the kids there too, I had been tempted to go along. But solitude was becoming a habit, like the Pall Malls, and I indulged them both that evening, sitting on the front porch and watching the cars go by as I listened to the occasional shrieks of laughter coming from the pond—Junior's, for the most part. Then I heard the back screendoor slam and a second later Sarah came out onto the porch, out of breath and dripping water all over the floor.

"Come on, Greg, you gotta come. Wontcha please, huh? Wontcha, Greg? Come on, wontcha?"

How could one resist such a petition? Shrugging agreement, I gave her little butt a swat and left her jumping up and down on the porch. When I returned, in my trunks, she took a firm grip on my index finger and marched me back past the barn and down the path to the pond, where we found everyone in the water except Cliff. Looking pale and cold, he sat shivering on the edge of the dock. Mother, in her perennial black suit and white bathing cap, was peacefully treading water while Junior squealed happily from his perch on Kate's shoulders. Seeing us, Kate promptly dove under water and came up separated from her little brother, who appeared to have swallowed some of the pond in the process. While he coughed, Kate swam to shallower water and stood, Venus rising in a bikini, a Venus who baby-talked.

"Well, widdo Sawah got her big bruvver to come after all, didn't she? And my, how bwown and hard he wooks." She turned from us to Cliff, saying that if he too wanted to have a beautiful tan, he was just going to have to get out of the Eskimo more often.

Cliff grinned at me. "No thanks. Not if it means building fence."

I asked my mother how long she had been treading water.

"Hours," she said.

"What a lady."

"*Nonsmoking* lady," she pointed out.

Sarah still had me by the finger. "Come on, you get out in the water and stand with your legs apart. I want to show you something."

I obediently dove in and took a position, legs spread apart, about ten feet from the dock. The water by then was roiled and dark and I told Sarah to be careful, but she dove in anyway and swam right into my knee. By moving fast, though, I was able to make it appear as if she had indeed swum between my legs. And that naturally was an accomplishment that Junior could not let go unchallenged. He had me back up another five feet, until my head was almost under water, before taking his shot. And when I saw that he was going to miss me altogether, I must confess that I didn't sidle over to where he was—little Sarah needed all the victories she could get, I figured.

Coming up, Junior at first claimed that he had made it through my legs and when Sarah called him a liar he started to bitch at Mother, claiming that I had cheated for Sarah and that Mother should make me admit it. When he got nowhere with her, he carried his appeal to Cliff, who characteristically gave him a sop of sorts.

"The water's too muddy, Junior. Try it someday when it's clear. Then you'll make it."

"Well, it was muddy for me too, and *I* made it!" Sarah said.

Junior screamed back at her. "I went twice as long under water as you! And Greg cheated! He moved!"

That was enough for the rest of us, and especially for Mother. Getting out of the water, she put on her robe and told Junior and Sarah that it was getting dark now and was time to go. At their duet of complaint, she said there would be no bedtime cake or milk for anyone who complained. The voracious little buggers fell silent at that and glumly followed her as she left.

"Have fun," she called back. "And watch out for the dragon."

It was a family joke, one of Kate's childhood inventions to

keep the Regan kids from using our pond. "I guess it isn't really a dragon," she had told them. "But it looks like one and it can bite off your foot. You've really got to watch out for it."

Alone now, the three of us fell into a somewhat uneasy silence, as if we knew each other only casually and could not think of a thing to say. Kate had gotten up onto the dock and was drying her hair with a towel — why, I don't know, since she soon went back into the water. Perhaps she only wanted to fluff it and make it prettier, or perhaps she was calculating enough to know how she looked standing there above us in her bikini, with her arms arched gracefully over her head. At the time I had no idea how ineradicable from my mind that scene in the dusk would become: Cliff lounging back on the tire tube, looking over his bony knees at Kate on the dock, our armed Venus smiling slightly, as if in contemplation of some delicious act of mischief, while behind her the sky and the great old oaks were slowly darkening. I hear the frogs croaking and the cicadas in their furious song, and I see the water and the dock and of course Kate. Over and over, all this quarter century, I see Kate standing there in the dying light.

"Well, good," she said. "Just the three of us again, just like old times. Isn't it too freaking neat for words?"

I could see Cliff's consternation: Why was she being so sardonic? It *was* neat, he undoubtedly was thinking. It would always be neat.

Kate dropped her towel and came to the edge of the dock. "And to have Greg here too. The Great Haybucker. It's just too freaking much."

"Glad you realize that," I said.

"Oh, I do. I do." Smiling, she looked over at Cliff, still floating on his tube. "Well, let's have fun!"

With that, she dove into the water and came up under him, capsizing him and his tiny craft. Breaking the surface, she let out a shrieking laugh and threw her arms around Cliff's neck, making him work hard to reach shallower water. All the way she kept clinging to him and laughing, as if she thought Cliff too was having the greatest time of his life. And even when they were both able to stand, she still held on to him, indifferently pressing her breasts and legs against him.

"All right, Kate, that's enough," he said, prying her arms loose.

She immediately jumped back and threw up her hands in mock horror. "Oh, I am so sorry, Mister Kendall, sir. I simply forgot all about your sweet little Sally and that no one else is even allowed to touch you anymore, not even your sister."

Cliff looked embarrassed. "Oh, come on, Kate. Knock it off, okay?"

But she already had turned away from him and was moving in my direction. "What do you think, Greg? You think brothers and sisters should be allowed to touch?"

I swam over to the dock and climbed out of the water.

"I asked you a question, twin," she persisted.

"And I just decided I get enough exercise during the day," I said. "Swimming is for you softies."

"You leaving?" Cliff asked.

"Yeah. I'm really bushed."

"I've been up since five myself. Why don't we all go?" Cliff looked hopefully at Kate, who was still gliding around like an otter, with only her head above water.

"If you have to leave—go ahead," she said. "I'm staying."

"Come on, Kate," Cliff pleaded. "We can't just leave you here."

"Why not? I'm a big girl now. And anyway, I know you're not that tired. If I were Saccharine Sally, you wouldn't be going anywhere."

Cliff was standing on the grassy bank now. He looked over at me. "What do you say? A little while longer? I suppose we could handle that, eh?"

I had already tossed my towel over my shoulders. "Not me. I'll see you two later."

As I stepped off the dock and started around the pond, Kate emitted a sharp little laugh, like the bark of a terrier. "There he goes," she said. "The great haybucker and builder of crooked fences."

"That's me," I admitted.

"Have fun in your little basement room, there all by yourself."

I heard Cliff groan. "Kate, you go too far. You always go too far lately."

Just before I went out of view I glanced back at the pond and saw him reluctantly wading again into the water, where Kate was still swimming, with only her head visible. I could see her hair radiating out from her, moving like kelp on the water's surface, and it struck me as almost funny that where a minute before I had seen her as a kind of Venus, now she seemed more like that frightening creature she had conjured up for the Regans. And without thinking, I stupidly repeated my mother's warning.

"Watch out for the dragon!" I called.

After showering and raiding the kitchen (at that age, I think I ate my weight every few days) I went down to my room and pretended to read, when in fact all I was doing was listening for Kate and Cliff to return. It wasn't that I thought the same thing might happen with them that had happened between Kate and me, even if it was her wish that it did. I knew that Cliff was probably the last person in the world who could have entered into such a relationship, even without design, as in my case. But I was not sure that Kate knew this, not anymore, not as she was now. So I was worried—no, terrified, sickened—at the thought of what Cliff might be learning about his sister, and possibly about his brother as well. Nevertheless I kept on reading, wandering aimlessly through the forests of Faulkner's *Bear,* comprehending nothing. And in time I heard them: the back screendoor whining open and slapping shut, followed by the padding of bare feet on the kitchen floor, then their voices, both of them, as well as Mother's, all unexcited, normal. And I *breathed.* For the first time since leaving the pond, I relaxed sufficiently to empty my lungs and fill them again, long and deep, the breathing of a man reprieved.

Such a development required celebration, I felt, so I closed my Faulkner and lit a cigarette and smoked it down, trying my best to avoid the thought that one could not go on forever living in the expectation of being reprieved. Sooner or later, the way Kate was carrying on, Cliff was going to learn what had happened between her and me — and then what? What would he do? Or, more to the point, what would it do *to him?* The realization that I had no answer to that question frightened me more than anything else. By then, as I've already said, I had come to accept that the terrible secret eventually would come out and that Kate and I would have to pay the price for it. And I saw nothing unfair in this, for we after all were the ones who had stepped over the line, *way* over the line, and therefore could not very well expect anything except condemnation and ostracism. But the thought of Cliff and Mother and Jason suffering similar penalties — that hurt me more than I would have dreamed it could. Yet I had no idea what to do about it, other than just to stay on and wait for the inevitable to happen, then leave under my own true colors, such as they were. Perhaps that way the three of them would be so filled with revulsion toward me that they would go easier on themselves, for a while anyway.

The grandfather clock had already chimed one o'clock when I heard someone on the front hall stairway. I heard the screendoor being unhooked and opened and then the squeak of the porch glider, and I assured myself that it had to be Cliff, because Kate would have sat on the swing. So I got out of bed, taking my cigarettes, and went upstairs as silently as I could, carefully peering out onto the porch before opening the door. And I saw that I had been right: Cliff was sitting on the edge of the glider, with his head in his hands.

"Mind a little company?" I asked, going over to the railing.

"Hell no. But what's keeping you up? I thought you were so bushed."

"Foreign affairs," I said. "Ike needs me."

"You too?"

"Sure. Where would he be without us? Caught in a sandtrap somewhere."

Cliff got up and came over to the railing too, to stare with me out at the lawn and the road. Banter out of the way, neither of us said anything for a time. In the silence, I lit another cigarette. Finally I spoke:

"You worried about Kate?"

"What do you mean?"

"How different she is."

"Yeah, I guess so. And the funny thing is the last couple of weeks I was thinking she'd really straightened out. I mean, she stopped being such a loner, you know? Dating Sally's brother and all. I thought she was on her way."

"But now you're not so sure?"

He shook his head, almost angrily. It was not easy for him, I knew, talking about our sister.

"Well, you know — like down at the pond tonight," he said. "The way she tries to keep a guy guessing all the time. You never know what's going on inside her head. It's that way when we double-date too. One minute she can be so damned nice to Sally and Arthur — has them eating right out of her hand — and the next she's giving them a shot. Especially poor Arthur. Just when he thinks everything's going fine between them, she drops him flat on his face."

"That's what's worrying you?" I asked.

He became defensive. "Well, what else? That's what the problem is. That's how she is."

I dragged on my cigarette and flipped it out into the yard, only half smoked. "You forgetting what she said about me?"

"Of course not. How could I?"

"Well, you don't act like it. If what she said was true, I'd think you wouldn't even want to talk to me."

In the streetlight, I could see his desperation. "But why would she lie? I still can't see that."

"Maybe she was covering up."

"What does that mean?"

At his look, the terrible dread I saw edging into his eyes, I backed away. "I don't know. I'm just talking through my hat.

Everything's so goddamn confusing, I just talk. I don't even know what I'm saying anymore."

But he wouldn't let me off, not that easily. "Come on, Greg. You started to say something—just like that other night. So say it!"

It was like being wedged between a bull and a corral; there was no way out. I thought of Kate and how my real need was not to expose her but to hold her, love her. And all I could do was shake my head.

"What's the matter?" Cliff asked. "What are you crying for?"

"I'm not crying."

"The hell you're not! What is it? Tell me!"

But I could not. Instead I just stood there, wet-faced and humiliated, gripping the railing so he would not see that I was trembling as well as crying. He put his hand on my shoulder, but I shook it off. I pushed him from me.

"Go to bed," I said. "Get the hell away from me."

"I just want to help, Greg."

"Then help *her,* for Christ's sake! She's the one that needs it!"

After that outburst, I knew he was not about to let go. So I ran like a branded calf. I plunged back into the house and down the stairs to my room. And if I slept at all that night, I don't remember it. What I do remember are the cigarettes and the silence and the grandfather clock measuring the hours of my life.

It seems to be dawn, though I can't be sure. I am lying with Toni in our upstairs room and I hear a distant urgent whispering that causes me to unbraid my body from hers and to put on my robe and leave the room. I follow the whispering sound into Jason's bedroom and see him through oak branches lying very still in bed, most of his body covered by the snow that has blown through the shattered wall, covering almost everything in the room. Outside a small black tramp with a toothless grin stands behind a broken tombstone staring in at Kate who is sitting on the edge of Jason's bed in a bikini, gently stroking his forehead and whispering words I can't make out, but which have set the old man's eyes blazing in the cold white deadness of the room.

Hearing me, Kate turns and smiles. "He's paralyzed now," she says. "He can't speak. So I told him all about us. And about Cliff and me too. He doesn't like it, but what can he do?"

In a rage I go to the bed and seize her. I pull her up and drive my mouth into hers as my hands tear at her bikini. I clasp her buttocks and pull her against me, and she is amused. She pulls her mouth free and looks down at Jason and says, "See? What did I tell you?"

But I can't stop. I get her down on the bed, in the snow, on top of Jason. And I strain, I plunge, in desperation, because I know I am losing it now. I know it is going. I fight to stay there, with her, but it is like trying to hold on to the wind.

Twelve

Sarah's room is like no other in this house. Instead of the solid semi-antique furniture that crowds the rest of the place, her bedroom set is of recent origin, a white French provincial group probably purchased from Sears or Levitt's. The floor is carpeted in beige and three walls are painted in "salmon" while the fourth is covered with wallpaper in a fleur-de-lis design that reappears in the drapes and in her bedspread. As such, the room strikes me as an unfit place for a man to sleep, let alone die, though I never say this to Jason, who undoubtedly has more important things on his mind than the esthetic qualities of a room that I increasingly fear may be the last place on earth he sees.

Yesterday morning he sat up in bed and let me feed him some oatmeal and toast and a few sips of tea. Afterwards he asked me to sit down in the chair next to his bed because he wanted to "get a few things said." Normally I sit down without being bidden and we exchange a few words about the weather and how he's feeling, or he simply rolls away from me and I get the message and leave. This was different, however. Just in the way he laced his fingers across his shrunken belly and glared up at Sarah's too-cheerful wallpaper, I could see that this was not to be any ordinary conversation. And so it turned out. As he spoke—in a whisper—he kept clearing his throat and every few seconds he would have to pause and catch his breath. Seeing what the effort was costing him, I suggested that he wait and tell me some other time, when he was more rested. But that only made him angry.

"It's now or never!" he said. "I've got to explain!"

"There's no need."

"I'll decide that."

"Explain what?"

"My life."

I smiled at him. "You sure we have time for all that?"

"What *all that*? We both know there hasn't been much to it."

"Come on, Jason. You had a big family and none of us ever went hungry. You produced some of the best cattle in the country and you've probably read more books and understood more things than—"

His hand feebly waved me quiet. "I'm talking about *my life*. My doing *nothing* all these years. Didn't you ever wonder about it?"

"I never thought of you as doing nothing."

He shook his head in regret. "I never intended it that way. I came here to prepare myself. I thought my work would be in politics."

"I know that, Jason."

"A congressman, I thought. Or senator."

"You'd have been better than most."

He gave me a scalding look. "Don't interrupt. I must get this said."

I gestured agreement, giving him the floor, and he went on in a rush, as much of a rush as his frail wind would permit.

"So, when the political thing didn't pan out, then I thought, well—I would write. I'd become a writer on social and political matters. And I tried that too. There are manuscripts up in the attic right now—one I even finished, on the evils of the mobile society. But no one was interested. The publishers just returned them."

Even whispering, as he was, he did not have the wind for this and he kept having to stop. Each time he did so, he would lie there glaring up at me in a rage of infirmity, and I would wait until he had breath enough to go on again. To silence him, I thought of getting up and walking out. But I knew that that would only have infuriated him and taxed his heart even more.

"So here I was," he went on. "A man nearing forty. My ambitions dead. What could I do? Go teach school somewhere, like Sarah? Get a sales job or go to work in a bank—I, who had studied at Yale and the Sorbonne?" By now, tears were rimming his eyes. "Oh no—not your father. He was too proud for that. He was too great. Too special. So here I sat, reading books and fumbling around in my library, like an old man."

"It wasn't like that," I tried.

"Oh yes it was. And I know it's one of the reasons you children never cared for me as you did for your mother."

"That's not true."

"Yes it is. Especially you and Kate. Oh, you may have felt for me as a father—but you never liked me. You never loved me. I always knew that."

"You're wrong."

"You laughed at me," he said. "Both of you."

I stood up. "Jason, this is ridiculous. You can't do this to yourself. You've got to rest."

"Like that," he said. "Like calling me Jason. You never called Mother Emily, did you? No, because you loved her. But me— by your teens I was always Jason. I thought of making you stop, but it would have been like begging."

I told him that I had to leave him now, that I had to check the fire, but he wheezed on, oblivious of anything except his need to get it all out.

"All those years what I really wanted was to be close to all of you, as Mother was. But I didn't know how. I pretended that I stayed in my library because I had important work to do. But all I really did was hide there. I spent my life hiding in that terrible room."

There was no way I could have left him then. I sat down on the edge of his bed and tried to console him by telling him that few people ever really thought they had lived successful lives. I pointed out to him my own case, that here I was at forty-four, unemployed and living off him, twice divorced, the father of young girls I seldom even saw. But he heard none of it, so intent was he on sucking in enough air so he could get out a few more words of self-destruction.

"One last thing—that night you came to my room and threatened me, you said that I killed Cliff." Coughing now, he had to break off again. And while he waited, he kept staring intently at me, with eyes that looked as if they might combust at any second. "You tell me the truth now. That, I demand. Call it a dying demand."

Helplessly, I nodded.

"*Why?*" he got out. "Why did you say I killed Cliff?"

In this extreme hour of his life, I found that I was no more able to lie to him than to look away from his consuming stare.

"Because you were so strict with him," I heard myself say. "Because you were so demanding. He lived for your approval. After what happened to Kate—while he was was driving—"

"Rather than face me—he did what he did."

I nodded just as his gray face began to crumple, to implode. And he nodded too, as though in agreement with my terrible charge. But if he was willing to accept it, I discovered that I could not, and I seized his wrists with such force that he looked up at me in sudden fear, as if he thought I might indeed kill him after all. Instead I pulled him to me. I put my arms around him and hugged him and said that he was my father and that I loved him and would not leave him. And finally I felt him break too and begin to weep, and I think I even felt some pressure in his bony old arms as he tried to hug me. Crying freely, I kept saying the same thing over and over.

"You're my father. And I love you. And I won't leave you."

The Saint Helen's Hospital Ball was easily the most misbegotten annual social event in the county. Ostensibly organized as a charity affair to raise funds for Saint Helen's Hospital, its true purpose seemed more along the lines of stimulating business for the hospital's detoxification and psychiatric wards. The lethal character of the affair came about, I believe (with the benefit of grown-up hindsight) mostly as a result of the dance being held at the nearby Elysian Fields Country Club, which was probably the most exclusive and certainly the most luxuriously housed and maintained private club in the entire southwest suburban area. With its large membership roster of Chicago millionaires, it had no trouble maintaining a seventy-two-hole golf course as well as an Olympic-size swimming pool and a cluster of tennis and handball and other courts, all discreetly laid out around a sprawling ivy-covered Tudor manse that fairly exuded the rarefied air of old money and social prominence.

For Woodglen's hustling middle class, it must have been a heady challenge, the prospect of donning formal wear and dancing in such a setting, possibly even rubbing elbows with club members who just might be highly impressed with you and invite you to—well, there was no end to the flights your fancy could take. It was simply a helluva fine opportunity and anyone worth his salt would have been a fool not to take advantage of it, even if the affair did tend to be much too wide open, full of lowlife and teenagers and the like, in fact anyone with the price of a ticket.

So each year the dance apparently excited a fever of anticipation in the hearts of the locals, especially the socially ambitious wives of our more prosperous plumbers and dentists and hardware merchants, such as Mr. Fielding. And I imagine that that fever must have mounted into pure terror by the time they drove up to the clubhouse on the winding drive through the trees and gave over their Chevrolets to liveried parking attendants and then ventured on red carpet into the beautiful building and out onto the dance floor, all so luxurious, so perfect—and finally, so brutally disappointing. In no time at all, their girdles must have been killing them and their husbands must have begun to resemble waiters (who danced like farmers). Most likely, the only people who spoke to them were ones they already knew, from business and church. And worst of all, there were those goddamn teenagers everywhere:

pimply, greasy-haired boys and impossibly firm-armed, small-waisted girls without a wrinkle on their empty faces. So it was bottoms-up: martinis and manhattans sliding down like lemonade. And even before the band's first break, the squabbling would begin, marital spats that had a way of developing into shoving matches between the men and hair pullings between the women, often followed by the feckless losers vomiting either right at their tables or on the way to the rest rooms. And finally there was the magnetlike appeal of that huge, unused swimming pool, gleaming like a sapphire in the lantern-lit night.

That at least is how I see the affair now, from the vantage point of a quarter century later. But even then the ball did have a certain fame as an annual local calamity not to be missed if one could help it. In the Kendall household we had heard about it for years and I even had gone to see for myself the year before, hoping my date would become sufficiently infected with the general mood of bacchanalia to get tight herself, and thus hopefully a little loose as well. Instead she professed shock at the whole affair and had me take her home before midnight, still every bit as sober as she was chaste.

This year, however, I never would have gone to the dance if it hadn't been for a girl named Barbara Polanski, whom I met one afternoon at the Farmer's Lumber Company. New in town, and newly employed there as a clerk, she was about twenty and struck me as very friendly and sexy, so I engaged her in conversation and finally asked her for a date, forgetting for the moment that I wanted to have nothing to do with women or a social life. It developed that she had two tickets to the ball (given to her by an uncle, who owned the lumberyard) and I readily agreed to escort her. At the time I didn't know that Mr. Fielding, the hardware merchant, had been similarly dragooned into buying tickets by the hospital auxiliary and had given four of them to Arthur and Sally, which meant that Kate and Cliff would be going too.

Thus, in the days following the discordant little scene at the pond and my hopeless conversation later on the front porch with

Cliff, the three of us had been innocently pointed toward an August Saturday evening and the Saint Helen's Hospital Ball, unaware that for us it would be more like a battle than a dance, a battle not all of us would survive. For me, they were days of blessed routine: long hard hours in the sun followed by solitary sessions scratching deathless thoughts and intriguing lists onto the pages of my yellow pads. During those days I had as little to do with Kate and Cliff as I could, yet I saw them often enough — at dinner, mostly — to notice that they were not themselves at all. In Kate's case, this meant that she had dropped one of her more recent poses — that of the radiant junior prom queen — in favor of a brooding melancholia that she seemed almost to revel in. She stopped setting her hair and wearing lipstick. And on one occasion, when she left the house wearing old jeans and a workshirt, I might have cheered had it not been for the fact that she was going out on a date with Arthur.

It was the deepening change in Cliff, though, that worried me more. Always so steady and cheerful, he now almost never smiled or laughed. And for the first time in his life, he had difficulty getting up in the morning and making it to work. The reason for this, I knew, was that he was awake a good part of every night, or at least on those nights when I intentionally had lain awake and listened for the inevitable whisper of his feet on the front stairway as he went out onto the porch, where he would sit alone for hours thinking — what? Was he brooding over my reckless slip of the tongue: *Maybe she was covering up?* Had the look of dread in his eyes become conviction in his mind — because Kate herself had confirmed it? Was it that he, like his mindless younger brother, could no longer think of her as his sister?

No, it had to be something else, I told myself. Something simple and feasible, such as that he and Sally were having problems. Perhaps they'd had sex together and he was feeling guilty because of it. For some reason, I just could not accept it that the similarity in Cliff and Kate's demeanor, that somber depression they both now shared, might have meant that they shared something else as well, some new and crushing burden. I could not accept it then and even now I don't know that it was so. I only know that in the long dog days leading up to the dance, the Kendall household was steeped in silence and misery, as if we were already grieving for our dead.

On the night of the dance, I bathed late and stretched out on my bed downstairs, waiting to hear Cliff and Kate leave before I started to dress. Mother almost spoiled my plans by bursting in and breathlessly announcing that I had to come upstairs and see Kate before she left.

"She looks so beautiful in her gown, Greg! You've just got to see her."

I pointed out that I wasn't dressed and that I would be seeing her soon anyway, at the dance, which drew from Mother a weary toss of her head.

"I don't know what's got into you lately," she lamented.

"*I'll see her,* Mom. Later."

As she went back upstairs I could hear her gaining speed with every step, for Kate and Cliff were still in the process of leaving. They were going to the Fieldings' first for some sort of pre-dance party — punch and cookies, most likely — so I knew that I still had plenty of time to get dressed and pick up my date without being unconscionably late. Because Sally and Arthur's parents were also going to the dance, and taking their car, Cliff and Kate had had to use ours for their double-date with Sally and Arthur, which left me with nothing except our ratty old pickup, a calamity I unenthusiastically had explained to Barbara Polanski on the phone, only to learn that her generous uncle had already offered her the use of his car — a two-year-old Buick — for the affair. All I had to do was drive the pickup to her place and from that point on we would travel in style.

·So I finished dressing, got Barbara's corsage out of the refrigerator, and recklessly ran the gauntlet on the front porch. Jason and Junior managed to contain their enthusiasm better than Sarah, who gave me a bear-hug, and Mother, who exulted that all her children were so good-looking that she couldn't tell which of them was best. Junior obligingly came to her aid by claiming that he was the fairest of all, which at least allowed me to leave them laughing.

As I drove the truck out onto the road and waved back, I had no idea that it would be the last time I would ever do so or that I would remember that moment all of my life, see the four of them there on the wide front porch of the big white house framed by the shaded lawn and the leaves of the elms, all of it eerily like an old *Saturday Evening Post* cover, a tableau from an America whose loss seems more and more to have been a fatal one, for all of us.

Spruced and ignorant, I drove to Barbara's and the two of us went on to the dance in her uncle's Buick. And as we treaded up the red carpet and entered the castlelike clubhouse, I don't believe either one of us felt any more social anxiety than grazing cattle, probably because we enjoyed that best of all status symbols: youth. The ballroom itself was huge and nicely decorated, with an abundance of potted palms and bunting and Japanese lanterns and the like, especially outside on the sweeping patio and pool area, where most of the guests were dancing. Inside, at the dozens of tiny cocktail tables, each covered in white linen, the serious drinkers were already beginning their desperate pursuit of happiness. For myself, I was more interested in getting my date into my arms as rapidly as possible and we immediately took to the dance floor.

Barbara Polanski was a tall large-boned girl with a small waist and abundant breasts that she seemed quite willing to press against me. The music, which was being played by a Chicago dance band called Marty Moon and the Meteors, seemed adequate to my half-tin ear. And in fact almost everything struck me as just fine, with the possible exception of my plain blue suit, for I was surprised to see that most of my peers had gone to the expense of renting tuxedos. Barbara kept joking about those who wore them, saying that they looked like penguins and apprentice waiters, but I didn't doubt that if I had been similarly attired, she would not have minded at all. As it was, we got along well enough and in time were enjoying ourselves. The few numbers we didn't dance to, we sat out with some of my high school friends, drinking punch and Cokes spiked with rum that had to be smuggled in, because the waiters were so zealous in carding the young. Not wanting to cadge drinks all evening long, I located the official dance "pusher" — none other than our one-time victim, Joey Regan — and bought from him two pints of rum, brown bags and all.

We had been at the dance for almost an hour before Kate and Cliff and their dates arrived. And the moment I saw them, I no longer had to wonder who was the fairest of all, and not only of the Kendall siblings but of everyone at the Saint Helen's Ball. I knew that Mother had made a special dress for Kate, but until now I hadn't seen it, a floor-length black velvet thing, simple to the point of severity, yet just right for my twin with her lovely figure and carriage, her perfect arms and shoulders and her blond hair spilling free. To me, she looked heartbreakingly beautiful and I virtually had stopped dancing to gaze at her, a lapse that caused Barbara to smile ruefully.

"Who's that?" she asked. "An old girl friend?"

"No. My sister."

"You're kidding. Boy, she's a knockout."

"Yeah, I guess so."

The incident embarrassed and angered me unreasonably, made me feel almost as if I had been caught at my favorite vice. And from that point on I began to feel things slowly coming apart, as though having a good time were like playing superior tennis or golf, a touch one suddenly could lose.

For a time, Barbara and I joined the four of them at their table, where unspiked punch was the drink of choice. But the mood there was so prickly and cheerless that we soon danced away and for the most part stayed by ourselves the rest of the evening. And I must confess my spirit had been buoyed temporarily at least by what I had sensed at the foursome's table — and by what I saw later on the dance floor — for it was obvious that Kate could not abide her devoted Arthur. He watched over her like a Versailles footman, and for his trouble

206

appeared to get nothing but contempt. At the table she barely spoke to him and on the dance floor she kept a good six inches between them and almost never even looked at him. When the band started a new number, "The Anniversary Waltz," she steered him over to us and asked Barbara if she would mind changing partners for one dance.

"I want to talk to my brother," Kate said, as if the matter were already settled.

Barbara gave me a wry look as Arthur dutifully waltzed off with her. Out on the floor, Kate did not bother to hold to the six-inch distance she had maintained with Arthur and I had all I could do to keep from closing my eyes and dancing off into some dreamscape where one could have everything he wanted, and the hell with the world.

"I hate it here," Kate said.

"It shows."

"Let it. All these drunks, they disgust me. Especially the women. They're obscene. Fat old loudmouthed freaks."

"That's what's bothering you?"

Suddenly she smiled warmly at me, and I realized that we were dancing past the table of the elder Fieldings.

"There!" Kate said. "Let them know I'm not sour all the time, just when I'm with their pride and joy."

"Arthur? Why, I thought you two were meant for each other."

Her fingers dug sharply into my shoulder. "Don't be smart."

"Sorry."

As the strains of the waltz continued she dropped her head against my shoulder and for a few seconds I felt the coolness of her nose and forehead nuzzled against my neck. Then I caught myself.

"Kate, for Christ's sake."

She looked up at me with surprise and puzzlement, as if she could not understand my reaction. And her eyes suddenly went moist.

"I don't want to stay here anymore," she said. "I want to leave. Will you take me?"

"Kate, I've got a date, remember? And so have you. If you want to go home, Arthur will take you."

"I don't want Arthur. And I didn't say home.'

"You can't be serious."

"Can't I?" She just stood there looking up at me, not dancing now, her hand barely touching my shoulder, the determination in her eyes edged with desperation.

"The answer's no," I said.

And she immediately turned from me and swept off the floor, weaving her way rapidly through the dancers and on past the tables of those obscene old drunks she could not abide. I assumed she was heading for the ladies' room and that is what I told Arthur when he asked where she was. He gave me a disapproving look.

"Well, what happened?" he snapped. "Did you say something?"

I smiled pleasantly. "I must have, eh?"

He wagged his head peevishly and took off through the tables, heading for the ladies' room too, evidently to stand guard outside the door until Kate emerged. Meanwhile I took Barbara by the hand and led her back to a corner table on the patio, not far from the potted rubber plant where I had stashed one of my pints of rum. (The other was in the car.) I got a plateful of hors d'oeuvres and two large paper cups of punch, which I laced liberally with Barbara's approval. A normal healthy Pole, she obviously was no stranger to demon rum.

"Can I be nosy?" she asked.

"Sure."

"What did happen with your sister?"

"Nothing much. She's just not too pleased with Arthur. She wanted me to take her home."

"Why? She afraid of him?"

"Of *Arthur?*"

She smiled. "No, I guess not. But why then?"

"No reason. That's just Kate. She gets a bee in her bonnet every now and then."

Barbara said that if I thought we should take Kate home, it would be all right with her.

"It's still early," she added. "We could come back afterwards."

"No, it's okay," I told her. "Kate will be fine."

And so she seemed to be. When I saw her after that on the dance floor or sitting with Cliff and the Fieldings at their table, she did not seem particularly distressed. One reason for this might have been that she was dancing with partners other than Arthur now. Two of them were boys from our class; another looked like a forty-year-old La Salle Street banker; and I even saw her in the arms of a grinning Joey Regan, his evening's business evidently completed. Finally I saw her dancing with Cliff to the strains of "Stardust." I remember the number because Barbara, on hearing it begin, took my hand and pulled me onto the dance floor.

"We can't miss this," she said. 'Stardust' is *my* song."

As we danced, I found myself steering her so that I could keep Kate and Cliff in view, remembering how Kate had behaved with me earlier. And what I saw did nothing to put my mind at ease. Cliff had never been keen on dancing, but now with Kate he was hopeless, so stiff he seemed almost incapable of movement. But what unsettled me was the way he and Kate kept looking at each other, staring into each other's eyes not like lovers so much as strangers without a common language, lost souls trying to find meaning through the nebulous and uncertain windows of each other's eyes. Occasionally Kate would say something and Cliff would close his eyes and move his head in what I could only read as a gesticulation of helplessness and futile denial.

But the floor was crowded and I could see them only now and then. And also Barbara had begun to hum close to my ear, at the same time pressing her body tightly against mine, with the result that I was rapidly losing interest in everything but her. I do remember the last time I saw Kate and Cliff, though — remember it as those in Hiroshima must have remembered that last clear doomed morning. The two of them had stopped dancing and just stood there looking at each other for a few moments before starting off the dance floor, with Kate leading the way. I remember the golden flow of her hair against the black velvet of her dress and the determined thrust of her chin and the long lovely line of her neck and of her arm reaching back as she held on to Cliff's hand. About him, I recall mostly in that moment that he looked both miserable and resigned, as if he did not want to go with her but knew he had no choice in the matter, which only reinforced that air of fatal nobility and decency he always carried with him, like a tattered flag.

That is what I remember of those few moments. Only that. At the time of course I thought the two of them were just going to their table, and as a result I did not continue to gaze after them. Then too I was increasingly absorbed in trying to keep an incipient erection in its place, a task that Barbara Polanski seemed intent on frustrating. So I was not even aware that they had left until Sally and Arthur came steaming over to our table and demanded to know where their dates had gone. A great wit even then, I asked them if I was my brother and sister's keeper.

"That's not funny," Arthur said.

"Are they coming back?" Sally asked.

I told them that I didn't know and in fact wasn't even sure that they had gone.

"Well, they have!" Arthur snapped. "And let me tell you, Sally and I have had just about enough of you Kendalls."

"I'll drink to that," I said, lifting my paper cup.

When they were gone, Barbara leaned over as if to tell me something but instead put her tongue in my ear. Under the table my hand crawled onto her leg and she left it there.

"Maybe we ought to go too," she said. "After one more drink, okay?"

"I'll buy that."

As I refilled our cups with punch and came back to the table and spiked them, the ball had already begun to unravel. At the poolside a fortyish woman kept drunkenly pulling on the sleeve of her husband's tux, trying to get him to break off a conversation he was having with another man, and he peevishly slapped at her hand but missed and toppled her into the pool. The man he had been talking to immediately began to laugh like a lunatic at the poor woman sloshing about in the shallow water, trying to work her sopping gown back up over her suddenly bared breasts, and this in turn prompted her husband to shove the laugher into the pool after her. By then, the tables were emptying and there was a lot of shouting and laughter as the crowd began turning itself into a mob. From the splashing sounds I knew that others were going into the water now too, but I couldn't see them, except for the inevitable atavistic flapper who had scrambled up onto the high board and now began to strip to the accompaniment of a bump-and-grind number Marty Moon and the Meteors just happened to have in their repertoire. The girl unfortunately never made it down to her altogether, prematurely falling off the board as she struggled to undo her brassiere.

By then Barbara and I were already making our way to the door.

"What a great dance," she said. "It's really been fun."

I drove us to the forest preserve and headed for a remote stretch of bridle trail that I knew the sheriff's patrol never checked. And even before we got there Barbara Polanski had me convinced that I was finally going to establish my sexual independence from Kate. (The incident in St. Louis did not apply, as far as I was concerned.) Sitting tightly against me, Barbara kissed me and nuzzled my neck and I felt her hand come to rest on my bulging lap. By the time we parked, I had unzipped my pants and she had begun to caress me with her hand. What I really wanted, though, was for her to go down on me as the black woman had, but she made no move in that direction and I lacked the nerve to ask her to do it. Instead I took her in my arms and unclasped her dress in the back and worked it down. But all she let me do finally was mold and kiss her breasts. The rest of her, she said, was off limits.

"I've already gone that route," she told me. "And I just won't let myself be used anymore."

As I kissed her, she explained. It seemed that in high school in Waukegan she had dated a "good Catholic boy" for three years, but had remained chaste all the way till graduation, after which she had thought they would marry. So she had let him make love to her "all last summer," expecting to get an engagement ring from him at any time. But all the fellow did was give her a goodbye kiss and move on to Notre Dame, free as the wind. Since then, she had wised up, she said. She would give a boy pleasure if she liked him, but that was all.

"Until I get that old wedding ring, these legs stay crossed."

By then I was already past controlling myself and I ejaculated all over her hand and dress and a windshield towel I belatedly had snatched off the floor. But that did not bother Barbara in the least. It was what she expected, she said. What she wanted. To give me pleasure and "maybe kiss a little and have a bit more rum," that was enough for her.

Only slightly disappointed, I obliged her on all three counts. And in time I asked if she agreed with leading sexologists that unless a man ejaculated inside a woman, they were not having true sexual intercourse. The woman might come herself, but that didn't matter, I informed her. To the experts, she was still pure.

"Like right now," I went on. "Right after the guy comes. He could do it and a girl wouldn't even have to worry."

"What girl?" Barbara asked.

"Any girl."

Her smile was dubious and knowing. But for some reason, she did not laugh. "How could the girl trust this guy?" she asked.

"She wouldn't have to, because it'd be too soon for him. He couldn't come even if he wanted to."

"Some could."

"Not me."

"Really?"

212

"Honest."

Thus did I occupy myself during those crucial minutes and hours when my brother and my twin needed me more than at any other time in their lives. But then, ever since leaving the dance, I consciously had tried not to think about them: why they had left together and where they had gone and what they were doing. Perhaps I sensed that this would be the night when it all came out into the open, when my life would change unalterably for the worse. So why not take it in stride? Why not just lounge back and give myself a few final hours of innocent pleasure? Who could it hurt? Yes, that could have been my reason. Or then again, maybe it was only that I didn't care enough, not enough anyway to let it inhibit the free and noble exercise of my libido.

Whatever the reason, the thing I remember about that very special span of time is Barbara moving onto my lap and presenting her breasts to my mouth one at a time. And above all, I remember that as she arched backwards to change the angle of my penetration of her, I could see over her head in the darkness the radium glow of the dashboard clock's hands pointing to one-fifteen — approximately the time that Cliff and Kate in the family Packard were going through the guardrail above Thorn Creek and slamming into the trees beyond. And I never did understand that. All my life I have heard stories of siblings and twins who seemed to share the same nervous systems, who felt pain when the other was hurt and who sometimes even died when the other died. But me — I felt nothing at all. In his mind my brother already was dead and my twin sister lay broken beyond all mending, and the only thing I felt was the silken secret heart of Barbara Polanski sliding back and forth on me. So don't sing me songs about no man being an island. I know better.

Incredibly, seventy-two hours have passed since the storm ended, yet the roads remain unplowed and we are still without power. The days have become clear and sunny but so cold the snow has not even begun to melt. Sometimes I wonder if there has been a nuclear strike or some otner cataclysmic event, rather than a simple snowstorm. Occasionally from upstairs I can see in the distance some of our neighbors — an old Mexican woman and two black youths — trying to dig out of their homes. But since the road is still closed, it would appear they dig in vain.

Meanwhile I keep the fire going and I write these pages and I look after Jason, who seems to be weakening with every passing day now. He sleeps most of the time, taking catnaps interrupted by feeble bouts of coughing and an occasional need to urinate. I force-feed him soup and water but he is strong enough to take only a little at a time. And his grip on reality seems less sure each day, to the point now where he sometimes doesn't remember who I am or how we came to be alone together in this cold and silent house in the snow.

Thirteen

Last night, while I slept, my father died. I woke at dawn and stirred the fire into life and fed it a few more split logs from the dwindling pile in the living room. I tried the phone without any luck and then I used the bathroom before going upstairs to check on Jason. At first, I thought everything was all right, because he was lying on his back, as he usually did, with his head propped up on pillows. But he made no movement and then I saw that his eyes and his mouth were slightly open, as if death had surprised him by coming while he was asleep. I felt his forehead and found him already cold, so I closed his eyes and pulled the covers over his face and opened the window to let the room get even colder than it was. Then I shut the door and came back downstairs and washed my hands.

I still find it hard to believe that he is gone, even though I knew he had been slipping for weeks now. But yesterday he had seemed no worse, even taking some soup and trying a bite of toast, though it also should be noted that he barely spoke all day long, just lay there in Sarah's bed gazing out the window at the now-blue sky. The last time I checked him was at eleven last night and he was sleeping then. The room was about as warm as I could get it, probably close to sixty degrees, and I had him wearing his usual two pairs of long johns under a good half-dozen covers. Because of this, I don't feel that he could have died of heat loss. And I know that I have been diligent in trying to get food and liquids into him.

So I tell myself as I sit writing this that I am not to blame. I did not let my father die. Yet when I found him this morning, what I felt more than anything else was anger — at myself — as if I knew that I had failed him once again, bugged out on him one last time. And somehow the fact that I know this is not true doesn't change a thing. Nor does it make any more endurable this terrible isolation. I thought it was bad enough before, to be snowbound with a dying old man in the midst of a suburban ghetto. But now, sitting here alone, with the phone and electricity still off and food and firewood running low and my only companion a body lying upstairs under a sheet in an open-windowed room, I begin to understand the meaning of the word *isolation* in its more exact dimensions. And I don't much care for it.

At times I wonder if the phone and power companies and the street department are all locked in some dark conspiracy of inaction undertaken for the sole purpose of giving me time to finish this record, its completion being of such vital importance to the world at large. Maybe once mankind learns all about Kate and Cliff and how I came to flee to California they will renounce their old habits of greed and intolerance and bellicosity and lay down their arms in favor of brotherhood and sweet discourse. And if not that, then maybe they will push a few dollars my way. Whatever. That is probably the chief advantage of writing in isolation: that tiresome old lock on reality begins to slip and you never even know it. You forget that most people do not eat straight out of cans or yell obscenities into a dead phone or stand at the open door calling for persons already dead for a quarter century. Nor do they keep returning all through their days and nights to a messy kitchen table and a dog-eared stack of legal pads, to scratch in them a few more words of infinite superfluity. But then not everyone knows what is real.

After Barbara and I got back into our clothes, I started the

Buick and turned on the headlights. And I saw, glaring down at us from a tree limb about a hundred feet ahead, the round yellow eyes of a great horned owl. The bird immediately took off, but so slowly, its great wings barely flapping, that it seemed as if some force other than flight were lifting it up through the trees into the darkness. I looked at Barbara to catch her reaction to the owl, but she had been fastening her hose to her garter belt and had missed it. So I said nothing. By then I was not feeling very talkative anyway, having just "established" my sexual independence only to discover that everything remained exactly as it was before. My life was still about to blow up in my face. And in my own mind, I was no less a pervert, no less a slave to my twin.

I followed the bridle trail to the main forest preserve road, which took us past the formal parking area above Sauk Lake. I saw a few cars there and later I would wonder if that was where Kate and Cliff had gone after leaving the dance. Now, however, I went past it without a thought and turned onto Reardon Road, which ran west for about two miles between the forest preserve on one side and a series of small farms on the other. It was a curving two-lane blacktop, out of the way and lightly traveled, which made it a favored race course for area hotrodders. Its sharpest curve was at the point where the road passed over Thorn Creek and the rocky, tree-lined ravine that bordered the stream. The guardrails there had been breached more than a few times and I myself remember signing the impressive casts of the Camelli brothers when they returned to school weeks after surviving a crash at the site.

So as Barbara Polanski and I sped along the road, heading for her home, I was not surprised to see up ahead in the darkness, among the lights of other parked cars, the red flasher of a police cruiser stopped on the creek curve.

"It might be someone we know," I said to Barbara as I pulled in behind the other cars and parked.

Getting out, I took Barbara's hand and we made our way along the shoulder of the road, past the other parked cars, toward the ravine ahead, which looked eerie in the web of lights playing on it. We came to the torn-up guardrail and I saw the broken tree halfway down and then the car itself, mangled against the base of a second tree, a huge oak that had neither bent nor broken. And it was then, as I dropped Barbara's hand, that I recognized the car. I vaguely remember scrambling down the side of the ravine and pushing past the others gathered around the wreck and even shoving a policeman out of the way.

"It's okay!" a voice said. "He's her brother!"

But someone else was trying to pull me away and I had to fight him off until finally I made it to the car itself—to what was left of it—and looked inside. And I can remember that first blow as I saw her, as if someone had hit me in the spine with an ax. I dropped to my knees, I tried to breathe, I tried to climb through the flattened window frame into that bloody labyrinth inside, wanting if anything just to cover her, to hide her monstrous injuries from the world as well as from myself. The car seemed to have fit itself around her like a garment, the passenger door and post pushed tight against her back while the dashboard and engine embraced her from the front. Most of her dress had been torn from her and her limbs hung broken and askew and she was covered with blood and her face was unrecognizable, with her left eye exposed in that terrible way. It did not occur to me any more than it did to the police or to the others there that she could have been alive. And I remember screaming at them to let me cover her as they pulled me from the wreck again.

"You can't get in there," one said. "We got to cut her out. The fire truck's on the way."

And then it struck me that I had not seen Cliff. I began to yell at them to let me go, to let me see my brother, but they said he was gone and that they were searching the woods for him.

"He musta been throwed," one of the policemen said. "We found half his bloody jacket—it was caught in the door."

Then suddenly Tim Regan's weasel face was in front of mine, flashing on and off in the crimson light.

"Willard Emry was the first on the scene," he told me. "Willard says he saw someone run across the road and head into Jurgen's place. Could've been Cliff."

"No way," the same policeman said. "No one in a wreck like this is walkin' anywhere. He was throwed. He's near here somewhere. We just gotta keep lookin', that's all."

But that was something I could not accept. Pulling free, I remember yelling at them that Cliff was not there, not dead, and that he was waiting for me. A week later, at a bar in town, Tim Regan would tell me that I ran through the creek then and scrambled up the other side of the ravine like a wild man. He told me that I raced across the road and dove over the barbed-wire fence there and bounced to my feet and "just kept right on goin', like it was daylight, for Chrissakes." But I don't remember any of that and I remember the rest of my journey home only vaguely, more like a single moment drawn out and repeated over and over, so that in the end the whole long desperate sprint now seems timeless: a few seconds or half an hour during which my feet keep pounding against the hard August ground and I keep tripping and falling and picking myself up, my heart thrashing in my neck, my voice whimpering like that of some frightened child trailing at my heels.

All that way I doubt if one coherent thought passed through my head. At the most, I had some sort of inchoate notion that I was trying to find Cliff, though in reality I imagine all I was trying to do was put distance between me and what I had seen in the car, that *thing* which I knew to be Kate but could not accept, not then anyway.

So I ran on, across Jurgen's farm and Detweiler's and Regan's, until I reached our own land. My side ached and I was sobbing for breath as well as for myself, and I remember hearing the word *no!* moaned over and over as I stumbled on, walking occasionally, tripping still over roots and branches not visible in the quarter-moon light. I came to the pond and ran past it, unable even to glance at that place where Kate and I had loved. Slowing to a walk again, I became aware of a dog barking somewhere in the darkness, growing louder as I kept on. Then, reaching the corner of the barn, I saw Junior's mutt Jocko standing near the open doorway. He came whimpering to me, then immediately ran back to the doorway to bark again, but with a greater boldness now. And for the first time since I saw our car down in the ravine, something like thought took place in me—but it was a thought that sucked the air from my lungs and jellied my knees.

One step at a time, I forced myself on into the barn, into the stillness of that vast dark vault lit here and there by the polelight outside: shafts and planes of light slanting like lasers through the windows and cracks. And there in the center of the vault, at the edge of the opening to the mow, I saw Cliff hanging at the end of a rope, not turning at all, just hanging there in the roaring silence. I don't believe I even cried out when I saw him. All I remember is going into the equipment room and getting a scythe and cutting him down. And then I must have picked him up and carried him over to some hay bales and sat down with him in my lap, as if he were a sleeping child, for that was how they found the two of us at dawn, when the police and volunteer searchers came crowding through the barn doorway like awed and excited children. I learned later that they had to pry my arms from around him.

My parents were not notified of the accident until four in the morning, after Kate finally had been freed from the wreckage and taken to the hospital, and long after I had found Cliff in the barn. It is a terrible thing to think of them being wakened by the police and told of the accident and then dressing and calling Mrs. Detweiler to come and stay with the children while they went to the hospital with the police—all while their oldest son lay dead in the arms of his brother not two hundred feet away, without their knowing it. For myself, I neither saw nor heard a thing, probably because I was in a state of shock by then, indifferent to such matters as where I was or what I was doing or what I should have been doing.

Jason and Mother were told only that Cliff had wandered away from the scene of the accident and that I was one of those out searching for him. So all their concern at that time was for Kate, as well it should have been, for she was already in a coma when she came out of emergency surgery that morning. Later

Mother would learn from a nurse she knew that no one at the hospital had expected Kate to live and that the surgery that prolonged her life—as well as her suffering—had been undertaken only because the surgeon on duty that morning was young and inexperienced. An older man would have recognized that the case was hopeless, the nurse said (which should remind us all not to suffer serious injury near a hospital where such "older" men are regularly on duty).

In any case, Jason and Mother did not learn of Cliff's suicide and my having found him until seven that morning—almost an hour after Kate had been wheeled out of surgery, with a fractured skull and brain damage and crushed legs and a face that was all but destroyed. How my parents were able to survive successive blows such as those I really don't know, other than to recognize the fact that human beings have been managing kindred prodigies of suffering and endurance since time began. Yet I still find it phenomenal that they somehow got through those crushing days one by one, week after week, until I was gone and Kate finally had joined Cliff in the ground. Only then, I imagine, did their faces set and their lungs fill, the terrible anxiety finally over and only grief to bear.

If funerals are for the living, then I must have missed something at Cliff's. Throughout the service, my feelings of sorrow and loss seemed to coalesce under my breastbone into a steady, twisting pain that made me wonder if some monstrous thing were not growing there and about to break through at any moment, as through the shell of an egg. I gulped and swallowed tears and wiped my nose, and still the rivers ran.

I remember the church being filled to the walls and spilling over, with mourners in the basement as well as outside, under the portico and even on the front sidewalk. And I remember Reverend Sunbeam breaking down at one point himself as he insisted to the crowd that his words on this occasion were not the usual polite and proper eulogy, "because Cliff Kendall was purely and simply the very best—the finest—the nicest—and, yes, the most Christian young man" he had ever known.

The Reverend asked the crowd if there was "anyone among us, anyone here, with a heart so slow or eyes so blind that they did not love this boy? Love him as a friend or as the son, the grandson, they had always wanted and never had?" At that, a wave of grief swept the crowd, especially among our high school friends, who at that point undoubtedly were beginning to deal with the chilling realization that to bury another youth meant that they themselves were not immortal after all.

Later, getting out of the cars at the cemetery, I wondered if I would even make it up the hill to that distant open grave, with Cliff about to be lowered into it. By then, I was dizzy with the pain and my legs felt like rope. Yet it had been given to me to hold up my mother, just as it fell to Jason to hold on to Sarah and Junior — a trick, I wondered, to keep the two of us on our feet?

At the graveside, I remember looking up and being surprised at the great throng of mourners (including an entire troop of Boy Scouts) spread out over that same gentle hillside where the stones are now graffiti-covered and a grinning old black man hides behind a tree. The elms were still flourishing then, so almost everyone stood in welcome shade as Sunbeam went through the rest of the ceremony, not once mentioning how Cliff had died. At the end, I held on to Mother while she placed a single white rose upon the casket and then we left, moving slowly down the hill toward the waiting limousines, we who were condemned to life.

The two weeks I was to remain at home seemed to go on forever. I did only the farm work that had to be done, and spent most of my time in long solitary walks or lying alone in my basement room staring at the plank-and-rafter ceiling as if I hoped to find in its cryptic symmetry some clue as to how I would go on living in this new and empty world. Barbara Polanski and the Regans and other friends called on the phone, but I declined to go out at all, except by myself. Occasionally I would drive into Aurora and find some seedy little bar where I could have a few drinks in solitude, then I would drive slowly back to the farm, always taking the long way home if there was a choice.

Jason as usual kept to the library and Mother busied herself with Junior and Sarah, trying bravely to show them that life would go on just as it always had. But I could see that she had been mortally wounded, that the light was gone from her eyes for good. And she must have sensed a similar thing in me, for we rarely spoke.

On two occasions I went with her and Jason to the hospital. The first time all we saw through the window of the intensive care unit was a patient bandaged like a mummy. There was no way of knowing whether it was Kate we were looking at or some other unfortunate creature. The second time we happened on the scene when the doctor and a nurse were changing the bandages on her face, and what I saw then caused me to run from the window like a child. Somehow I held my vomit until I was outside, crouched and hiding between cars in the parking lot, begging God to let me forget what I had seen.

On the way home, Jason said that he and Mother had spoken with the doctor and that the man still did not know if Kate would ever come out of the coma.

"He said it might be better if she didn't," Jason went on. "She might be—well, you know."

Yes, I knew. A *vegetable*. And at that moment, I think, the change in me began. For the first time since the accident I felt not grief so much as anger, a cold and burgeoning rage at my own repellent impotence and vulnerability. I felt like a dog so used to being kicked that it virtually asks for more abuse just in the way it crawls. And I vowed to myself that this dog was not going to crawl anymore. No, it was going to run.

Even now, sitting here at this cluttered kitchen table a quarter century later, I still don't know why Cliff did what he did. I know that a number of people had seen him and Kate leave the dance early, abandoning their outraged dates, but I never heard of anyone drawing any inferences from this other than the obvious: that a dutiful brother had come to the aid of his unhappy sister. As far as I know, I am the only one who ever took note of the fact that the crash occurred almost two hours after Cliff and Kate left the dance, which of course could have given rise to all sorts of speculation. In fact I can almost hear the wheels turning in your head right now: Two hours? Alone all that time, parked somewhere? Well, then, of course they did it. Kate must have gotten to my brother just as she did to me, and as a result he was so devoured with shame and guilt that he crashed the car in an unsuccessful murder-suicide attempt, after which, thinking his sister dead, he limped home to finish the job by hanging himself.

It is a plausible scenario, I will grant you. It *is* conceivable that Kate could have caught Cliff off-guard, breaking down with tears and anguish defenses she never could have breached any other way. I will admit that he was vulnerable. For one thing, Cliff had always had a somewhat unbrotherly attitude toward Kate, a sensitivity to her moods and a concern for her welfare that would have been better placed in an uxorious young husband. Her eccentricities in high school had always caused him inexplicable pain and worry, just as her recent ephemeral rejuvenation as a shiny young deb elated him unreasonably. So, admittedly, there was that predisposition in him, that *weakness,* if you will. There was also the fact that they had begun double-dating with Sally and Arthur that summer, coming home alone together night after night in our car, probably growing closer all the time. And I don't doubt that Cliff found himself glancing over at her more than once as she lounged back in the green glow of the Packard's dash, or that Kate may have used those occasions to unsettle her too-saintly older brother, mischievously touching nerves in his psyche that he had not even known existed. It certainly does not beggar belief to speculate that Cliff may suddenly have found himself comparing his Sally to Kate, to the former's disadvantage. In any case, it was during this time that his attitude changed so radically, as he slipped into the relentless depression of his last few weeks. And then too there is the simple fact of his being male, the unappealing statistic that almost all persons prosecuted for incest are male, suggesting that it is only the innate probity and coolness of the female that keeps the act within bounds and that when such an inhibiting factor is missing or indeed is turned upside down by someone like Kate, then the father or brother simply doesn't have much of a chance, his sex drive being what it is.

So, yes, I will admit that a case can be made that Cliff was no better than I, only more remorseful. And if you choose to believe it, I can understand. But I can also assure you that you are wrong. After living eighteen years with Cliff, I think I knew him well enough to state categorically that he would never have been *able* to commit incest. For me, this is simply a given, much as if I were to say that I know lambs are not predators. So I have always accepted it that all Cliff did with Kate that night was talk. At the same time, I realize that I must also accept the possibility that she may have *tried* with him, tried to find that intimacy she no longer could with me. And failing in that, as she had to, I imagine she then must have told Cliff about the two of us and how I had not been as strong or as "cold" as he was. Knowing her state of mind that night, and in fact all that summer, I would judge that she told him what had happened between us not as a confession but as an act of intentional and even calculated cruelty—though the style of it matters little, I know. It was the content that Cliff had to deal with and the evidence is that it pushed him over the edge. In destroying his perception of the two persons closest to him, Kate destroyed him as well.

Shaken and bewildered, Cliff must have started for home, driving as we all have driven on occasion: recklessly, unconsciously, so lost in thought we barely remember later having driven at all. And he must have gone into the curve faster than he should have and, losing control, sailed through the guardrail and crashed. Thrown from the car as it glanced off the first tree, he probably came upon Kate in the wreck just as I did later, with that same terrible vulnerability, totally unprepared to find instead of the live and lovely girl of a few seconds before that heinously mutilated *thing* inside. And unhinged by it, decimated by both guilt and shock, he immediately must have started running for home, heedless of his own serious injuries, driving himself with the singlemindedness of a lemming seeking the sea.

And that is all there is to it, as far as I am concerned. Cliff did not touch Kate, nor did he intentionally crash the car. All he did was kill himself.

As for Kate herself—why she did what she did, why she was as she was—I really don't know. For years after I left here I consciously tried never to think about her or what had happened between us. And then later, as a young fool steeped in Freud and Jung and other vices, I convinced myself that the whole thing had been merely a matter of sickness, that it all had happened only because Kate had been emotionally ill, a victim of drives and passions she could not control or comprehend.

But as the years have passed, and with them my certitude about almost everything, I find myself wondering more and more if it wasn't I rather than Kate who was the sick one, in that I denied my own nature, chose pale convention over the urgent bidding of my heart. Why is it so reasonable, I ask myself, to see Kate's problem as a manifestation of emotional illness rather than as a case of simple honesty, the actions of a girl who had the will and spirit to go where her heart took her, no matter how alien or forbidden that place might have been? Often I wonder what would have happened if I too had had that kind of blazing honesty. Would our passion have consumed us, or would it simply have burned out in time, leaving the two of us to go our separate ways? Or just might it have endured, annealed us into hardest steel over the years? And I wonder: would she then be with me now, as old as I am to the hour, lined and heavier, but beautiful still, probably even more beautiful? Could it be that we might have survived it all, trampled the world with our love?

I don't know. In fact, I don't even know that she loved me. And that I guess is the problem, that I never know, that instead of answers I have only theories and explanations. But then even those are better than lies.

It was almost September when I left, on a night so hot and humid that I was afraid Jason or Mother might be awake and hear me leave. But if they did, they made no move to stop me. I packed my duffelbag and left a note, saying that I would not be coming home but would stay in touch. Then I walked to the freeway and hitched a ride going south to St. Louis, a route I had to take in order to follow Sixty-six west to California. But I had no plans to stop off at the riverfront and take in the strippers at the Lucky-O or to try to find my way to the bed of Black Mama again. For the time being, getting drunk and having sex were not so all-important. What I needed now was to be on my own, just me, alone. And as long as I could manage it, I didn't want to know anyone and I especially didn't want to love anyone. It was a callow thought, I know. But at eighteen, it seemed no less than the most basic condition for survival.

fourteen

It has been three days since Jason died and over a week since the storm hit and the phone and electricity went dead. There was a one-day thaw but now it is cold again and the snow remains drifted at roof levels in most places. Still, this unprecedented breakdown in utility services remains a galling mystery to me. All I can figure is that there must have been an apocalyptic ice storm associated with the snow, possibly in the Ohio Valley, wiping out entire grids of phone and power lines — something like that. But as for the snowplow that never comes, that I can't understand at all, except perhaps as a logical culmination of the breakdown in municipal services that has been plaguing most of us these past years.

Nevertheless I am not without hope. I keep believing that one of these days — one of these minutes — the phone is going to ring and it will be Sarah or Toni, first one and then the other, each saying that she has been trying to reach me ever since the storm hit. Sarah's affair most likely will be over and she will be waiting for a bus home, hopefully not too much sadder and wiser than when she left here.

As for Toni, I have assumed for some time now that Junior probably dumped her the second he hit L.A., his hemorrhoids in irresistible itch to begin their inflamed tour of the gayer

Hollywood bars. So by now I figure that she most likely is in Venice somewhere, staying with friends until she gets a job or maybe a modeling assignment or even a bit part. And I will admit it is my expectation that when she does call, it will be to beg me to come to her — because if she doesn't, then I'll just have to do the begging myself. Either way, I figure I can't lose.

And if neither of them ever calls? Well, then I guess it will just be a matter of muddling through here: eating all the ketchup and peanut butter and sugar and whatever else there is, and keeping the fire going even if I have to start burning furniture eventually. But in time the snowplows *will* come through and the electricity *will* come back on — certainly that isn't too rash an assumption, is it? And when those things do happen, then I can begin the long process of getting out of here, probably by borrowing against Jason's estate so I can afford to bury him and return to the Coast to settle my problems there. Because I have no previous criminal record, I wouldn't be surprised if all I got was a probationary sentence, which means that I could be out on the beach again in no time at all, strolling in the cool salt air past all those tanned young goddesses and idly trying to think up some get-rich-quick scheme (such as a horror script) so I could go on strolling there forever, with a goddess of my own at home, in the person of Toni.

But all that is still very much in the future. For now, there is only this littered kitchen table and the open-stove firelight spilling across the legal pad, turning it into something molten and shimmering, investing these words with magic of one kind anyway. As I write, the side of me that faces the fire is hot, while the other is cold. I hear the wind picking up again, singing under the eaves like a choir of castrati. If I go to the door and shine my dimming flashlight outside, all I will see is snow, light sprays of it exploding in the wind, adding to the great drifts against the house and the outbuildings. Above the door icicles hang ready to be picked, a Siberian's fruit. And thinking of ice, I remember that earlier, when it was still light, I went upstairs and checked Jason's body once more and found it beginning to putrefy in spite of the cold. So I packed it in snow, right on Sarah's bed. (If and when she returns, I imagine she will want a new mattress.)

I can't believe I am so close to the end of this record. It makes me wonder what I will do tomorrow night and the nights after that, especially if there is still no electricity and I can't watch television to learn what has happened to us. The prospect of one day doing only that — sitting back and relaxing with others, talking, watching an electronic box — fills me with a minor terror, for I guess I have come to enjoy this silence, this oddly appealing communion with my own life. I will miss the darkness and the firelight playing in it, raising ghosts in every corner: Mother doing dishes at the sink, turning to say something to me or the kids; and Cliff standing there in embarrassed pride in his scout's uniform, almost trembling for his father's approval; and Kate — *everywhere.* In the lambent light, I see her lying in grass chewing on a haystem and I see her nude in front of the bathroom mirror and coming up out of the water and disappearing into my arms. And I ache for her, even now, after all these years.

Sometimes what I see in the light makes me weep and all I can do is settle back and give in to it, letting the tears come and come, as if they might wash the images away. And then there are other times when the images make me smile. I sit here with my pen lifted and my mind gone as suddenly I am a child again, running hand in hand with Kate and Cliff down the hillside through the high summer grass. Strangely, there is no laughter or in fact any sound at all, and the hill does not come to an end. The grass just goes on forever.